3

Hideous Creatures

Hideous Creatures

S. E. Lister

First published in Great Britain in 2014 by Old Street Publishing Ltd
Trebinshun House, Brecon LD3 7PX
www.oldstreetpublishing.co.uk

ISBN 978-1-908699-56-5

Copyright © S.E. Lister, 2014

10 9 8 7 6 5 4 3 2 1

A CIP catalogue record for this title is available from the British Library.

Printed and bound by pb print in the Czech Republic.

To my parents, with love and gratitude.

I with my hammer pounding evermore
The rocky coast, smite Andes into dust,
Strewing my bed, and, in another age,
Rebuild a continent of better men.
Then I unbar the doors: my paths lead out
The exodus of nations: I dispersed
Men to all shores that front the hoary main.

I too have arts and sorceries;
Illusion dwells forever with the wave.
I know what spells are laid. Leave me to deal
With credulous and imaginative man;
For, though he scoop my water in his palm,
A few rods off he deems it gems and clouds.
Planting strange fruits and sunshine on the shore,
I make some coast alluring, some lone isle,
To distant men, who must go there, or die.

Emerson, *The Seashore*

Part One

1

In the Water

With the earthquake came the storm.

Arthur was drenched already. He lay flat on his back, blinking the rain from his eyes. Beneath him the earth rumbled as rock strained on rock, deep in the world's belly.

And he remembered.

"Shelo," said Arthur aloud. He heard stones clatter down the bank behind him, the creak of tree-roots, a curlew shrilling in alarm. "Shelo…"

The ground bucked him with the force of a mule. He was thrown back and sideways, cursing as he scrambled for a hold. The air was strange, dusky, and overhead he saw for an instant what seemed to be a towering figure in the sky, robed in billowing black.

"Shelo!" he cried again, but the figure dissolved into swathes of storm-cloud. His cry became a howl, a thin thing lost in the rising wind. He could not hear himself, could not feel his body shaking because the world was shaking too. The water rose in the lake below, waves swelling and breaking against the banks. Arthur snatched at stones which skittered from his grip, thrown from side to side at the mercy of the quake.

Shelo was gone in the water. His body was sunk now into the silt; face, shoulders, chest, caressed by weeds, tracing along the intricate inked lines which covered his bare torso. He would grow soft there, cold and soft to the touch, his flesh disintegrating like sodden paper. The fish would eat his awful eyes.

Arthur crawled, half on his belly, half on his knees, to the lip of the lake. The world was still trying to dislodge him from its surface, gouging the skin from his hands as he clung to it. He flung himself forward so that his face was inches from the water.

Weakened, he lay still for a long time. The earthquake finally rumbled itself into exhaustion, reduced to a quiver, and then eventually a desolate hush. The noise of the rain seemed muted, and even birds did not stir. Near Arthur's head a spider clung to a reed, so still it might have been caught in amber.

"Please," whispered Arthur into the silent, iron mass of the lake. "Please… give him back…"

It was his fault. This dawned over the space of the stretching minutes, and slowly Arthur sat back, breathing hard and fast. He closed his eyes.

He imagined that Shelo fell away from him still, limp in the dappled underwater light. Fell away from him through the water, sinking ever deeper, his black eyes open and clear as glass. He was swallowed by darkness.

This will never leave me.

Arthur watched the dim reflections of clouds ripple and distort in the pouring rain. He would stay, he decided, until his body was eroded and washed away.

Lightning lit the world bone-pale, and he saw a human movement in the corner of his vision.

"Arthur! *Arthur!*"

Sliding through the mud towards him was a small shape… not Shelo. He did not raise his head. Her muddied boots and trembling knees soon filled his line of vision.

"Arthur, get up!"

"Go away," he moaned. She bent down to shake him and he snapped at her like a trapped fox. "*Go away!*"

"Please, please get up, you're soaked through, and – " Thunder drowned her out. She sounded weak, petrified. "Where is he, Arthur?"

"Leave me!" he gasped. He somehow ended up looking at her — boots too heavy and too large, borrowed clothes sodden and bulging where her side was bandaged beneath. Her eyes were round as wagon wheels. He did not intend to catch her gaze, but she forced it upon him, and he could not look away.

"Where's Shelo?" she gasped. "I woke and you was both gone…"

"Gone." His voice did not sound like his own. "Gone in the water." He broke off into a wail. He had heard such sounds from his father's dogs when their pups were thrown in the rain barrel.

The shaking in Flora's knees spread to her whole disheveled outline. She tried to touch him but he pulled violently away from her, scrabbling into a huddle further up the bank.

"It's my fault." He swallowed mouthfuls of rain with sobbing. "We fought. I pushed him."

"You know Shelo like I do," Flora cut across him fiercely. "He wouldn't be drowned in no lake unless he wanted to be, make no mistake."

The water below them seemed to hold a malevolent consciousness, a gaze. It was Shelo's resting place. It was poison, now, through and through.

"Get up, Arthur," Flora said again, with the hint of a plea. He shook his head, biting hard into his knuckles and staring out over the lake. "You can't stay here," she persisted. "You're gonna catch your death, and anyhow…" She cast an anxious glance across the lake, down to where the valley met the woods. "Reckon even now, they ain't stopped searching."

The earth rumbled. As Arthur curled his body over his knees, Flora looked around desperately, hopelessly. Her drenched hair straggled around her face. "*Please*, Art! It's bad enough him gone in the water without you leavin' me as well!"

"Go on," he mumbled. Water spilled from his lips. "Go on with you."

She dragged him, in the end. Cursing like the outlaw she was, she burrowed her hands beneath his arms and forced him up the bank and away from the trees. He staggered, unseeing and uncaring. Arthur knew that the storm was against them, that it would pursue them wherever they ran. And sure enough, the thunder and the lightning drew closer together as they fled the lake, the wind plucking hysterically at their backs.

"It's Shelo's storm!" he screamed. "It's going to destroy us! Let me *go*, devil have your eyes, let me…"

The thunder sounded so close and deep that it seemed the earth was shaking again. He realised that Flora had led him to the cliff face, and he scrambled over the rocks at her prompting.

"Up there!" she gasped. "Looks like a cave!"

She pushed him into a fissure, which widened as he crawled. In the sudden absence of rain and the muffling of the noise, he realised that he was breathing in great, lung-ripping gasps. His feet were searing as though branded.

They tumbled together into the dry inner space and lay panting. Arthur's arms were trembling convulsively with the effort of the climb.

"It's like that place of my daddy's," said Flora, gazing around at the walls of the cave. She was drawing breath with difficulty, clutching at the place left of her heart, where a bullet had lodged just days before. "Back at the great river. You recall it, Art? Where I first saw you."

Slowly, groggily, Arthur sat up. Rain coursed down the cliff face inches away from them, filling the cave with rippling shadows. They lay fighting for breath in their own spreading puddle.

"Your *feet*," said Flora. He clenched his jaw and forced his numb legs towards him, hands shaking uncontrollably as he pulled one foot into view. The flesh of his soles had been cut to ribbons upon the rocks. Crimson blood trickled sluggishly away to mingle with the water.

Flora was watching his face. "It ain't so bad," she ventured. "We can clean it up, and…"

"And what?" he threw at her. Panic was pulling him under. "I won't be able to climb out of here, Flora!"

She opened her mouth and closed it again. "It'll get better," she said dumbly.

He turned his back on her, not easy in such a small space, and let his head sink into his hands. Now that the shock was fading, his body was beginning to remind him of different pains – the heart-deep cold, the rawness of his skin beneath sodden clothes, the agony in his feet. And worst of all, the dull ache in his innards. The pain his body couldn't hold, that shook him loose from himself.

"It won't," he said, and found himself rocking back and forth, hands clawing and clinging at his torso, wailing like a baby again. "It won't… get better. Shelo! Oh, Shelo!"

There was no awkwardness in Flora. She took off her coat and tried to cover him in it, but he resisted. She knew far better than to try and put her arms around him, but she took a grip on his elbow and wouldn't let go, tugging doggedly until he fell still.

"It'll get better," she said again. There was something strange in her voice.

"You are glad," he breathed. "You are…" He could not bring himself to say *relieved*.

"'*Course* not." Flora's freckled face flushed pink. Her small hands clutched at his arm all the more fiercely. "'Course not, it's just that… Arthur, he…"

"Speak it."

"In some ways…" She swallowed. "It's a mercy."

It was right and terrible and unthinkable for her to have said so, and he cursed her with words he'd learned aboard the *Head of Mary*. She flinched at hearing such oaths on his tongue. The absence of Shelo gaped inside him. Finally, when the last spark of energy in his body was spent, Arthur fell back against the cave wall.

"What are we without him?"

Lightning thrust a glare into their dimness, then withdrew again. Flora whispered, "I don't know."

§

Night engulfed them. It would have made sense to huddle together, drenched as they were, to share what little warmth they had. But neither even made the attempt. When the storm began to wane, what must have been hours later, they were still sitting in torpid silence. Arthur didn't dare close his eyes. Behind his eyelids, Shelo fell away from him in the water, endlessly, his hands outstretched.

Flora was completely still in the shadows, and he thought she was asleep. But then she spoke up, unprompted, as if continuing halfway through a conversation.

"So what's to be done?"

He shifted around, gaze averted from his mangled feet. "Go back," he said dully. "Go back to the freedman-farmer, and never think of me."

"But Art, we…"

"There is no longer any *we*," he said.

With a peculiar gnawing pain, he watched this dawn on her. Her mouth fell slightly open. The steady drip-drip of water from her hair into her lap continued, one drop poised at the end of her reddening nose. If he did nothing, he knew, she would stay at his side and share whatever dark end awaited. It would not do.

His body convulsed. His tongue spoke words that were not his.

"You are of no use to anyone. Truth be told, you never were."

She gasped, recoiling as though another bullet had just lodged between her ribs. Her eyes were wide as pennies, her hands pressed to her still-bandaged wound. "Art…"

"Shelo cared so little for your life, he would have left you to bleed."

"Then don't ask me why he chose you, neither!" she cried out, spindly arms now hugging her body protectively.

"He needed me." The old refrain. "He called me from across the sea."

They looked at each other through the dark.

"The eyes of Shelo," said Arthur, "saw through us like the eyes of God. It was me he wanted, me he chose and treasured…"

She began to cry, something he realised dimly he had not seen her do before. Her tears were not fathomless and weakened, like Hannah Hallingham's, or stormy and defiant, like Harmony's. Instead they seemed incidental, an inconvenience, rushing silently down her face, more quickly than she could wipe them away.

"There's something so badly wrong with you." Sobs twisted her voice. She was huddled against the wall of the cave, as though the stone itself might be her last hope of comfort. "With both of you. I wish I never met you. I wish my daddy was still alive. I wish I never been born. If Shelo chose you, Arthur, it's 'cos you're the only one he could find who'd gone as badly wrong as him."

There was a pause, in which Arthur turned his gaze back out into the storm-tossed night. Then he asked, "What do I have to say to make you leave?"

"I heard it all," whispered Flora. She wiped her nose on her ragged sleeve. "Ain't nothin' hasn't been done to me, ain't no name I haven't been called."

Far below, the surface of the black lake seethed and writhed. Arthur hardened his resolve, drew breath for the final blow. "And it will always be so, Flora Barber. You will die on some dirt road, or with your neck in a noose. For you will never be another kind of creature."

The silence was deep and severing. Misery had leeched Flora dry of tears, the white tracks stark on her face. Her thin chest was heaving. She got to her feet, bent-backed beneath the rock ceiling, gathering up her sodden coat.

"Oh," she whispered, "Oh, Arthur Hallingham. I know all about what you are, and I never cared. I never thought you was less than human, 'til now. I wish you'd drowned with him."

It was drizzling, now, and a butter-coloured moon was just visible behind the thinning cloud. Arthur watched her climb out of the cave's mouth, and felt the same relief that he had heard seamen experienced as their wounded limbs were sawn away. He was shaking, blood pounding in his ears. Darkness pulsated all around him.

"My feet," he said aloud, to himself. He couldn't climb down, he was entombed here alone. *And the worst of it... the worst of it...* he swallowed, and let his eyes slide closed. Shelo had sunk into the silt, Silas was long gone. Harmony was further than an ocean away, so diminished now with distance that the pieces of her face refused to form together in his mind.

Flora was right to wish him drowned. It would have been a better death.

§

"Arthur."

His eyelids were lead-heavy. He groaned and stirred himself, drenched and frozen still, bruised from lying among the rocks. For a moment, he could not begin to fathom whether he had been here for minutes or weeks.

Then he heard the last choking of the thunder, miles away, and remembered the storm that had been dying outside the cave. He could not have slept for long.

He could see almost nothing. The sky was clearer now, but the moon and pinprick stars barely penetrated the surrounding shadows.

Then white lightning voiced itself, and everything was illuminated.

It was Shelo, made of water and of darkness, made of ashes and of bone. Arthur's whole body leapt as though electrified, limbs flying, scrambling back from the appalling vision. Far below him, outside the mouth of the cave, the lake glimmered silver.

"Arthur," Shelo said. He did not appear faint and ghostly, but real in all his grimy solidity. His smile was a yellow wolf smile. His skin had the sheen of water. He was a drowned man.

Arthur's chest fought to draw in air. He knew that he must be sleeping still, or else turned wholly mad at last. But despite himself, he crawled out from between the rocks, and shuffled inches nearer on his knees.

"I'm so sorry!" he breathed. "So sorry!"

Shelo's tongue caressed the tips of his sharpened canines, one at a time. He seemed to be considering. "Sorry, Arthur? Sorry that I am dead?"

"So sorry!"

Shelo laughed. "I cut out the heart of me," he said, "and locked it inside a tree."

He placed a hand on his bare torso, on the left side of the ribcage, where a scar contorted the skin. "If you do not believe," he added softly, "then touch me."

"I cannot stand," whispered Arthur. Shelo's gaze fell on his tattered feet, and his lip curled. Slowly he descended, until they were crouched on a level. Arthur trembled. Their faces were inches apart, but he could not feel Shelo's breath.

"If you do not believe," said Shelo again.

Arthur tried to steady his hand as he reached out, but he could not. Neither could he bear to look into that ravenous face. The inked lines that traced Shelo's shoulders, his neck, his chest, were hypnotically intricate. He followed their loops and twists until they led him to the dead blackened bloom of the scar. His fingers hovered fearfully.

Shelo covered Arthur's hand with his own, and pressed it to his chest.

Breath snagged in his lungs like a feather on a branch. The skin was neither warm nor cold, but had an unworldly, sinuous feel; made of water, made of smoke. Behind the ribs there was no heartbeat.

And after all, reasoned Arthur, after all, why should death, why should water, hold him under?

"I never meant for you to drown!" he sputtered, mindless with terror. "Down there... in the dark..."

"I was born in darkness beneath the world," said Shelo. "And crawled from the water into daylight. My eyes first came to see without sun or moon."

His face had become monolithic, sombre. Arthur could see the dirt in his every pore. And yet, he realised, there was no smell. The odour of Shelo, that rich stench of deep-forest earth and the buried remains of things, the musk of crushed powders and drying fungi, the sour note of sweat, was missing.

He pulled his hand away, and Shelo watched him.

For the first time since Arthur had been woken by the earthquake, something else loomed larger even than Shelo's death. He recalled the moments before he had pushed Shelo backwards over the bank of the lake. The reason they had fought.

He swallowed back a baffling tumult of feeling. Shelo's new body dripped like a stalactite. Water formed a skin over his features. He was unreachable. He was silent. Arthur wished that Shelo had a heart, so that he could see into Shelo just as Shelo saw into him. "We did a great thing," said Shelo. "Me and you, Arthur."

"I sent Flora away."

Shelo looked down at him. He did not even seem to have heard. "We did a great thing. For so many. In all the ages of man, who could have dreamed it? Before us, how many died crying out for it?" His head was shaggy with its mane of oiled black hair, heavy and brutal as a lion. "You saw how they came, Arthur. Swarming out of the night like insects drawn to lamplight. Paupers and whores and kings."

Outside, the wind whined against the cliff face. And suddenly, Arthur thought of the Atlantic. It loomed unthinkably huge, and behind it, a half-forgotten life. Footsteps echoing in fire-lit chambers, sugar heaped into teacups, steam rising from a copper bath. Rain on glass panes, and the deep throb of a cello. All drowned now, all sunk in the ocean. Gone in the water.

"I have nowhere," said Arthur emptily. "I have nothing. Now that you are gone."

"Then follow me one last time."

Bewildered, weary beyond words, Arthur raised his eyes to meet Shelo's. "My feet," he whispered. "I cannot walk."

"Show me," Shelo demanded.

Obedient, Arthur shifted from his knees, sticking out his legs in front of him like a child proffering bootlaces to be tied. Slowly, intently, Shelo knelt. Arthur did not dare to breathe. Shelo's hands touched his soles. He felt nothing; he felt the damp chill of mist. Shelo's fingers covered his wounds.

"Close your eyes," said Shelo.

2

Breath of the Almighty

The New World had first been suggested to the minds of men, so Arthur had heard, by two corpses washed up on the western beach of a Portuguese isle. Their raft had been made from bamboo pieces of extraordinary size, and their decayed faces were unlike anything that had been seen before. They were clothed in strange skins. They had perished drifting upon swift currents from their native shore, journeying outwards from their known world. Even in death, they told of a country beyond all maps.

He himself came to Virginia on a tide of blood, on the boat called the *Head of Mary*. His sister had once shown him an experiment in which two magnets were drawn irresistibly together, flying with urgency across the table until they collided. The continent beckoned him in this way, with ever-strengthening force.

By the time the *Head of Mary* came to harbour, he knew that its every timber was rotten to the core. There were worms in its wood, and a thousand barnacles clung to its belly. But despite everything, the sight of land finally rising up towards him from out of the low fog brought a choked hope to his throat. Through all the terrors of the crossing, one thought had sustained him. If there was any place that held life for him still, it must be this.

§

Three thousand miles before, the crew had gathered round him as the ship left its African port, exclaiming and handling his strange body as they might a beast at market. He was of far more interest to them than the cargo below deck, whose colour and form were no longer any novelty. Arthur was whiter than the whitest of the crew, and not proportioned, somehow, like other men. His limbs did not know when they ought to end, and his hands and feet were too large. His rust-coloured hair grew in uncertain tufts.

The sailors murmured to one another that he was stricken by a curse or contagion. They demanded an answer from him until he offered the only one he had.

"Since I was a boy," he whispered, "something has been amiss." Arthur had tried to speak of it once before, to his sister, but on that occasion too, language had failed him. It was only that his skin had never seemed to fit his frame; that from his earliest hours, the sickness in his spirit had entered his flesh. He was certain that no physician could put a name to what ailed him, much less cure it.

When he spoke, the English crewmen laughed aloud. *What are you doing here?* they demanded of him. *What are you doing here, your Lordship? Did you fall out of your carriage and land on our deck?*

Before boarding, he had never so much as lifted a cloth or a broom. His hands were softer than fish-flesh. But he had traded the promise of labour for his passage, and was set to work with a bucket and mop, with heavy ropes he did not know how to tie. He quickly lost all sense of night and day, subject instead to the rhythms of his bewildered body and the demands of the duty roster.

He tucked a crumpled handful of letters into the frame of his bunk, and cocooned there at some odd hour, dreamed of what awaited. Outside a storm cradled the ship and fires flashed down from heaven, whilst Arthur dreamed of jungles. He had been told that there was a country in Spanish territory, far south of where the *Head of Mary* was to drop anchor, where the trees grew with such speed and vigour as to resemble animal life, rather than vegetable.

In his dreams, green tendrils sprung up from the earth to wind themselves around his limbs.

Disturbed by the ship's rolling motion, he sweated and cried out, thrashing in his bed like a drunk. His cabin-mates tied his wrists together while he slept, the better to spare themselves from his fists. As he was too long for his own bunk, they bound his ankles to the next man's headboard, and stuffed a cloth into his mouth. He awoke in choking confusion, cold and soaked and surrounded by chaos.

He soon learned that the *Head of Mary* never slept. The ship was a breathing organism, ever feeding, ever defecating and crawling forwards on its belly.

§

Standing watch in the salt-swept darkness, he half-thought he heard his brother's wrathful cry on the wind. Months before, the sound had rung in Arthur's ears as he fled into the night from Harcourt Hall. Now he turned his head and found that it had faded from his hearing at last, drowned out by the lapping of the waves at the prow.

He looked up at the shrouded stars. He thought of taking a new name, and for a moment felt hope rise in his chest like an anchor from the deep.

Somewhere far beyond in the water, a great shape stirred. Its bulk sent out ripples which rocked the *Head of Mary*. Arthur's breath whitened the air as he gripped the side of the ship and craned forward. The beast sent a spout of water high into the black sky, and on the other side of the deck the crew cried out, leaping to their feet and calling for lanterns. Arthur did not move. He wondered if it might be a devouring fish, sent from God to swallow him down into its belly for daring to think he might escape. The great fish, like the crew, knew that he did not belong here.

The creature followed close by them for the course of many days and nights. It groaned along with the living cargo, as though it felt the same pain. The noise was deep and wide and terrible, like nothing Arthur had ever heard before. The groaning of the great fish and of the cargo shook the timbers of the ship, vibrating through it from below, and stealing into his sleep.

Sailing into a blood-red sundown, they passed some distance from a ship that had been set ablaze. Flames devoured its sails and darted down the mast like devils. Smoke poured into the scarlet sky. The stricken ship listed in the waves, its reflection writhing beneath it. Aboard the *Head of Mary*, a cry went up as the crew dashed for a closer look, gawping and hanging off the side of the deck. Some shouted to the captain, calling out for him to turn closer and look for survivors.

He would go no nearer, and as the *Mary* left the burning boat in her wake, Arthur saw why. Shadows of men leapt out of the flames, legs flailing, suspended in the glowing air before crashing into the waves below. Their heads were thrown back and their arms thrown wide, welcoming the deep. Their skins were black as ash.

Arthur stood on deck as the wind rained cinders down around him. They landed on his shoulders and in his hair. The scene before him seemed to blur and recede, and he felt himself swaying, his legs weak as saplings.

He thought that he would fall. But a hand steadied him, pressing between his shoulders until he stood straight again. Night gathered, and the light of the mutiny-fire shrank into the distance. Arthur's comforter, an old sailor with a league-long face, did not say a word.

§

Silas, like most of the *Mary*'s crew, was a jailbird. Thirty years for his debts had gnawed his youth away, and no other employer would have him. His whole free life he had known nothing but the ships along the sugar routes, which he had sailed more times than he could count. His hands were hard as leather. He had few friends among the crew, and no family back on shore.

He had not been amongst those who gathered around Arthur to examine his curious body, that first day aboard in the scorching sun. The old sailor kept to his own company. When others followed Arthur across the deck, mimicking his awkward movements, or his silver-spoon speech, Silas watched from the sidelines. He whittled birds and fish out of driftwood with his pocket knife. These hung from the low ropes of the rigging, a grainy, mismatched shoal, swaying gently in the wind.

One early watch when the roster had twinned their names, they paced together for many hours along the back quarter of the deck. The sailor seemed to be ruminating on something: and it struck Arthur that he had been forming the same question for the past thousand miles. Silas pushed the words around his mouth, testing them with his tongue, making certain that they had ripened.

"You'll forgive me," he said, at last. "But what need has a man of your breeding to labour his passage on such a ship?"

Arthur's swollen tongue filled his throat. He had scarcely spoken a full sentence since first departing his home shore for Africa, uncounted weeks ago. Had any other asked it of him, he would have made no reply.

He licked his salt-cracked lips. "I am unwelcome in England," he said hoarsely. Cold dawn light stung his eyes, and he closed them, feeling the dipping motion of the deck beneath his body. "In the house of my father."

"Is that so?"

"There was a night... my brother, he might have killed me with his own hands..."

"You must have given dreadful offence."

Arthur barely heard him. "Fled by moonlight," he said. "Rode to the land's end in the rain."

He could not have gone on, had Silas pressed him — could not have told more of Harcourt Hall, or of his time in the unsleeping African port, living in the refuse beneath the harbour. But he was questioned no further. The old man rested his elbows on the side of the boat and chewed at a mouthful of tobacco.

Days after he had stood with Silas and watched the mutinied ship sink into the dusk water, Arthur found a tiny carved statue in the bottom of the water-barrel. It was made from a beast's claw, and crowned with bright feathers. It did not look like Silas's work, but nevertheless Arthur sought him out, finding him scrubbing dishes below deck.

"Witch-work," said Silas. "From the cargo's hands, not mine." He muttered and shook his head. Veins pulsed in his rough forehead. "Seen it before. They think it'll bring a curse down on all who drink it."

"A mutiny?" asked Arthur.

"Of sorts. Toss it overboard, seaman, and say your prayers."

"Should I tell the captain?" he said.

Silas looked at him sideways. "There's powers in this world much to be feared. Spare them in the hold another beating, won't you?"

In the dead of night, Arthur cast the tiny statue into the waves. He did not pray, as he had no wish to draw the attention of the Almighty. But he trembled with holy fear. He dipped his hands feverishly into the washing bowl, afraid that the little idol had left some stain upon his skin. He went back to Silas, who seemed sure to know of such things. "Is there truth in tales of witchery?" he asked.

Silas looked at him, eyes sunk like wrecks into his face. "Oh, your lordship," he said softly. "Ain't their witchery we got to dread."

Arthur did not dare ask him what he meant, and did not find out until some weeks later, when an outbreak of sickness in the hold took more than thirty of the cargo, young and old alike. Their bodies were rolled across the deck and into the waves without ceremony. Even the grown men were so starved as to weigh almost nothing. The children were all bellies and limbs, flies settling on their still-warm skin. Once the last of the dead had been swallowed into the deep, Silas rested his elbows on the railing again, and took his cap from his head. When Arthur drew alongside him, he rubbed one filthy hand slowly across his face, and did not speak for a long while. Finally he muttered, "We shall be damned for what we have done."

"What?" Arthur's body was gripped by a chill. He had heard these exact words in his own home not so long ago, on another man's lips.

"It occurs to me," said Silas, whose voice was so low now as to be almost inaudible, "that this here work has sealed His judgment. That these poor beasts – that they do have in 'em the breath of the Almighty, after all."

Arthur shivered. Beads of sweat appeared on Silas's forehead, and ran down his cheeks.

§

The *Head of Mary* set a course through miles of featureless ocean. Many days passed without any glimpse of an island or a distant ship, or so much as a cloud at the horizon. Heat lay thickly over them, and no rain came. The crew panted and sweated and grumbled at the skies, while a sour stench rolled onto the deck from the hold below. Soon it became so unbearable that no crewman could stomach it without growing faint. They drew lots to decide who would feed the cargo, then bound their faces with rags dipped in rum. They staggered back up the steps again, babbling fearfully.

Arthur dreaded the day that the lot would be his. From below deck, reddened eyes gazed silently upwards. Silas muttered of a sickness he had seen on past voyages which stole men's sight away, passing first amongst the cargo and then spreading to the crew.

"It began this way," he told Arthur. "With the reddening of the eyes. And in ten days the captain bade us cast half of 'em overboard, unsaleable as they were. In twenty days, five of the crew was entirely blind, and ten half-sighted..."

Arthur's hands flew to his own eyes.

Silas shook his grizzled head. "I might tell you of the time," he said, "when I was aboard the *Blackbird*. We passed through a fog so thick that no one could see his own hand before his face. From the heart of this mist came upon us another ship, unexpected at our starboard side. We couldn't see nothing but its shadow." He shuddered. "We were afeared that it was some foe come to board us. They had no such intention, but by heaven! The terror their tale struck through us, I would rather they had fired cannons."

Arthur leaned in to listen, despite himself.

"We heard their voices through the mist," said Silas. "Driftin' to us from their deck to ours, though we never once saw their faces. To my knowledge they may have been wicked spirits sent to taunt us, things without bodies nor any form at all. Their cries was horrible to hear, more pitiful than lost lambs. *Sailors!* they cried, *sailors, won't you take pity on your fellow men? We are the crew of the most accursed ship* Temperance. *Won't you drop anchor beside us for a while?*

"Natural, our captain called back, askin' what their misfortune had been, and what we might do to bring aid. But after they gave their answer, he hauled up anchor and threw wide our sails to catch the fastest wind he could. *Oh,* they cried to us, *oh we have been struck by a terrible contagion! Some red plague has taken from us that which is most precious, and now we are at the mercy of the blowing winds. Oh mercy, oh our fellow men, not one soul upon this cursed ship can see!*"

The *Head of Mary* swayed on the crest of a wave. Below deck, the eyes of the sweating cargo blinked slow and hopeless.

"Oh, you can be sure, we made good speed from that ship," said Silas. "You may think we was at fault not to take pity on them poor devils, but it was never in question. Sailors know when something unnatural's afoot. We made haste away from that cursed vessel, and never again did I hear of the *Temperance,* or what became of it."

The old sailor looked out to sea. "I'm half-minded to believe it's still out there somewhere, lost upon the seas with its cargo of the blind."

§

The day that Arthur drew the shortest straw, his body descended downwards into the hold, though the rest of him did not seem to follow. He remembered little, afterwards, of that place. He remembered dark bodies with reddened eyes. He remembered bodies stacked one beside the other, and the floor slippery with blood and waste.

He remembered the living shackled to the dead.

§

The weather broke at last with violence, scattering hailstones like the seventh plague. They tore through the sails and hammered down onto the deck. The *Head of Mary* reeled drunkenly, and Arthur was crippled by nausea.

Confined to his bunk, he drifted through scattered thoughts of the shore that awaited him. In the library, a lifetime ago, wind had caught the pages of Lucas's book and turned them frantically, scattering maps and paintings, showing glimpses of thick tree roots and the scales of sliding reptiles. It was these pictures which returned to Arthur now, unfolding in the recesses of his head. He thought that he smelled the fruits of strange trees, unpeeled green skins with his fingernails. He grew ever more certain that a dark winding form moved towards his bed. A pair of awful eyes blinking in the dimness.

"Silas," he gabbled, staggering out onto the deck with his boots on the wrong feet and his shirt unfastened, his panic overcoming his sickness. "Silas, there are beasts down below…"

The storm washed his words away. Arthur bowed his head beneath his shoulders and yelled into the shrieking wind. The cry rattled in his ribcage. Waves towered on every side, tossing the *Head of Mary* between them like cruel children. When the hail died away, the air grew thick with a pulsing charge, and lightning pierced the clouds.

§

Arthur's stomach lurched independently of the ship's motion.

That night in the library, the breeze had blown open the window, scattering dead leaves among the dusty tomes. It had brought the scent of deep-forest earth, of a sour, ancient musk. It was in that moment, before there had yet been any cause for flight, that Arthur had first known where his running must take him.

"The continent called out to me," he whispered, later in the night when the wind had calmed and the *Mary*'s crew sagged, exhausted, onto the sodden deck. The old sailor looked askance at him. "That I might have some fresh purpose there. Some new beginning."

"Yes, your lordship. If you say as such."

The air felt heavy and hot. When a fiery glow descended from the heavens to rest upon the mast, the crew fell trembling to their knees, save Arthur, who could not have moved for all the world, and Silas, to whom no wonder was new. *The Holy Ghost*, cried the crew, *the candles of the Ghost!* The water beneath, far stiller now, shone with weird luminescence. Fish weaved and flickered, their shadows elongated. The blue fire sputtered like an Indian signal, and it seemed to Arthur in his feverish thoughts that it was meant for him.

In the wake of the descent of the Ghost, the crew grew ever more subdued. The captain tried to talk them round, but they knew what they had seen, and there was no turning their mood. A large parcel of the cargo had perished during the storm, suffocated by the closing of the portals or finally succumbing to the red-eye contagion. When it came to putting the bodies overboard, all were suddenly afraid. What power from on high, or from the African shore they had left behind, might be watching?

In the end, the captain threatened beatings, and they obeyed. The ocean swallowed the dead as though they had never been.

§

Arthur's body, always a stranger to him, worsened as they neared shore. He lost control of his limbs, noises escaping him like flies. The crew crossed themselves and murmured nervously to one another. They no longer followed behind him, flailing in imitation as they had done during his first days at sea, but gave him a wide berth.

In his bunk he drifted in black liquid spaces, cold and alone, curled in on himself like a thing unborn. All sound was muffled, and all light was far away. He scratched through his shirt and dug scarlet welts into his own skin. He bled onto his blankets.

Flesh dropped from his frame, until he crouched at the ship's bow like a leper, scabbed and skeletal, unshaven and unwashed. His tongue thickened, and for days at a time he forgot how to form words. He lapped rank water from a bowl, and spooned down grey gruel. When the cargo began to refuse food, he found that he could stomach nothing either. They sat in their filth and clenched their mouths tight shut as they were beaten. Arthur shuddered and picked absently at the scratches on his body.

In the end, fearing that he was in the throes of some madness, the crew looped a rope around his wrists and bound him to the mast. He sat with his back flat against the sturdy wood, his eyes searching the sky, straining to recall the thought of the new green country which awaited.

"Your lordship," said Silas in his ear, when no other would come near him. He slipped him a flask of water, hard bread wrapped in cloth. "Your lordship. Don't be going too far from us, now."

In the deepest watches of the night, Arthur heard himself howling. He rocked back and forth to try and break his bonds, but they would not loosen. He glimpsed a solitary sailor creeping below deck to where the women of the cargo were held.

His howls were answered by a muted echo, and he shuddered in the sickly moonlight. Faintly, he grew certain that if the ropes around his hands and feet didn't hold him, he would hurl himself headfirst into the sea. It might, after all, be a better death.

Before he sailed the Atlantic, he had not imagined that there could be a place on earth as appalling as the confines of his own body. He had been wrong. Aboard the *Head of Mary* he had found a horror without which surpassed the one within.

The groaning from the hold continued long and low. To Arthur, it sounded like the familiar sobbing song of a cello.

§

By the time the New World rose before them out of the west, his body had exhausted itself into stillness. His limbs fell motionless, and his throat grew too hoarse for crying out. He hung from his ropes, all his struggling spent, and looked towards the oncoming land.

It was Silas who eventually cut him free, in the dull dawn before they put down anchor, hacking through the cords with his pocket knife. Fog lay thick over the *Head of Mary*, obscuring the tip of the mast and turning the approaching shore into a mass of shadows. Silas helped Arthur to his feet and across the deck, where he promptly leant over the side of the ship and vomited into the waves. Arthur's eyes followed the drifting progress of the scum in the water, until his gaze was drawn gradually upwards, and he caught his first near glimpse of the new continent.

Gulls passed overhead, with their scythe wings and hoarse screams. They gathered at the *Mary*'s prow and cut a curving course through the air. They squabbled over fish scraps and defecated on the deck. The ship arced around green islands

Silas watched Arthur from the corner of his eye, his mouth slightly open, questions clinging to his tongue like barnacles. They stood together at the edge of the deck, salt spray whitening their faces, and watched the horizon. Arthur found that he was trembling as though he had awoken from a long fever, and leaned weakly forward onto the railing.

"You got letters, your lordship?" asked Silas, at some length. "Names, addresses. Some place to head for when we land?"

"Nothing of that kind," he whispered. Crumpled in his bunk were notes from Lucas, addressed to men in Africa who might have welcomed him. Arthur turned his eyes to the coming horizon, and for a moment his heart strained towards the New World, gripped in a vice, threatening to burst from his chest with its pounding.

As the fog parted to reveal the sails of twenty more ships, all tethered at the harbor and letting off a stench so thick that it was almost visible, Silas laid a hand upon his shoulder. Neither of them moved, though the captain had begun to shout orders. Arthur closed his eyes, and wiped his mouth weakly on his sleeve. A choked hope caught in his throat.

"Silas," he asked, "will you leave me when we land?"

"No, your lordship," said the old sailor quietly. "Not if you don't wish it. I shan't leave you."

3

Black Bloom

Whenever Lucas, Arthur's childhood friend, had spoken of the New World, he'd spoken of skies. He'd fallen head-over-heels for the sight of a wide sky rolled open over the continent like a parchment, the emerald grass beneath it. His letters had grown lyrical and expansive. *This is God's own land*, he had written, *made from the finest of His materials. I have seen such wonders here, that I do not know how I shall tell you of them.*

He wrote of forests broader than all of England, of great lakes into which London might be sunk. He spent words lavishly on the land's clear rivers and virgin-white shores. *This shall be some better home for man. Here we shall begin anew. I truly believe it.* His brash, exuberant handwriting covered side after side.

Lucas was no great artist, but as he journeyed south he had begun to include drawings in his missives. He had a botanist's eye for detail, and his outlandish birds and beasts and flowers seemed to writhe on the pages, pinned down but very much alive. At first there were crested finches, coloured startling scarlet, narrow firs, delicate wildflowers. These gave way to stump-legged swamp lizards, sultry white orchids.

Back at Harcourt Hall, Arthur and Harmony had pored over every page, binding them together in one volume which grew and grew. They stowed the makeshift book in the library, and returned to it on rainy afternoons. Arthur moved his hands across its cover, touching traces of foreign earth. Each time it fell open he breathed in the smell of its dust, of the long miles it had travelled.

As the string of Lucas's absence stretched ever tighter, his letters came less frequently. His handwriting diminished. He journeyed southwards through French territory and into Spanish, drawing tangles of bloodwood roots, plump *camu* fruit, coiled snakes.

There is something that begins to trouble me, wrote Lucas. *I shall say no more of it here. But my heart is strangely heavy. I think of you often. I think of my return.*

§

In the cool part of the day the *Head of Mary* came to harbour, and just hours later, a great fish was beached upon the same shore. It drew crowds from the town; women who covered their noses, children who gasped and pointed. Men with muskets came to jab at its grey flesh. It lay upon the sands, a motionless mound, water streaming down its skin. It did not die until evening. The whole day through, as the *Mary*'s crew laboured to unload, it filled the air with clicks and moans. An eye the size of a man's head rolled queasily back and forth.

As the cargo were led away to their holdings, gulls landed upon the fish's broad back, burying their beaks. They tore through the fat to the blood beneath, and lifted heads that were stained with gore. The crowd soon followed suit, taking knives to the beast's belly and squabbling over the meat. Long, thick tendons swung like ropes. Somebody pierced its head, spilling a fountain of white oil. The sand grew slippery and stained.

"I have heard of such things," murmured Silas. "The fish what carries its seed in its brains."

He took Arthur to an inn where he lay flat on his back and soaked the hard mattress with sweat. The wind carried in the reek of fish-flesh from the beach. Flies landed on Arthur's body. He watched them creeping over his white arms, did not move when they landed on his face and crawled into his beard.

The old sailor sat in a low chair beside the window, and cradled his pipe in the palm of his hand. "There have been boats sunk by such creatures in the last throes of life. I met a man saw one do battle with a mighty sea-serpent, not so far from this very coast." He poked tobacco into the bowl as though feeding a fledgling. When he lit it, a new pungent smell filled the dim little room. Silas inhaled and blew out a plume of smoke through the shutters into the foggy dusk. The glow from his pipe stretched across the hollows of his face.

He disappeared when dark fell, leaving his coat and pipe upon the chair, and a lit candle on Arthur's bedside table.

Arthur knew that Silas had gone to drown the memory of the voyage in a deep tankard. He licked his own cracked lips slowly with his tongue. They still tasted of salt. He raised himself onto his elbows, too nauseous to sit upright. The shutters rattled and blew open. Past the shingled rooftops, the last of the light lapsed into the sea.

He inched a hand inside his filthy shirt, and withdrew the thin envelopes that he had kept in his bunk through the long voyage. He was not sure why he had not cast them overboard, tattered and useless as they were now. *Ask at the port. There will be refuge for you.* In the candlelight, he could make out the names and the African places that Lucas had so diligently traced out for him. He held the paper near the flame.

On the night he had departed England, in their race to the southern coast, the two of them had left their horses foaming at the bit and staggering with exhaustion. Lucas, he remembered, had looked pale and drawn in the early morning light. Arthur's last sight of him had been from the deck of a cloth-ship, a slight figure of a man whose hand was raised in dazed farewell.

He hesitated, and then slid the envelopes back beneath his pillow. The candle oozed white wax and a deep-sea odour.

He might have stayed in Africa: might have crawled to the door of some acquaintance of Lucas's, been offered bread and shelter, perhaps pity. But it would not have done. He had known in his bones that Africa was not far enough.

Night was broken by rumbling from the harbour, and by all manner of cries and howlings from the woods outside the settlement boundary. "Silas!" Arthur whispered, when he became aware that the bed on the other side of the room had been filled. The old sailor's feet protruded through his threadbare socks. "Silas! Do you hear the beasts beyond the walls?"

Silas stirred. He pushed up his nightcap and looked blearily through the dimness, a flicker of alarm passing over his ruddy countenance. "Now, your lordship," he said. "There's no storms in here, no fearful things to find you. Won't you rest easy?"

§

Silas left each day to spend his earnings in taverns and tobacco-houses, but at first Arthur would not set a foot out of doors. Once he had slept away the worst of his exhaustion, he took to sitting at the window, picking at the unhealed sores upon his chest.

Tides half submerged the corpse of the great fish, then retreated again, leaving it prone on the shore. Even when the meat turned putrid, the townspeople did not leave it to lie. They processed to the seafront with buckets. They carved more holes in its monstrous head, and caught the pale liquid which spilled forth. Fires were lit in the shipyard, and great vats of creamy oil bubbled and seethed, sending a cloud of dirty smoke high above the settlement. The whitish mess turned solid over the chill autumn nights, and was

34

pressed through layers of sacking until a pure wax trickled forth.

The candle at Arthur's bedside guttered and smoked. He understood now why it filled the room with such a strange, pervasive smell. The light of the New World had been harvested from deep in the belly of the ocean. From his room at the inn, he could see points of brightness in the windows of every house, and in lanterns along the uneven streets. One winding alleyway, leading up the cliff-side away from the sea, had lamps which glowed red.

§

He grew accustomed to the sight of new sails appearing at the horizon, of vessels winding along the shoreline before coming in to dock. Herds of skittish sheep were driven down ramps and onto the harbour, where they were penned between barrels of pickled fruits, stacked rolls of cloth. The same ships were replenished with lumber, with molasses rum, Indian corn and salt cod.

The country past the boundary of the settlement was wild with thick woodland and fast rivers. Daily, men departed the gate, mounts heavily laden, or else hauling carts behind them. Some were accompanied by their thin-faced wives, by children who had long since cried themselves into quiet. Arthur watched them take their leave from the port town, heading west over the hills, and realised how little thought he had given to certain vital matters.

"I take it, your lordship, that you have in mind some manner of occupation." Silas watched him shrewdly. "Seein' as you have come here without so much as a friend to meet with, or a coin in your pocket."

Slowly, reluctantly, Arthur shook his head. "No. No occupation."

"No form of trade at all that you are familiar with?"

He had never tilled a field, nor lifted one stone atop another, nor so much as buttoned his own shirt until recent months had demanded it. He only thought, somehow, that the land would enfold him into its arms. Where he might go, or what he might do there, was beyond him.

With the thought of looking upon the road that led west, he left the inn at last and took himself to the town gate, treading a little cautious way into the woods. It was evening, and the path was quiet. The wall bore the scars of storms and of the native's fury, long swathes of timber scorched and rebuilt in haphazard fashion. The forest creaked and muttered, and Arthur turned his head sharply as scarlet finches flitted between the trees.

"Show me," he whispered into the half-darkness. The wind picked up, and Arthur's hands worried at the skin beneath his shirt. "Show me my way. My new beginning."

As though in immediate answer, something shifted. From the corner of Arthur's eye he thought he saw a shape slink downwards from the branches of a tree. The silhouette of a huge man crouched upon the forest floor, hands buried deep in the greenery and rotting litter, a shaggy mane of hair hanging from his head.

Arthur heard himself whimper. He clasped his hand at once over his mouth, but the crouching figure made no movement. Arthur looked for a fraction of a second into a pair of awful eyes.

Then the shape vanished into the trees, and the certainty of Arthur's first impression — that this was, indeed, a man — evaporated. It moved more like a great black hound, or a wolf, or like the panther that he had seen at a menagerie one long-ago rainy day. The sound of its panting was wet, animal.

He stood frozen, a thin mist settling with the night, the church chimes ringing out far behind him for the closing of the gate. On the wind came a scattering of dead petals, the scent of deep-forest earth. Of an ancient, acrid musk.

§

Sleep deserted Arthur for weeks on end. At the inn, he fretted, still filthy with the dirt of the voyage. Silas brought him bread which he did not eat, razor blades and clean clothes which sat unused at the foot of his bed.

He did not dare return to the boundary or go out into the town alone, but waited instead for Silas to come in from the taverns each night, tongue loosed by ale. In melancholy moods the old man murmured of his prison days, of those he had seen drowned on long-ago voyages. In livelier tempers he recounted tales heard from men who had ventured deep into the continent, journeying up into the cloud-forests or outward to untouched isles.

"There are savages to the south without heads, with eyes and ears what are hid upon their chests. There are those what commune with dark gods, and eat the hearts out of their foes." He settled into the chair before the window and lit his pipe, laying his feet upon the sill. Arthur closed his eyes as Silas breathed out soft words with his pipe smoke, the room filling with a yellow haze. He imagined firelight upon naked skins, glinting upon the sharpened points of spears.

"These I have heard told," said the old sailor. "And as to those things... those things I have seen..."

His merriment escaped him with the coming of the midnight hour, with the last of the smoke from between his lips and the chiming of the far church bells. He fell quiet, and Arthur opened his eyes to see Silas sitting forward in his chair, gaze fixed on the dark harbour far below the window. His face, ruddy by daylight, was a tallow mask. The whites of his eyes showed, shot through with bloody tendrils.

"Who will bear it away from me? I never much thought of them poor Afr'can beggars, so many years on the ships. But of late their voices sound loud in my ears, even when I am ashore. Who will bear it away from me, before I am dead and damned?"

His shoulders bent. The sea that had borne him so many times beat ceaselessly against the cliffs. He tipped the ash from his pipe into the street beneath and rose, turning to Arthur, unsteady with ale and remorse. "Might a man make amends, your lordship? Might all his wicked life in this world be washed away?"

"I cannot tell," whispered Arthur.

"And yet I must take another commission, and pile hot coals upon hot coals." Silas staggered to his own bed and with some effort pulled away his boots, casting them into the corner. "I will sail again, and your lordship, you must not follow me."

He fell still, staring at Arthur across the dim room. "We will find you some better occupation," he said, with deep urgency. "An honest livin'."

Arthur tried to contain the nervous trembling of his limbs, but found that he could not. He wrapped his arms around his ribcage, wondering what possible use his weak body and addled mind might be put to. He had hoped, knowing all the while the vanity of it, that Silas would not leave him.

§

The sailor took him the next day to a tavern behind a nearby marketplace, to meet with men who were gathering supplies in readiness for the journey west. They had spread their maps upon a table and were talking over the routes through the hills, while their wives busied themselves darning shirts and wrapping food into parcels. Arthur hung back, scratching at his unkempt beard as Silas bent the ears of his drinking mates. The men listened with courtesy, but as their eyes strayed over Silas's shoulder their expressions changed.

They looked Arthur up and down, the tangle of his hair, his filth-encrusted shirt. Beneath their gaze he shrunk, all words receding from his throat. He shifted from one foot to the other.

"He has no trade to speak of," Arthur heard Silas say, "but he is book-learned, and most willin' to be apprenticed."

"What palsy does he suffer?" asked one of the men, who had turned entirely from the map to stare at Arthur.

"No palsy. I cannot say that he is strong, but he will work for his bread."

The man's wife, child on her hip, took him by the arm and spoke in a low, rapid voice. As the child's face creased and reddened, she gestured towards Arthur, and against his will the distressed noises which escaped him grew louder. He bit into his lip until he tasted blood.

"Our roads will be hard from the first," said the man, "with much danger from savages, and outlaws, and foul weather. It is not good that there should be any infirm man in the party…"

"There is a want of health about him," interrupted his wife, more fiercely. She jogged the child upon her hip until its squalls were silenced. "A godforsaken look. I would not think him of much use, nor trust that he might not bring bad fortune."

Silas began to counter her, the others around the table raising their own voices in question or dissent, and Arthur could stand it no longer. He made for the door and stumbled outside, where he was swallowed at once by the marketplace crowd.

He had followed Silas on their way from the inn, but in his absence could not find his bearings. A butcher was crying his wares at a deafening pitch, slamming slabs of meat upon his cart amidst a cloud of flies. Arthur backed away, only to find that he had knocked into a stout man who had been standing close behind him.

To his alarm, the stranger did not move away but instead drew yet closer, looking him up and down. He had the uncomfortable impression that the man had watched him enter the inn, and had been waiting for him to emerge.

"I believe, you are he," Arthur's assailant declared, checking a piece of paper from his pocket. "Came to shore on the *Head of Mary*. You lodge now at the Yew Tree, with an old ship's hand."

Arthur nodded breathlessly. He swallowed the urge to call for Silas. "You are even now in search of employment," said the man. His breaths were laboured and wheezing, and an unpleasant smell hung on him, old sweat mingled with a bitter iron tang.

"How…?" began Arthur.

"Just a messenger, mister, from one who is most interested in your affairs."

He had the look of an aged cherub, his fair curls greasy and graying. His round face was filmy with sweat. Arthur fought a wave of disgust.

"He wishes to meet with you, that you might be of some assistance to him in his work."

"What manner of work?" The stranger did not answer, but instead pulled out a second piece of paper and tucked it without preamble into Arthur's pocket, his stubby fingers dexterous.

"Come to my establishment, and he'll have words with you himself." He tucked in his flapping shirt-tails, and turned, stepping back into the crowd. "If you've the stomach for it."

§

Arthur paced the little room at the inn, his thoughts running wild until the old sailor returned. Silas sunk down into the chair before the window, but did not light his pipe or remove his boots. He looked bleakly across at Arthur, rubbing his stubbled chin with his hand.

"I don't know what's to be done," he said. "Only that we might persist, 'til some other party is willin' to have you…"

Arthur barely heard. His mind had carried him out to the wood beyond the walls, and the eyes that had stared into him from the shadows. "Silas, what appears like a man, but runs like a beast? What has the semblance of a man, but is incorporeal as the air?"

"Your lordship…"

"The land itself called out to me," intoned Arthur. He clasped the scrap of paper, with its scrawled address, tightly in his perspiring palm. "Saw me, and knew me, before I ever set sail."

He noted dimly that Silas was now staring at him with alarm. "Put away such thoughts, your lordship," he said. "Be assured, there's no good to be had from them."

Arthur barely heard him.

Staggering outside later in the night to relieve himself, he returned to find something tucked into the buttonhole of his shirt, which he had left hanging on the bedpost. Silas slept on unawares. It was a large flower, crisp in death and dark as ash, the strangest of calling cards.

He dashed at once to the window and pulled back the blind, leaning out for the sight of a retreating figure. But the street below was silent and empty. He seized the candle at his bedside and flung open the door, to find the crooked landing bare. He had passed nobody on the staircase, and there were no footsteps upon the filthy floor.

Letting out a breath, he took the dead flower in his hand, as tenderly as though it were a token from a ghostly lover. It seemed somehow to pulse with a beat like a heart. It insinuated things he could not have begun to name.

4

Such a Look

Before dawn, he left Silas sleeping and made for the street where the red lamps hung. Checking the paper in his hand, he moved towards a crooked house where a solitary blue light shone from the attic window. As he approached, two women in a nearby doorway turned their heads, but did not call out after him. Their paint-rimmed eyes weighed him, and found him wanting. They hitched up their skirts to scratch unthinkingly at their thighs, their perfume hanging in pungent clouds.

The door was heavy, and behind it a narrow room, unfurnished save for a counter of sorts at one end and a stool in the corner. Dust lay thickly over everything. Behind the counter sat a lank-haired woman occupied scratching figures into a ledger. She addressed him without so much as glancing up.

"How far gone is she? If it's after the quickening of the child, it'll cost you extra." She licked the end of her quill, revealing sparse teeth. "More'n four months, can't be sure she'll live."

The door swung closed behind him, disturbing the dust on the floor. The only illumination was the pale light from outside. Arthur wiped his sleeve across his clammy forehead.

"I am looking for a man…" he began hoarsely, and did not know how to go on. The room swallowed his words whole.

The woman paused in her work, fixing Arthur with a glare. Her small eyes took in his filthiness, his bloodied shirt, the lice that burrowed in his beard. Her gaze lingered just south of his belt, causing Arthur to shift uncomfortably.

"If you mean him what sleeps upstairs," she said, "he ain't here." Her eyes crept upwards towards his midriff, then raked the whole height of him, to the peak of his rust-coloured hair. Arthur shuddered. He could not have felt more invaded had she run her hand across his skin.

A pair of cockroaches scurried unhindered across the countertop, inches from her elbow. When Arthur did not leave, the woman leant back, and hollered through the door behind her.

"Samuel! *Sam!* Is a gentleman here after Shelo!"

The stout man from the marketplace entered the room, wheezing with each step. When he saw Arthur he stopped short, wiping his hands on his apron. "Our lodger ain't here," said Sam. "He'll be back in due time."

The two of them stared at him, reptilian in the gloom. Sam's tongue flickered across his lips.

"Listen. I ain't his keeper, though he lays his head here. You may wait in his rooms, if you wish, or return here when you please."

Arthur, entirely tongue-tied now, looked between them. The woman licked the end of her quill once again, ink glistening upon the page.

"I would wait," she cautioned, "were I in your place. 'Tis best to cause Shelo no displeasure."

There was no light in the crooked stairwell, and Arthur ascended blind, Sam's broad backside before him. The walls sagged inwards on every side. A stale odour which had been faint in the front room grew ever more pronounced. It had a metallic edge to it, like old blood.

Behind a closed door to his right, Arthur was sure he heard somebody cry out. But Sam kept climbing, grunting with effort as the stairwell grew increasingly narrow. Arthur lowered his head, dust and crumbling plaster coating his hair.

"Here." Sam kicked open a misshapen door at the very top of the staircase. He pressed himself against the wall to let Arthur pass. The doorway was so low that he had to bend almost double to enter.

He was in a small attic room, the sloped ceiling just high enough for him to stand, a blue lamp hanging from the timbers like a cold star. It cast a ghostly glow upon the strangest sight that he had ever seen.

Arthur's breath stopped in his chest. Shelves covered every inch of wall, and upon every shelf stood jars arranged in immaculate rows. These were filled with a sticky liquid, thinner than blood, thicker than water. Suspended at the centre of every jar was a curled object.

At first he thought that they were tadpoles. Releasing his breath, Arthur took a step closer. His body began to shiver uncontrollably. And as he drew near to the tiny, translucent creatures, it dawned on him. Many had limbs, pink feet, miniscule fingers held anxiously in mouths below their oversized eyes. Others were so malformed as to be almost unidentifiable. They were wrinkled like pickled peaches.

His breath misted the glass. His throat closed.

"My collection," said Sam, offhandedly.

"What manner of establishment is this?" asked Arthur.

Sam did not answer. Peering into the attic from the threshold, he indicated a heap of rags and blankets on the floor. "He'll come back, when it suits. He comes and goes as is his will, to business of his own."

"I shall wait," Arthur said. The tiny bodies drifted all about him.

§

His brother had mocked him for saying it, and so he had stopped saying it many years ago. But Arthur remembered being born. More than that: he remembered the time before. He had floated in the liquid dark, webbed hands reaching imploringly into the emptiness about him. He remembered a place of coldness. He had known, even then, that he was unwelcome.

He lay on Shelo's blankets amongst the unborn dead. He could not see that the man had any possessions, save for his bedding, and the bundles of dried herbs and leaves, which were strewn across the floor. He appeared to have been crushing seeds with a pestle and mortar. Empty bottles with indecipherable labels were scattered carelessly. Broken-necked birds were strung up along a line tied between the timbers, their feathers plucked, little legs bound with wire. Beetles and smoke-coloured moths were pinned to a board.

He had barely acquainted himself with this strange space when he was disturbed by a commotion below. There was a pounding at the door, followed by a convergence of voices which gradually grew in pitch and volume. One was Sam's, low and wheezing, while the other was higher, hard with despair. Arthur took himself to the stairwell and inched down towards the half-open parlour door. Through the crack, he saw Sam in a greying nightshirt with a lamp in his hand, talking with a woman whose face was concealed beneath her hood.

"Twenty," Sam was saying, "and I will take no less." His back was facing Arthur, his bulky form in shadow. The woman was agitated, cloak held tightly about her body, voice growing fainter by the moment.

"Ten now, ten in the coming month! I swear—"

"I won't be paid in promises."

"Have you no ears to hear me? I shall be turned out to the weather and God's pity!"

"So I am told, a dozen times each night." A damp panting, and it dawned upon Arthur that Sam was laughing. "If only you had stopped to think of ruin before you fell into it! But since I am a merciful man…"

There was a pause. The woman in the cloak was breathing hard and fast. Feeling now like the worst kind of intruder, Arthur edged back up one step.

"Ten now. A further twenty-five before these two months are out, else it's an increase of five each week my due is not delivered. Is that agreeable to you?"

Arthur inched upwards again, back towards the attic, but he could still see the woman's stooped shape through the crack in the door. One hand was at her hood, the other brushing across the place where her belt was bound loosely over her skirts. He did not hear her reply.

He lay down again upon Shelo's bed, knees pulled up against his chest. Soon after, a ragged moaning began to rise through the floor, and Arthur set his teeth together. To drown out the sound, he recalled what had been murmured over him in his cradle, time and time again. He formed the words dumbly inside his mouth.

Oh, Master Arthur. Such a look you had, when you came into this world! What a look of fury, and of devilish intent! No small wonder, that you were the death of my lady.

§

It seemed to him, at Sam's establishment, that he was surrounded on all sides by an encroaching fog. Steam from pans of brewing rootbark in the kitchen seeped up between the cracked floorboards. At all hours of the day and night, women came to knock upon the parlour door. They were whores and beggar women, merchant wives and the daughters of governors. They came dressed in veils and hooded coats, clutching their purses. Sam and his wife ushered them in from the street, sent them on their way again in the hours before dawn.

Arthur watched through the attic window as they limped away down the street outside. The sight of them sent his thoughts spinning, and he became convinced, in feverish moments, that a woman was standing over his bed. Her greying hair hung in tangles, her nightdress trailing upon the floor. She gazed at him imploringly, tears flowing down her face.

After four days, Silas came knocking. Plainly discomforted at even setting foot in such a place, he was allowed in under the sharp eye of Sam's wife, and crouched awkwardly in the doorway of the attic. His gaze wandered to the jars that lined the walls. It occurred to Arthur that Silas must have knocked on many other doors and asked many questions to find him.

"Your lordship," he said softly. "Won't you come back from this place?"

"Silas," pleaded Arthur. "Silas. He has for me some manner of employment."

The old man's league-long face was solemn. "Employment? Him they call Slitwire Sam, of this establishment?"

"Not him. Silas." He faltered. "Like a beast… incorporeal as the air…"

Silas wore the look of one who has sailed beyond the edge of his map. His eyes ranged again around the dim attic space, this time taking in the slaughtered birds hung by their feet, the scattered bottles, the blue lamp.

"Wait here with me," asked Arthur helplessly.

"I have been to this town many times," muttered Silas, "and know something of what is said to dwell in it."

For the first time since he had glimpsed the creature in the wood, Arthur began to wonder whether the answer might not be tucked beneath the old sailor's tongue, like a pearl in an oyster. He sat up, fully alert. Silas braced himself against the doorway, leaning forward as he spoke, as though trying to impress upon Arthur the full weight of his words.

"I heard that there was a man who came out of the forests deep in Spanish country, and was said to be living among the natives here, ten year or so ago. One tale says that he was born of the savages, but his own people turned him from among them, such a savage that he was. And these northern natives were also in fear of him, and would have nothing of him either." His voice dropped even lower, taking on a tone of warning. "They say this exile lives now within the city walls, and hides his face from daylight. I heard he hates the white man, and is ever scheming against him. I heard it is within his power to bring about all manner of fearful witchery. Some name him an omen of fire, or shipwreck, or all kinds of calamity…"

"Do they say that his eyes are like the eyes of God?" whispered Arthur.

"You have seen such a creature?"

Arthur nodded fervently. Silas drew back into the stairwell. He was looking at Arthur with great pity and alarm.

"Listen," he began carefully. "I been told of a vessel at harbour what's found herself short of crew." When Arthur did not reply, he prompted, "A goods boat, quite unlike the *Mary*. Captain's carrying some unlawful cargo and is hiring without questions."

Arthur looked blankly at him, and Silas stepped down from the doorway, rubbing his hands together. He did not seem able to spend more words in persuasion. Backing into the stairwell, he hesitated before turning once more to Arthur.

"You know where I can be found," he said. "Come back from this place, when you are returned to your senses."

§

It gradually met Arthur's notice that there were those who, though they came knocking at the parlour door, did not leave. Sam's wife burned bloodied sheets in the backyard at dusk, and he thought he glimpsed the pair of them bearing the odd bundled body into the night. He could not be sure, but he suspected that these were tipped from the harbour into the dark water, washed away by the same current that carried in the ships.

"Ain't this one a beauty?" murmured Sam, who shuffled up the steps to the attic with little cloth-wrapped objects in his hand. He slipped these into empty jars, and pressed his face close, tongue sliding over his lips. "Ain't this one an ugly beggar?"

He seemed to sense Arthur watching him, and turned, unabashed. "There's no cruelty in it, mister."

"Do you think," asked Arthur hoarsely, "that they were sensible of anything?"

"No. It were better for these, that they were never born."

When he had gone, Arthur burrowed into the pile of rags, his arms tucked close to his chest. He remembered the moment that he had first emerged into the world, sodden and bloody and screaming. With his first gulps of air, he had understood his own hideousness. The hands that pulled him forth had gripped loosely, seeming to fear what he might be. Then he had been laid into arms which only shuddered, ready to drop him from their grasp, and did not hold him close.

§

Through his childhood, Emily Hallingham had been ever-present in her absence. Her pious portrait hung upon the main wall of

Harcourt Hall's long gallery. As a boy, Arthur had never liked to pass by the gallery door, certain as he was that her eyes looked upon him in accusation. He had been the death of her.

God-fearing soul as she was, and you bringing on such a nervous condition in her... such a look you had, when you came into this world! What a look of fury, and of devilish intent!

Each night he had tiptoed past the gallery door on his way to bed, dust beneath his bare feet, and glimpsed her through the darkness. Once, dared by his brother, he trod closer to look her fully in the face. She was tall, regal, clad in a dress which fell to the floor in heavy folds. She was black-haired, like Edward and Harmony, with fine eyes and an upright bearing. Close-to, she did not immediately appear to him so frightening as he had always thought her. In fact, it seemed that she looked down upon him with a forgiving tenderness, as if she had been hoping that he might pay her a visit. But then the moment passed, and insidious as woodworm, the truth began to gnaw at him once again.

Oh, Master Arthur. What sorrow you brought into this house. What sorrow you brought upon us all.

§

Shelo came at last in the night, when a salt wind from the ocean was howling through the streets and rattling the roof of the attic. The jars on the shelves clinked quietly together, and the extinguished lamp swung to and fro. A shadow appeared in the doorway. Believing that he was still asleep, Arthur sat up and watched it creep across the wall. It came nearer, until it was stood over the bed. He clasped the blanket to his chest, staring blearily upwards through the dark.

And then he smelled it. No dream could carry so powerful an odour, of rich earth, of spices, of forest rain. Shelo emerged into the dim attic, and Arthur scrambled backwards, barely able to believe the sight before him.

Every visible inch of the man's skin was inked with intricate lines, from his feet to his fingertips, ascending his neck and covering his entire face. His lips and eyes stood out startlingly from the elaborate mask. It looked as if a creeping weed had sprouted from his navel and grown unhindered, its tendrils winding around each part of him. His oiled hair hung thick and heavy, each limb sturdy as a young tree.

Arthur got to his feet. He felt that he might break down and weep. His sight splintered, and he turned away, shamed.

But Shelo drew close, examining Arthur first from one side, then the other. He sniffed at him, then reached out a rough hand to take him by the chin. He tilted Arthur's face back, staring at it intently.

"You are just right," said Shelo quietly. It felt wrong that this outlandish being should speak in a familiar tongue. His voice was low and resonant, with an untraceable accent. He formed each word carefully, with his whole mouth, as though spitting out bones. His eyes, which moved deep in his face like beetles burrowing into dead wood, were the most appalling things that Arthur had ever seen. "The time is just right. Now, the old things can be burned away and cast aside."

His hand lingered on the side of Arthur's face before letting go, and Arthur fought the urge to rest his head against the man's shoulder. His body pulled him back, stiff with horror. Close-to, Shelo's familiar scent had a decayed, putrid edge. It was almost overpowering.

"What do you make of me?" asked Shelo. They were stood inches apart, not quite forehead-to-forehead. Arthur was thrown back to the moment that the *Head of Mary* had come within sight of the new continent. The sense of a looming hugeness close at hand, of unexplored wilds, of a land lying in wait. "Speak."

"I…" He swallowed, and tried again. "I have heard…"

When Shelo showed his teeth, Arthur saw that they were pointed at the tips. "Do not believe any tale you hear," he said.

Arthur remembered the two magnets that had rushed together across the table to collide with such force. Inside his chest, a surge of hope was matched by a cold wave of terror. Tentatively, he raised his gaze to meet Shelo's.

Nobody had ever looked at him as the man with the inked skin was looking at him now. There was ravenous hunger in it, and triumph, and knowingness. And Arthur was utterly sure that Shelo *saw*. His eyes had pierced through skin and flesh to the secret things beneath. There was no hiding. The sensation of nakedness was unbearable.

"I saw you from across the sea," said Shelo. "I called you to myself. Do you believe me, Arthur?"

He was visited by the strange thrilling notion that the tide which carried him had flowed at Shelo's bidding, that the wind which blew in the *Mary*'s sails had been Shelo's breath. It was not possible. And yet, helpless before the man's will as a sapling before a gale, Arthur knew he had only to overcome his unbelief.

"I came so far," he whispered.

"I know," said Shelo. His lip curled. "I know. I have been waiting."

He drew a small flat knife from his belt, and Arthur flinched back. But then he found that the blade was being proffered to him, handle first, with an inclination of Shelo's great head.

"Now, go and clean yourself, Arthur, and cut off your hair and beard. We can talk of nothing while you still carry the stench of that ship."

5

Beneath the World

When he awoke, the storm outside the cave had passed, and Shelo was gone. Water trickled in thin rivulets down the face of the cliff to the bottom of the valley. All was calm and still. It was as if the earthquake, the deafening thunder, the torrents of rain, had never been. His feet were whole and healed.

Recalling why he was alone, he felt a faint hope that Flora might have come crawling back in the night, forgiving all. Against his former reasoning, there came the selfish thought that he did not want her gone.

But there was no sign of her. It was so unlike her to actually follow through on a threat that he spent some time tramping around the soft grass at the edge of the lake, calling tentatively for her. He knew where she would have headed, but wounded as she was, she could not have got far. He half-expected to find her curled at the base of a tree, averting her stubborn gaze, ready to rise and follow him again once his back was turned.

The night's rain had washed away her footprints. At the lip of the lake, Arthur crouched and dipped his hands, splashing cool water over his face and hair. A blackbird sung in a nearby tree. He could not believe that it had been mere hours since he and Shelo had tumbled into the depths, locked together in their fury. His memory of the previous night was somewhat hazy. Shelo, he knew, had risen from the waters. They had spoken together.

As his head cleared, he thought that the wind carried with it the distant sound of voices. It struck him with alarm that Flora might not have disappeared through her own volition. They had evaded Barber's men for more than ten days, but the storm could have driven them to seek shelter in the valley. There was no sign of a struggle, and nor could Arthur remember hearing one, but he still felt ill at ease. If they had come for her, she would not have been able to run away.

Without his boots, which had been sunk in the lake along with Shelo, he was similarly helpless. Torn, he padded across the wet grass, leaves clinging to his heels. Reeds brushed the length of his legs. "Flora!" he called, as loudly as he dared. "*Flora!*" He had nothing else besides her name. He did not know how to form even the thinnest of apologies.

The voices, unmistakably male, grew louder. Somebody was approaching from the far side of the opposite bank, below the line of trees. He knew instantly that he did not have time to make it back to the cave, and dived instead for the shelter of the long reeds. A startled bullfrog shot into the water. Arthur wavered, ankle-deep in thick mud, and watched as two men topped the rise not far away.

It was Ripstone and Harpey. They both appeared past exhaustion, their feet dragging, their faces unshaven. They were plainly so dispirited that Arthur felt relief slow the rhythm of his breathing. They did not look like men who knew that their quarry was near. When they made it to the edge of the water, Ripstone sank down onto the grass, his head in his hands, diminutive frame hunched. Harpey, the more alert of the two, cast a wary eye over their surroundings.

They were snapping at one another, though Arthur could not make out their exact words. He willed Flora to run, to leave these weaker creatures in the dust. Ripstone, whose shirt was crisp with dried sweat, shuffled forward on his knees and stuck his head into the lake like a thirsty dog. Harpey sniffed the air, then spied the cave in the cliff-side above their heads.

He indicated this to Ripstone, and after some discussion, began to climb the rise towards the cave. In his companion's absence, Ripstone cast of his clothes, flinging them down into a pile and tugging off his boots before plunging headfirst into the lake.

For a moment, Arthur felt only horror at the prospect of a swimmer disturbing Shelo's grave. But then he recalled, with a tremor of unease, that Shelo's body no longer lay in the lake. It had risen from the water and come to him in the night, made of ashes, made of smoke. And then, as though some mind outside of his own had drawn his attention that way, he noticed Ripstone's boots, lying unattended by the side of the lake.

The swimmer had vanished underwater. Arthur knew that he had only moments, and tore himself out of the mud. In the time before Ripstone surfaced, he had covered the stretch of marshy ground and tugged the abandoned boots onto his feet. Sticky mud coated his hands.

"HALLINGHAM!"

The howl was Ripstone's. He was treading water near the centre of the lake, splashing in his panic. Before Arthur had even made it back into the reeds again, Harpey had emerged from the cave, and fired his pistol wildly into the air.

"*We'll have you!*" bawled the outlaw.

Arthur did not look back. He was not made for speed, with his awkward body, his too-long limbs. But now, terror drove him. Days ago, many miles from here, he had felt the shock of twin-fired shots rattling his bones. He knew that neither man would hesitate to aim at his retreating back.

Ripstone's parting cry echoed through the woods behind him.

"*We'll have you! Murderer!*"

§

Arthur ran for hours. In the woods, the sound of his tearing breath and uneven feet sent birds screeching for the canopy. He tripped on logs and fell to his knees. Ripstone's boots were far too small.

Shelo did not come for him until nightfall, when he had finally sunk down against the wide trunk of a saman tree. He knew that his pursuers would not rest, but he could go no further. When the sun dipped behind the flat-topped mountains, the tree's broad fronds folded in upon themselves. *Like a tired old man closing his eyes to sleep,* Lucas had written, beneath an ink-line drawing of its wispy blossoms. Arthur's head drooped.

Shelo came for him as the first stars appeared, cut like crystals into the clear sky above the canopy. Standing some yards away, he leaned against a tree. The breeze stirred in his mane of hair. He dripped lake water into the fallen leaves.

"Sleeping again, Arthur?" he asked softly.

Arthur stirred. The night lay thick as velvet. All around them, a soft chorus of amphibian calls was growing ever louder. "I came a long way."

Shelo turned his gaze outwards, towards the mountains. "They are coming for you, Arthur. They will not let him go unavenged."

"What do I do?" Arthur begged. "Please, Shelo, help me! I can't outrun them for long…" He squinted fearfully between the trees, half-expecting a barefoot and furious Ripstone to come crashing through the undergrowth. "Tell me what to do!"

"Follow the fish without eyes in the dark river beneath the world," said Shelo.

Arthur's stomach cramped with hunger, and he wrapped his arms around his torso. Anger flared in him, only to be swamped by resignation. He did not understand. But then, Shelo had so rarely required him to.

"Is it far?" he asked groggily.

"Across my broken back," said Shelo, "to where my heart is buried."

From nowhere, he was holding out a lamp, casting tangled shadows across the ground. It burned with a blue flame, like the light that had hung from their wagon – like the light that shone from Sam's attic, or the heavenly glow that had descended upon the *Head of Mary*, so many moons ago. In silence, and without looking back at Arthur, Shelo set off at a rapid walk.

Not wishing to be left behind, Arthur scrambled to his feet and followed after as quickly as he could. The forest was full of howls and deafening screeches, unseen creatures scurrying near his feet and in the branches above his head. He hoped that Flora had not come this way. He did not like to think of her alone in the darkness, fleeing those in whose shadow she had lived all her years. He hoped that she had made it somewhere bright and safe.

Shelo did not seem willing to slow his pace, or to make any further talk. His lamp drew entranced insects, their flapping wings huge in silhouette. He moved with complete surety. Arthur's own feet faltered. His sight became hazy. Shelo's light bobbed on ahead, growing ever more distant.

§

Arthur lost sight of his guide. He found himself at the edge of the trees, where a wide and sluggish river wound between its banks like a sun-dazed snake. Swarms of phosphorescent insects hung low over the water and flickered amongst the reeds. The horned heads of water-lizards sent ripples across the surface.

He clambered across a mass of tree roots, which dipped their tapered points into the river. A round moon was drawn onto the sky like a circle on a chalkboard, and by its light, Arthur could make out a little cluster of wooden dwellings. A platform of bound bamboo poles had been extended out into the water, and a few hollowed canoes drifted beneath it. Arthur hesitated on the brink of running. He had heard of shelter and sustenance being offered to travellers at such places.

Despite the late hour, a lantern was still burning in the outermost hut. An elderly Spaniard in monk's robes came to the door before Arthur had even summoned the courage to knock, and looked at him through the dark. For the briefest of moments Arthur saw himself as he must appear to this stranger: a bent-backed and wild-haired madman, eyes reflecting the innumerable darting lights.

The old monk addressed him in Spanish, but Arthur shook his head. The man smacked his lips and searched the air, then tried, "*Francais?* English?"

Arthur nodded emphatically, relieved. He mimed cupping water in his hands, raising it to his lips. The Spaniard nodded, and beckoned him inwards.

The room inside was clean and sparsely furnished, with nothing but a hammock slung between the walls and a stack of pots in the corner. From one of these, the monk poured Arthur a cup of water, and from another, brought him fish and cassava bread and plantain strips. He ate these ravenously, cramming them into his mouth with his bare hands.

At Harcourt Hall he had sat at a long table lit by chandeliers, with place settings of finest silver.

He had not filled his stomach since leaving Robert's farm, nearly two days ago. When he was finally sated, he handed the water cup back to the monk, wiping his mouth on his sleeve. He felt an untraceable trace of shame.

The monk began to speak in his own tongue, his meaning clear as he indicated the hammock. He nodded encouragingly. Arthur looked at it, sorely tempted.

As he glanced behind to where the rest of the little settlement lay sleeping, he realised that the monk was now looking him over intently. The old man seemed to be trawling the air for language. "*Cómo digo...?* You know...man?" He indicated a height several inches beneath Arthur's own. "Small man."

Arthur's heart jumped fearfully, and the prospect of a night beneath a real roof grew suddenly dim.

"He come, in day. He ask..." The monk indicated Arthur. "Tall, English, the hair of red..."

"I do not know him," said Arthur. He took a step backwards. Ripstone and Harpey must have split up, the former travelling at speed up the valley and along the riverbank. He had evaded the outlaw by a matter of hours. "Listen. I do not know him. If he comes again..." He pointed to himself, and shook his head rapidly. "You did not see me. Understand? You did not..."

The monk watched him carefully. Whether or not he had understood Arthur's words, he could not have mistaken his guest's sudden air of panic. He held up his hands, and nodded.

Arthur fled, for all the world as though Benjamin Barber's blood still stained his hands.

§

He disappeared into the trees once more, and ran until he was unconscious on his feet. He did not recall closing his eyes, nor crumpling into the thick undergrowth as sleep took hold. His

59

mind did not rest, but took him back to the twin gunshots which had rattled his very bones, and then he was holding Flora in his arms, powerless as her blood soaked the ground.

"Arthur," she said. "Arthur, help me." Her hands were searching her chest, baffled.

His shirt grew wet with her blood.

He could find no words to comfort her. His mouth gaped uselessly, and his body trembled. Her life leaked away into the grass, and with a shuddering shock, he awoke.

He was so deep amidst the towering trees that he could barely tell whether it was yet daylight. It came to him that, in his terror and exhaustion, he must have staggered far further than he had thought. He appeared to be in the heart of an entirely new country. Around him, the dense greenery seemed to breathe the heavy air. It creaked and groaned as if growing by the second.

Arthur realised that fine tendrils were wrapped around his limbs. He had fallen asleep against the bole of a tree, amidst its twisted roots, and a green creeper now bound him to the wood. With a yell, he wrenched himself free, and staggered upright. He was certain that the snapped strands of creeper caressed him like fingers before letting go.

He brushed himself off, unable to get rid of the crawling sensation that still covered his skin. A spider the size of a kitten picked its way across a log near his feet. A dragonfly slipped on the waxy rim of a jug-shaped plant, and fell in with a splash. Arthur had the impression of a hundred thousand lives all crammed in a space too small to hold them, bursting out, spilling over, unfolding on each other with predatory intent.

"*Shelo!*" he bellowed into the writhing greenery, forgetting for a moment all human peril. He kicked the ground with his too-small boots, uprooting a patch of bloated orange fungi. "*Where are you taking me, curse you?*"

There was no reply. A rustling in a nearby tree turned out to be a small monkey, gnawing at something held between its paws, unperturbed by Arthur's outburst. He had seen similar creatures in the African port, where they were sometimes trained for the entertainment of passers-by, or bought as curiosities for the wives and children of wealthy tradesmen. This one was buff-coloured, with a cap of black fur and pointed teeth. It finally stuffed the remainder of its meal into its cheek, which bulged grotesquely.

It began to climb through a web of creepers, and Arthur, lacking any more promising lead, followed after. The monkey emitted a chattering cry that seemed far too loud for its size, and was soon rewarded by an answering cacophony. Broken sunlight illuminated the clouds of moisture which hung in the uppermost branches of a towering fig tree.

Arthur recognised the bundles of fruit, though they were smaller and greener than those that his father, Jonas Hallingham, had imported from Italy. On every branch the miniature monkeys hung tenaciously, and crammed their mouths with unripe figs. The animals seemed entirely unafraid of him, and it occurred to Arthur that they had never laid eyes on a human being before. They did not dart back even when he approached the tree, and reached up to take the fruit for himself.

He crouched against the trunk, and ate the way they did, crushing the food in his fists and pushing it greedily into his mouth. Arthur knelt to drink from a clear stream that ran across the tree's spreading roots, cupping water in his hands and dousing his body as best he could. He was sweating copiously in the close, clammy air.

Everything was bathed in a low hum, tiny insects darting to and fro. Above him, green leaves stirred, and he lay back to stare up into the dappled canopy. Lucas, he suspected, had not made it this far south, this deep into the equinoctial forests. It was a shame. So impressed was he with nature's every working, with even the most mundane of organisms, he would surely have given his right hand for the sight of wonders such as these.

§

The noise of the monkeys, and of the water, was drowned out after a time by shrill bird-calls. Following the line of the stream, Arthur found that these grew ever louder, though he could see no sign of any birds. The stream widened, and he shuffled cautiously down a slope into a shadowed dip. Here, broad fungus shelves spiraled up the tree-trunks, and an endless centipede slithered across his foot. The stream, he noticed, had been joined by another line of water trickling down from the opposite slope.

A black bird flapped out of nowhere, and Arthur ducked, cursing. He turned his head towards the source of the now-deafening bird cries. To his right he could see what he had taken for a solid face of rock, perhaps all of fifty feet high, bursting with ferns and sapling trees and hanging strands of creeper. But then another bird shot out from behind the greenery, followed by at least a dozen others, and he realised he was stood before the mouth of a great cave.

The throats of the birds yawned pink as they snapped at insects. The stream, now a narrow river, flowed down the slope and vanished beneath the greenery into the darkness. Arthur balanced along the stones at its edge, his heart now beating harder. He could hear nothing above the din of the birds, but he suspected that the water grew yet wider and deeper beneath the ground.

He felt empty of courage, and yet had little choice. He tore a branch from a nearby tree which was dripping red resin, then crouched a little way from the cave mouth, searching out handfuls of dry twigs and leaves. Shelo had shown him how to do this, many weeks ago, on the long road across the grasslands. It had been easier there, where the sun baked the last drops of moisture from everything.

Here it took him several hours, with a selection of smooth stones and many hand-blistering failures, to achieve the same effect. Finally the kindling caught, and Arthur held the end of his stick grimly to it until the resin flamed. He held his makeshift torch aloft, and brushed back the curtain of creepers with a violently shaking arm.

"Shelo!" he called, into the blackness beyond. The echo was lost in the screeching of the birds, the panicked flapping of their wings. "Are you down here? Are you coming for me?"

A sudden gust of wind at his back threatened to extinguish his torch, and he stumbled forward, pressing his shirt sleeve against his nose. The cave was filled with a cloying reek. The thin flame illuminated birds crammed together in every ledge and cranny. Their droppings coated the walls and the sticky ground. Half-excluded from the daylight, the greenery persisted some way inside, hanging in damp fronds, growing ever paler and sicklier.

The hoarse din of the birds did not begin to fade until Arthur was almost beyond the reach of the natural light. He could no longer hold his torch up above his head, but was forced to lower it, taking care over each step. The rocks were slippery with a sheen of water and silvery mould. The bones of rats and fallen fledglings crunched underfoot.

Arthur tried reaching out his hands to find his bearings, but his body recoiled in disgust from everything it touched. Stagnant droplets landed in his hair and on his face. The torch sputtered, its rust-coloured flame growing fainter, and he clenched his jaw against the urge to turn back. Beside him, the river gathered speed.

He began to follow its murmuring sound, and as the cave grew narrower, the smoke from his torch obscured what little vision he had.

He began to imagine that he glimpsed daubings on the walls around and above him, blood-red lines which arched across the damp stone. And then, with creeping certainty, he realised that there were pale shapes in the water below. They darted along with the current in the rushing river, the banished phantoms of fish. He crouched down, compelled by horror, and in the little light that remained saw them all too plainly. Their smooth white snouts forged forwards into the blackness, their ghost fins trailing. They had no eyes.

A little way ahead, the roof of the cave dipped so low that the only way forward was in the river itself. It flowed into a tunnel just a few inches higher than its glassy surface, undulating sideways. The shape of this channel, just wide enough and deep enough for a man, was illuminated in front of Arthur for a few moments before his torch finally flickered out.

In the pitch dark, he rested his chin on his chest, and drew a deep, pained breath. He clutched at his knees, rocking back and forth. He whined at Shelo's cruelty.

It was no use going in clothed. Slowly, Arthur stripped off each of his garments, as he had seen Ripstone do on the shore of the lake. He laid his things in a careful pile, though he knew that he would not be coming back for them. Neither would they be found here, so far beneath the earth.

Naked, he felt his way to the river's edge. He whimpered, the sharp rocks painful to his hands and soles. When he found the water, he lowered himself in, feet, legs, waist, shuddering and gasping. Fleetingly, he recollected a picture hung in his father's study which had once terrified and fascinated him, depicting a river in a cavern just like this one, beside which departed men knelt to drink. Harmony had picked out the words below, reading them aloud. *Into the Lethe, into the river of forgetting go I, where all my life in the world is washed away...*

§

Chest, shoulders, head. The river wrapped him in its insistent chill.

He drifted face-down, half-submerged, a white body amidst white bodies. The blind fish brushed against his limbs. Together, they were washed beneath the world, carried on a swift current. He raised his mouth above the surface to swallow air, and scraped his head against the overhanging rock.

Under the water, he opened his eyes. At first he could see nothing, but he blinked stubbornly, and thought he saw his own white hands. They looked as translucent as the tiny bodies in Slitwire Sam's jars. He gasped for air again. The mouths of the blind fish turned downwards at the corners, an angered look.

Arthur did not know how long he was in the water below the world. He imagined the sun rising and sinking in his absence, night following day with ever-increasing rapidity as he drifted. His pulse slowed. It came to him that he could be on the brink of forgetting, of relinquishing all that he was. This was what he had crossed the ocean for, after all.

§

By the time he emerged into the languid light of a dappled pool, his senses were all dulled. Slowly, he flipped over onto his back. The blind fish darted fearfully back towards the shadows.

Weeping branches and delicate ferns trailed in the water. Above the moss-covered rocks where the water gushed towards the daylight, a woman sat washing her long black hair. She did not scream at the sight of Arthur, nor leap to her feet, nor show even the slightest sign of surprise. She lowered her comb, and gravely watched him float nearer.

Conscious now of himself and ashamed, Arthur let his body sink low, so that only his hair and eyes were visible. They looked at one another. She was a native, perhaps some years older than him, though it was difficult to be sure. Her brows were knotted with weariness. She was beautiful, still. Arthur lifted his mouth above the surface.

"Shelo?" he breathed, and all the darkness he had swallowed below the earth came spilling out with the name.

The woman above the rocks tugged a shawl around her bare shoulders. She did not say a word. She rose with heavy resignation, as though a bell had tolled the end of her time, and beckoned him from the water.

6

Tide of Blood

In Sam's tin bathtub, Arthur wiped away months of filth. So much did it pain him, he might have been ridding himself of his own skin. The long scabs on his chest stung; lice wriggled in the brown water. To see his body so very white again made him uneasy, and he hurried at it, scrubbing his limbs raw.

He remembered hot water being poured down his back in his own chamber at Harcourt Hall, steam rising to fog the windows that looked out across windswept lawns. He remembered how the warmth of it had never quite seemed to penetrate his skin.

Clothed again, in too-large garments belonging to Shelo, he stood nervously before a mirror and took the knife to his wet hair. He hacked away handfuls of the rust-coloured mop, and the man in the mirror began to look a little more familiar. He cut away the tangles of his beard, and lathered his face with soap. As he scraped the flat knife along his cheeks, Arthur Hallingham emerged before him: gaunter, sicker-looking than he'd ever appeared before, but Arthur nonetheless. What was the youngest son of an illustrious line doing, so poorly clothed amidst the grime of Sam's dwelling, hunched over a cracked mirror?

Unable to take his eyes from the sight of his own bare face, he cut off his nails and smoothed his remaining hair back with water. He was astonished at how young he suddenly appeared, and curiously, how like his father. He had seen Jonas Hallingham wear the same look that now stared back at him from the mirror.

Can it really be me, here in this body? Can it be that I have seen what this body has seen, done all that it has done?

§

"There is something else, Arthur," said Shelo.

He loomed over Arthur's world. When he lit the blue lamp in the attic window, his great shadow threw the whole room into darkness. Words dripped from his mouth like water from the roof of a cave. "You must burn the clothes that you wore across the sea, and also, that which you have carried from your own country. You know what I am speaking of."

Arthur had kept Lucas's notes with their African addresses folded inside the bundle of discarded clothing. Unopened though they were, and irrelevant now, he baulked at the thought of losing them. He turned them over in his hands when Shelo was not looking. He did not know what to do.

Daily, he looked out from the attic across the rooftops, and down to the white sails in the harbour. The weak sun played upon the water, blurring everything. When Sam's sour wife called him downstairs, Arthur was not at all surprised to find that Silas had come again, cap in his hands and resolve upon his face.

"Your lordship," he said. "I know now the day and the hour that the ship of which I spoke intends to sail." He appeared somewhat taken aback at the sight of Arthur washed and shaved. "They are still in need of hands. Will you not come?"

"Silas…" began Arthur, uncertainly.

"Listen to me," said Silas. There was a note of pleading in his voice. "I said I would not leave you, but I know only one means of makin' my way in this world. I must take another commission."

For a moment, it seemed possible. Arthur imagined himself on a new journey, boards once more beneath his feet, the ocean stretching out on every side. He smelled salt. Silas would not leave him, and they would come always to distant, nameless shores. His beard would grow long again, and his body would be broken by labour. After years in the endless emptiness, perhaps, he might forget his own name.

Then, even as he pictured it, he saw the old sailor's eyes move from his face to something over his shoulder. Arthur turned. In the doorway stood six feet of muscle and ink, barefoot and coal-eyed. Shelo stood over them like the Angel of Death, and Silas, veteran of a hundred voyages and as many unworldly marvels, turned pale.

Shelo picked a tooth lazily, then lowered his eyelids. For the first time, Arthur saw that these too were inked, bearing the images of two wide-open eyes.

The ink eyes flickered, then blinked shut as Shelo's real eyes fixed on Silas, who seemed to be summoning his courage. He tore his gaze from the apparition in the doorway and turned to Arthur again, deliberately addressing him as if he were the only person in the room. "Your lordship, the *Justice* sails ten days from now, at sunrise. It won't be like the *Mary* this time, I swear it."

Shelo advanced slowly towards them. Arthur could not speak.

"Old man," intoned Shelo. His voice was deep and terrible. "How many crossings have you made upon the tide of blood that washes here from Africa?" His mere gaze might have peeled back the skin from the sailor's skull. "Did you really think that by acting in kindness towards one soul, you could redeem all your years of wickedness?"

Silas's league-long face remained impassive. But he drew slowly back, like a tortoise shrinking its neck into its shell. He appeared suddenly ancient and fragile.

"On the road leading down to the harbour," he muttered to Arthur. "I'll wait, the hour before the *Justice* sails." He backed towards the door, and Arthur became faintly aware of a rising panic in his throat. "If I do not see you there, I shall be on that ship... and trouble you no more."

On a stove in the back room, Sam's wife brewed juniper with milk and black cohosh. The poisonous fumes killed the flies which landed on the sharp instruments upon the wall, buzzing around the bloodied sheets piled in the corner. Sam and Shelo constantly had their heads together, stripping bark from cotton roots, powdering dried tansy blooms. Shelo leafed through the pages of yellowing books, measuring out ingredients with utmost care. He brought bundles of herbs and jars of liquid to the attic, and by lamplight in the evenings, dissected what appeared to be small rodents.

Each night, Arthur slept at Shelo's feet like a dog, Lucas's letters still tucked beneath his pillow. His rest was uneasy, interrupted by the women who knocked upon the door downstairs. Shelo slept with his ink-eyes wide open, staring up at the attic ceiling. He murmured sporadically, kicking out at intervals and waking Arthur each time. Night after night, Arthur came to with a hazy memory of having seen Shelo sat watchfully over him. Then, he awoke with perfect clarity past the midnight hour to find Shelo leaning over him in the dark.

"Get up, Arthur. Put your boots on, and come with me."

They left Sam's by the back door, and Arthur followed Shelo down a series of twisting alleyways. Shelo's feet fell silent as snow. A dog started towards them, barking fiercely, but drew back when it caught Shelo's scent. It cowered and whined, its eyes rolling back.

The bloated corpse of the great fish was still rotting on the beach, and the night wind carried the flesh-stench to Arthur's nostrils, almost disguising the reek from the cargo ships. Waves broke rhythmically against creaking timbers. He recoiled, covering his mouth with his sleeve as he caught sight of the *Head of Mary* among the moored boats. Its stained sails fluttered in the moonlight.

"Shelo…" he began, helplessly. They were descending towards a cluster of barns built near the water.

Shelo looked back over his shoulder. A lantern burned weakly on a pole nearby, and the foamy sea slopped against the stones of the harbour. He said nothing, but beckoned forcefully to Arthur, who followed him as though there were no help for it.

He became aware of a murmuring which was not coming from the sea below, but from within the nearest barn. He caught glimpses of movement between the slats, and for a moment thought of livestock – cattle, perhaps, or sheep. The truth dawned upon him with slow horror. Shelo had already taken his flat knife to work upon the thick padlock at the barn doors.

"Shelo," began Arthur weakly, "I cannot…"

"Quiet." The lock rattled. Shelo rubbed something into it, and Arthur thought he heard a slow metallic *click* from within. He hung back, terrified.

A guardsman, slouched beside the wall of the barn opposite, grunted in his sleep. Shelo pulled back the door a crack, then slipped inside without a backward glance. Arthur followed after, his entire body in revolt.

When he had descended into the hold of the *Head of Mary*, the air had been heavy and thick with heat. The cold of the night on the brink of the New World cast the scene within the barn in a different hue. Moonlight shone through the slats onto five hundred bare skins, flayed and scarred and dull with sickness. Their breath clouded the air. Many of them were shivering, rattling the chains upon their hands and feet. They were packed together in cattle pens, old men and young, women with wailing babies at their breasts, blank-faced children.

71

There was a low murmuring as those nearest the door caught sight of Arthur and Shelo. One or two shook their neighbours and pointed, but most simply gazed, beyond all surprise or curiosity. Arthur let out an involuntary groan. *"Let's go, Shelo,"* he pleaded. *"Please, I can't..."*

Shelo was still as stone in the moonlight, bare feet planted on the filthy floor. When he finally moved forward in the darkness, Arthur saw him reach out to touch the wrists of the nearest men. It was hard to tell what had happened, but moments later there were exclamations of surprise, the clink of chains falling to the ground.

Shelo bent to see to their ankles, and then he was wrenching back the fence that held them in. Before Arthur was even certain of what he was seeing, slender figures were slipping past him and out of the barn door into the night.

"The guard!" he protested weakly. The noise was rising as more and more of the bound Africans pushed forward towards Shelo, wrists outstretched, suddenly animate in their desperation. Some trampled their neighbours in their haste, while others held out their children and their sick, begging in many different tongues. Arthur's head was whirling.

Shelo would not be distracted from his task until a cry was suddenly taken up by the guard outside, who had at last awoken. A light flared as he lit a torch, and he could be heard hollering indistinctly. The crowd in the cattle stalls flinched back, and Shelo turned his inked head.

He had not freed many, but those who had made it outside were already causing a commotion. Hurried footsteps suggested that the night guard's calls had summoned reinforcements from the town above. Without hesitation, and without glancing back at those who remained in their chains, Shelo grabbed Arthur by the arm and dragged him out of the door.

They crouched against the back wall of the barn, breathless in the long grass. Below them the rocks dropped away sharply to the sea, and behind them the harbour grew bright with torchlight.

"You saw them?"

"Yessir, ten or twelve at the least! Loose of their bonds and running hard!"

The guardsmen cursed and began to spread out among the buildings. Arthur heard a rustling in a clump of grass nearby, and saw one of the freed women limping away as fast as her feet would carry her. Her shaven head was ragged in the moonlight.

Shelo did not watch her as she ran. Nor did he search the night for signs of the others he had set loose. His eyes were fixed instead upon Arthur.

"Do you trust me?" asked Shelo quietly.

A powerful and profound emotion rose in Arthur's throat. He could not for the life of him have told whether it was adoration or deep distress.

"Do you promise not to turn to the right or left?" The light of the torches flickered between the buildings, and Shelo's breath clouded on the crisp night air. The bulk of him obscured the moon. He was not to be denied. "Not to leave me, or to love any other?"

Helplessly, Arthur looked up into Shelo's eyes.

"*I need you with me, Arthur,*" whispered the inked man, into the shell of his ear. "*I am going to burn down this whole order of things. Now that you are here.*"

§

He rid himself of Lucas's letters in the alley behind Sam's establishment, on the night before the *Justice* was to sail. Sam's wife set a fire there for some of the dirtied linen, and when she had gone inside Arthur cast in the stinking clothes he had worn aboard the *Mary*. They caught quickly, and Arthur crouched against the wall, turning the letters over and over in his hands.

Though Shelo was not watching, he knew that he was seen. He let the fire lick at the edges of the envelopes, then, in distress, blew it out again. To lose these scraps of paper would be to sever the last remaining cord that bound him to Harcourt Hall. To the possibility of return.

A little way down the cliff, he could hear gulls crying plaintively. Arthur dropped the letters into the fire in a single movement, almost catching his sleeve as well, and turned away before he could see them crumble to ash. The fire sputtered and smoked itself into the ground.

Shelo was absent from the attic that night, attending to some solitary business. Sam climbed the stairs to add two new jars to his collection, and stood back to admire the way they sat upon the shelf. The blue lamp swung to and fro, and Arthur stirred on his pile of rags.

"He ain't what you think him," said Sam. He scratched his backside, and laughed softly. "No kind of hero. Nobody knows who he is, nor what skin he has beneath all that ink, save Shelo himself. They say he crawled on his belly out of the forests deep in Spanish country, like a serpent."

Arthur curled his arms around his knees.

"He showed up on my doorstep one night," said Sam, "and told me he wanted to learn my trade. That creature, in my trade!" He laughed again, and shook his head.

The dim light reflected from the surfaces of the jars, and cast a greenish glow across Sam's face. "My services ain't talk for delicate ears like yours, mister. But he has been so very eager to assist."

Sam's fatly cherubic features had taken on a sly look.

Later, Arthur dreamed that Shelo returned, dripping with rain, oiled hair glistening with lights like stars. When he peeled away his wet shirt, the skin beneath writhed with living lines. They coiled around him, eyes and teeth and tails flickering between the tendrils. On the left-hand side of his ribcage, a black bloom unfolded its dead petals, opening up across his chest like a wound.

Shelo caught Arthur looking, and he bared his pointed teeth in a grin.

"I cut the heart out of me," he intoned, "and locked it inside a tree. Do you believe me, Arthur?"

The dream faded into dull confusion. Arthur whined and shivered in his sleep.

Shelo was still not there when he awoke, before dawn. He pulled on his boots quickly, and splashed water on his face. He had a sense that he was acting in disobedience merely by going to bid Silas farewell.

He left Sam's establishment by the back door, and clambered over the fence into the alleyway. An infant screeched in a nearby house, and a dog barked savagely. Though it was early, Arthur could hear two men scrapping just around the corner, perhaps still intoxicated from the night before. He gave them a wide berth, taking the path in the opposite direction and then doubling back down the hill towards the harbour.

It was a still morning, and the first streaks of light were just beginning to appear in the sky to the east. The sea was silver, then pale peach, then scarlet as the glowing orb of the sun appeared at the horizon. A bright planet hung low in the sky, ringed in red among the last faint stars.

He waited for Silas on the broad road that dropped down towards the harbour, at a point on the hill which gave him a clear view in all directions. He could see the *Justice* in the water below, its clean sails rippling. Men busied themselves about it, loading crates of cargo and loosening ropes. Arthur stared up the cliff towards the settlement, then down towards the water, but there was no sign of the sailor.

The sky grew ever lighter, and a faint salt breeze lifted Arthur's hair. And still Silas did not come. Disappointment settled crushingly on him.

The sun climbed slowly up out of the sea, and he continued to wait, gnawing his nails down to the quick. At first, when he caught the smell of smoke on the breeze, he thought it was a cooking fire from a nearby house. He ignored it until it began to grow persistently stronger, catching in the back of his throat. Dimly, from the direction in which he had come, he heard the beginnings of a commotion.

He turned, and saw a thick spiral of smoke rising into the dawn sky, a faint glow amidst the houses. It could have been any building in the straggling cluster that covered the hill. But Arthur's heart plummeted, and he simply knew.

By the time he had run back from the shore, the front of Sam's establishment was charred beyond recognition. The flames still had a hold, devouring the timber skeleton of the upper floors and licking at the scattered debris. Arthur gaped wordlessly.

A crowd had gathered in the street, chiefly composed of girls from the surrounding houses in their scant nightclothes. They crowed and pointed, barefoot and unselfconscious. A few of their better-dressed customers were attempting to slip away unnoticed, tucking in their shirts and straightening their hats. Nobody, it seemed, had made any move to throw water on the flames, or to run for help.

Sam's wife knelt among the wreckage in her yellowing night-gown. When she caught sight of Arthur, her eyes bulged, and she screamed incoherently.

Sam was hunched before what had once been the doorway, his hair grey with ash. He had not had time to dress himself, and his stout legs protruded beneath his nightshirt. He turned at his wife's cry, and his face grew as thunderous as hers. Before Arthur could back away, he had strode across and seized him by the collar, spittle flying as he raged.

"*You did this! You and that witch...*"

"I wasn't here!" cried Arthur. He wriggled as Sam's thick fingers pressed against his throat. "Let go, I wasn't..."

"Wherever you come from," snarled Sam, "wherever you *crawled* from, you might return there!"

The back of Arthur's head cracked against the wall, and his vision blurred. He thought he saw above him the shadow of a man, flickering in and out of view in the midst of the billowing flames. Smoke rose all around the towering figure, which stood where there was no longer any floor to stand upon. Its eyes glowed like embers.

Slowly, unmistakably, the shade of Shelo looked into Arthur, and raised a finger to his lips.

Strengthened by terror, Arthur wrenched himself from Sam's grip, and staggered away from the crowd. Smoke seemed to have filled his head as well as his lungs, and he could not think clearly. The panic that had been rising in him for days was released in full force. And he knew, with terrible certainty, what he ought to have done.

§

He came back to the harbour too late, as he had known he would, in time to see the *Justice* hauling up her anchor and moving out towards the sunrise. The dawn had turned to brightest gold now, streaks of mist hanging about the prow and in the ship's spotless sails. It was

77

too far away for the faces of the men on board to be discernible, but still Arthur hung over the wall, sea wind blowing fiercely in his hair as he searched out Silas. He did not know why the old sailor had not come to meet him. But he was certain that Silas was somewhere on that distant deck, headed now for another new shore.

Shelo found him there sometime later, as the town was beginning to awaken. The docks were filled with the bustle of cargo being loaded and unloaded, of tradesmen calling their wares. Not a hair was singed upon Shelo's head. He was leading a bony and balding horse, which had been laden for a journey.

Arthur turned reluctantly to face him. The shabby animal at Shelo's side appeared to be beyond any interest in its surroundings, head drooped, panniers swinging against its flanks. Protruding from the leather packs were around fifty of Sam's jars.

"I told you," said Shelo softly, by way of explanation. "The old things can be burned away and cast aside, now that you are here."

They looked at one another. Arthur nodded, but did not comprehend. Standing between Shelo and the sea, he felt endlessly small, ready to be swept away by the rising tide.

"That creature looks fit to drop," he said, faintly.

Shelo laughed. He rubbed his thumb against the animal's cheek, below its crusted eyes, which rolled back to show the whites.

"I have seen men break horses by frighting them half to death," he remarked, "then drawing them close with the smallest kindness. Here." He drew a jar from the horse's pack, and threw it to Arthur, who caught it nervously. "I do not need what's inside. We can lighten his load."

Down on the sands, in the sludge beneath the shadow of the pier, they crouched and emptied out Sam's collection, jar by jar. The sticky liquid clung to their fingers, and Arthur felt the last of his resistance drain away with it. The little bodies slid silently into the breakers.

7

Camphor

Arthur's brother, Edward, had been prone as a child to bouts of impotent rage. These would often find their expression in attacks upon his younger, weaker sibling – or, more frequently, in the destruction of Arthur's property. Their nurse, Mrs Walmsey, would scold Edward for hitting Arthur, but rarely noticed the breaking of toys or the tearing of bed sheets. When he was twelve, Edward had overstepped the mark, setting fire to the curtains in Arthur's room in an attempt to burn up a box of wooden soldiers. He had been roundly disciplined by their father, and afterwards repented tearfully. It was the last time Arthur saw any show of feeling from him before he withdrew into the sullenness of his adult years.

The memory of this incident came to Arthur as he was curled by the side of a dirt road, miles from anywhere and frozen to the bone. His head was at Shelo's feet, his back pressed against the horse's flea-bitten flank. His toes protruded through the holes in his boots, and the ground was hard beneath him. The night sky hung huge above his head, streaked with cloud and swathes of stars. He would have been fearful of the darkness between the trees, of the creakings and cries that surrounded them, had Shelo not been with him.

His whole life, his body had been shamefully weak. But now, in Shelo's shadow, he no longer felt it quite so keenly. Day by day, Arthur felt that he was vanishing into Shelo's strength, slipping it on like a second skin.

Beyond the woods, the road broadened, rising and falling over the hills. Deer and rabbits grazed the green slopes, scattering whenever Arthur and Shelo passed too close. It was too like England, too like the tranquil countryside which surrounded Harcourt Hall.

"Do not be afraid," murmured Shelo, as Arthur hurried to keep step beside him. The empty jars clinked noisily in the horse's panniers, padded out by bundles of pressed herbs, wizened fruits and dead blooms, bottles of dark liquid. "Do not be afraid, Arthur. They cannot reach you here."

§

The dirt roads wound through the hills for mile after mile, without sight of a single settlement. The land was wide and wild and untamed. The wind blew through endless fields of rippling barley and grasses. Every now and then, Arthur would catch sight of something he recognised from Lucas's sketches – little white flowers, angular as stars, trees in startling shades of red and gold.

He did not ask where they were going, or why. Wherever they stopped to rest, Shelo snared rabbits and field rats and thick-furred squirrels, peeling back their skin to reveal the raw pink flesh beneath. He stewed the lean meat with handfuls of herbs and leaves, and Arthur, who had eaten worse at sea, swallowed his nausea to partake. Shelo scraped clean the pelts of the animals he killed and hung them from the horse's back.

The empty miles rolled away from them on every side, and Arthur felt endlessly diminished in the face of so much wilderness. "You need me here, Shelo," he ventured after nightfall, when they lay in the cleft of a high hill beside the last embers of their fire. His words sounded tenuous and tiny beneath the universe of cold stars. "You called me here, didn't you?"

Shelo shifted his great bulk, and his voice seemed to rumble in the ground beneath. "Listen," he said. "I saw you from across the sea, and I knew you. I called you to my side. Now go to sleep, Arthur."

Forging deeper inland, they passed the remains of a large fire, which was surrounded by scuffed ground. Shelo paused there, kneeling to sniff at the earth.

"Natives?" asked Arthur fearfully, scanning the horizon. Shelo shook his head, his brow furrowed, but said nothing. Later in the day, kneeling to wash his face in a slow-flowing river while Shelo set snares further around the hill, Arthur saw something floating near the surface of the water. At first he thought it was a log, or perhaps a bundle of weeds – but then the current overturned it. He leapt backwards from the bank, yelping.

"Shelo! Shelo!"

"Stuffed with stones to make it sink, you see," Shelo explained, when he had dragged the remains of the body from the water with a long stick. Arthur, who had almost vomited into the reeds on its appearance, averted his eyes. "But then the flesh began to rot, and the stones fell away."

"It wasn't natives?"

"No." Shelo turned the corpse over with the stick again, and shunted it back into the river. It sank again with a dull splash, and Shelo cast the stick in after it. "They would not kill in that manner. This is the work of horseback robbers, road men."

Arthur grew cold at the prospect. "Are they many?"

"More than honest men in this land, Arthur." Shelo laughed his low laugh, and his teeth flashed yellow. He seemed to have caught the scent of something, his eyes suddenly alight. "They are the kings and governors here. Make no mistake."

§

Arthur had hoped they might make haste from the place where the body was sunk in the river, but it seemed Shelo had no such intent. He lingered, examining broken reeds and footprints in the dirt. When they moved onwards it was close to the line of the water, in the direction of the tracks that the killers had left.

In the days that followed they found more traces. The robbers built their fires carelessly at the roadside, not troubling to clear the ashes in the morning. The places where they made camp were invariably trampled and charred, scattered with the debris of the past night's revelry. When they had killed some beast or other for eating, its abandoned bones would draw rats and foxes. The tracks they left were plain as day, imprinted along the centre of the road, an invitation for those who wished to give chase.

Arthur's body grew rigid with constant watchfulness. They saw no other human soul for days – and then, passing close to the edge of a pine wood, came upon another gruesome scene. Their horse pawed at the ground and snorted its displeasure.

Two men and a woman hung from the high branches of a sturdy pine, swaying gently as the tree creaked beneath their weight. Their outer garments had been stripped from them, leaving their limbs exposed. Thick rope had been knotted around their necks, and their faces were puffy and bluish in death.

Arthur looked away as Shelo strode nearer, craning upwards at the suspended bodies. Then a strangled cry from the undergrowth caught their attention, and Arthur hurried to Shelo's side, quivering.

"Who's there?" called Shelo, drawing his flat knife from his belt. He licked the blade, and moved cautiously in the direction of the cry. "Who goes?"

There was another whimper. Shelo pulled back a tangle of

branches, and behind it, they saw another man lying amidst a wreckage of ransacked baggage. Shirts, stockings, bonnets and other sundry clothing lay strewn over the ground and snagged on the low branches of trees. Several cases had been broken open with some force, their contents snatched carelessly from them. The man was barely in better health than his hanged compatriots, clasping at a dark bloodstain which had spread across his chest and side.

Shelo crouched down beside him, pulling his hand roughly back to see the wound. The man groaned, thrashing helplessly. His words emerged through a foam of blood and spittle. "My master, mistress, their son..."

"All dead. Who did this?"

The dying servant coughed violently, gripping Shelo's arm as if it might be his means of rescue. "They shot me first. Took... everything of worth from my poor... mocked them most dreadfully... strung them high, and I could hear 'em crying out all the while..."

"Did you see a man in a red coat?" Shelo pressed him grimly. The servant's eyes rolled, and he gabbled in terror.

"Benjamin Barber! Terror of the roads! With my own eyes!"

Shelo prised the rigid fingers from his arm, and forcibly lowered the man's torso back to the ground again. The stricken servant convulsed, the grass around him stained with blood.

"Which way did they go?" asked Shelo softly.

"I am done for... please..."

"*Which way did they go?*"

His teeth locked together, the man raised a hand, pointing back down towards the river. Then he let out a sharp cry, and grew still without another word, still mid-grimace. The suddenness and brutality of his passing left Arthur numb.

Shelo immediately set about looking over the body, rolling it over and patting down the pockets. The robbers had clearly not thought the servant worth searching, but they had been mistaken. Shelo pulled a handful of coins from a pouch tied beneath the shirt, and pressed two of the smaller pieces into the dead man's eyelids. Pocketing the rest, he rose, motioning Arthur to fetch their horse from the road.

"Are we to follow?" asked Arthur with trepidation – and then, as Shelo made for the river-bank, "Should we not bury him?"

Shelo looked over his shoulder. "Are you hiding a shovel beneath your coat?"

Arthur cast his eyes down as he led the reluctant horse through the pines, forcing himself not to look back at the corpse in the undergrowth, or up at the three suspended from the trees. But as they neared the water, he could not help but glance back at the fearful patch of forest. Snow had begun to fall lightly from the white sky. A crow landed upon one of the hanging bodies.

§

They followed the curve of the river as it widened, dipping down through the woods and joining with other small tributaries. Brown leaves and swathes of snowflakes drifted into the water from above. Through the misted evening, Arthur glimpsed flat-boats, orange lanterns hanging from their prows, silhouette figures aboard dipping poles into the water. The familiar sound of waves breaking against timber made him feel ill.

The sight of these boats became more frequent, until they came within sight of a shallow estuary, where a solitary craft was being unloaded by lamplight. Shelo drew to a halt, stilling Arthur and the horse with a movement of his hand. He was barefoot, careless of the cold mud, and did not so much as shiver in his thin shirt. He beckoned Arthur close.

"If I give you words to say," he murmured, "will you say them?"

Arthur nodded. Shelo inclined his head, smiling a little. "It is not given to me," he said, "to wear a face that will be favoured by other men. Do you see?"

Arthur swallowed. He had the sense that he was being tested. Shelo bent close to whisper in his ear.

Horses picked through the mud towards the top of the bank, laden with tobacco leaf and bundles of timber. Shelo and Arthur lingered behind the trees as the boat was packed with new cargo. Money changed hands, and there was some brief talk among the men before those of the land party moved away, roping their horses together nose-to-tail and making for the road. They carried most of the lanterns with them, leaving the lone boatman to finish his preparations in near-darkness.

Shelo stepped into the open. Snowflakes settled around him like dust. Arthur followed obediently, and they led their horse forward until the boatman became aware of their presence. He was unwinding the mooring rope from a nearby stump and froze in the act, turning in slow dread to look behind him. What he saw there seemed to surpass his worst fears. For a moment, Arthur imagined the scene as this stranger must see it; an inhuman creature looming out of the snow, his ghostly companion, their half-dead beast.

The boatman crossed himself. Remembering his role, Arthur stepped forward, holding out his hand to Shelo, who placed the coins from the dead man's pocket into his palm.

"We are in need of passage," Arthur said. His silver-spoon voice rang strangely in the muted air. At the sound of it, and the sight of the money, the boatman's face changed. "As far south as you are going, sir, and I'll pay you all I have."

The man gave a perfunctory nod, but still seemed unable to speak. His gaze had travelled over Arthur's shoulder, fixing on

Shelo. His hand lingered uncertainly upon the mooring rope.

"I am in the business of selling medicinal supplies. Apothecary herbs, and remedies, and the like." Arthur pulled a bundle of pressed leaves from the pannier to show. "This is my servant."

"Does the man talk?" questioned the boatman, at last.

"He has knowledge of all manner of plants and their properties, and I keep him for it. Your pardon, sir – it is past dusk, and I have heard rumours of road men."

The boatman tore his gaze from Shelo at last, and glanced fretfully into the trees. "They say that Benjamin Barber himself is abroad."

Shelo shifted his great bulk, but made no sound. The boatman tugged his craft firmly back into its mooring, and opened his palm.

They drifted down the river through the night, heavy clouds hiding the moon above. Their only light was the lantern which dangled from the pointed prow, illuminating the snow for a moment before it was swallowed into the black water. The craft was laden with skins of every kind – heavy bear pelts, ragged wolf, white mink. Arthur and Shelo huddled among the furs, which lay in musty heaps beneath the shelter. Their breath mingled and turned to mist. The horse, blindfolded and tightly roped, scuffed its skittish hooves against the base of the boat. Its bony frame shivered in the chill air.

The boatman, shrouded in a beaver-hide cape, dipped a long pole carefully into the river, propelling them forwards. Each time he raised this makeshift oar, weeds trailed against the side of the boat. The sight of him in silhouette brought to Arthur's mind a picture from a book in his father's library, a half-remembered image which had terrified him as a child.

Beneath him, water lapped against red cedar. They slid smoothly along, journeying over glass.

§

Faint daylight, and smoke rising into a white sky above the pines. Arthur wiped his streaming nose on his coat sleeve, and emerged unsteadily from the shelter onto the deck. Shelo and the boatman were side-by-side on the prow, and beyond them, the riverbank. Women knelt in the mud, soap foaming at the water's edge as they scrubbed at their clothes. They raised their gaze to watch the vessel pass them by.

The boatman allowed Shelo to take over the oar, and sat wrapped in his fur covering, gnawing at a strip of cured meat. The shapes of settlements rose and fell away on either side, giving way to more woodland and frosted marsh. Arthur caught sight of fat silver fish below the water's surface, darting along on the current.

At around midday they encountered a vessel making its way upstream, manned by three traders each straining at a separate oar. Arthur and Shelo's boatman raised a hand, and the strangers manoeuvred their craft close to exchange greetings. The other boat was low in the water, weighed down by its cargo of limestone blocks.

They stared at Shelo like men beholding something from an unimagined world. They gave bread and a casket of ale for three rabbit furs. Gesturing back, they spoke of the river's widening, of a large town and a bridge which spanned the banks. "There will be good business for you. But go no further on these waters. Where the bank grows high and there are wooded islands and sharp rocks, there are outlaws."

"I have heard that Benjamin Barber is returned to these parts," said the fur trader. Arthur, standing close to Shelo, thought that he heard a rumble from deep in his throat. "I heard that he has reaped his fill of the roads and come back to the river."

They came within sight of the promised settlement before dark, and moored there in the shadow of the bridge. The boatman had his cargo brought to shore, and courteously handed Arthur back one of the coins he had paid. "You will have to find another to take you further down the river. If you are wise, you will journey by road from here."

To Arthur's puzzlement, Shelo did not head into the smoke and noise of the nearby town, whose high walls obscured its buildings from view. Instead, he tethered the horse to one of the bridge's timber supports, and removed its burdens, laying out the contents of the panniers on the grass. The horse stood listlessly at the lip of the water, flicking its tail against its flank.

A few hundred yards downriver, on the flats where the tide had drawn the water out, Arthur noticed ragged figures creeping down the bank from the settlement. They waded in the shallows and bent to pick at the waste which was half-submerged in the silt – broken cartwheel spokes, fragments of china, the beached bodies of fish.

Shelo drew out a lantern from the bottom of the largest pannier, and struck flint on steel to light it. He cupped his hand, and blew gently on the tiny flame. It burned the same cold blue as the light in Sam's attic window, as the luminescence that had descended upon the *Head of Mary*. Shelo hung it upon the underside of the bridge, and it cast a pale glow upon the muddy bank.

"You see them, Arthur?" asked Shelo softly. Beyond the sphere of light, a few of the ragged forms had begun to turn in the darkness, wary eyes blinking. Shelo licked his lips. "*Come to me, all you weary,*" he murmured. "*Come to me, you hideous and shameful and desperate. You betrayed, you full of bitter fury. Come to me, and I will give you a world turned on its head.*"

The shadowy figures crept nearer with caution, as though

catching a tempting scent on the air. A woman with a thin solemn face and a bent body stepped forward from the rest. She was gazing at Shelo, transfixed.

"You have much trouble in this world," he intoned. His voice appeared to wash over her, and she closed her eyes. Tears cut tracks down her unwashed face.

Shelo drew a small bottle from his pocket, uncorked it, and upended it with a handkerchief pressed to the rim. "All will be well," he said softly.

Then, in a sudden fluid movement, he took the back of her head in one huge hand and pressed the handkerchief to her mouth with the other. Before she could so much as struggle, her eyes rolled back in her head and she crumpled. Those gathered behind her scattered in alarm.

"Help me, won't you?" Shelo kept the handkerchief over her mouth, supporting her in the crook of his elbow. Arthur stared, and could not move.

"What is that?"

"Camphor. Take her legs, Arthur."

Shelo had laid out the horse's blanket on the frozen grass beneath the bridge. Together, they manoeuvred the unconscious woman onto it, while below, the dark river flowed blindly on.

Shelo knelt at the woman's head, surrounded by his supplies. With care, even tenderness, he brushed the hair back from her face. He looked up at Arthur.

"You will need to keep watch up on the bank, and call if anybody comes."

"What about them?" Arthur indicated the faint shapes outside the circle of the light, trying to hide the trembling in his voice. He did not understand what was happening.

"Let them linger," said Shelo. "The tales they tell will go before us."

§

In all the hours Arthur kept a wakeful watch, not a soul passed by. Dogs barked in the town above, the noise carrying sharply on the cold air. Water lapped against the banks, and night-birds exchanged calls close at hand. He felt as though he were back upon the *Head of Mary*, taking the midnight vigil up on deck. He imagined that a groaning arose from the darkness below.

Shelo emerged at sunrise, inked body quivering with a suppressed thrill. He was leading the horse, which had been laden once again. The woman was nowhere to be seen.

"Come, Arthur." Excitement, and a strange satisfaction, simmered beneath Shelo's surface. "I do not think it can be far, now."

"To where, Shelo?"

They untied the fur trader's boat from its moorings and made away with it, unsteady now upon the faster current. Shelo steered, weaving inexpertly in and out of the scattered rocks. Arthur huddled against the wind, nauseous, pressing his back against the horse's flank. The vessel lurched and spun as they passed wooded islands, buoyant now that its load was lightened. On either side of them, the banks of the river rose higher and higher, towering to limestone cliffs.

The sight of smoke from the settlement grew fainter. And Arthur heard, as he had in the night, the sound of birds replying to one another from somewhere downstream. The sharp noises were suddenly loud, then distant again, and he found himself turning his head uneasily. Frozen reeds stood to attention like soldiers.

Shelo crouched at the prow, lifting the pole from the water and letting the current carry them. Bare feet planted on the deck, he scanned the horizon. He tasted the air with his tongue. As he breathed, his wide shoulders rose and dropped tensely.

They passed beneath the shadow of a tall line of cedars along the bank, hemmed in by an island on their other side. A handful of small stones skittered down the cliff from far overhead, splashing into the water. A moving shape caught the corner of Arthur's eye, and as he turned to catch a better look, he heard again the sound he had taken for a bird call. It was all the warning they had before a man dropped down onto their deck.

He was young, smooth-faced and saucer-eyed, wearing a cap and an enormous coat that fell to his ankles. When he held out a pistol, it was with a hand that shook violently. He had seen Shelo too late.

Before he could make a sound, Shelo was advancing on him. The youth scrambled towards the prow, attempting to keep his pistol pointed in their direction. But he tripped, and hurriedly let out the bird cry again as Shelo's shadow loomed over him. The call was answered from just metres away.

Arthur's attention had been so entirely upon their attacker that he had not even noticed the two larger men who had dropped onto the back end of the deck. It came to him, as he stared down the mouths of their pistols, that this had been their intent. Their boots were muffled in strips of cloth, their faces tied round with scarves. They were lean and starved as wolves.

The taller of them, whose pale eyes stood out startlingly from his filthy face, stepped forward. He flicked back the catch on his pistol, and with his free hand, made a sharp gesture at the fallen boy. As he rose his cap was dislodged, revealing a head of long, tangled fair hair. Even amidst his panic, Arthur felt a faint tug of surprise.

The girl moved awkwardly around the horse, which had stiffened in fear, the jars in its panniers jangling. The boat tilted from side to side. With his shot now clear, the tallest outlaw trained his pistol upon Shelo, who had still not turned to face him.

"What cargo are you carrying?" he demanded. Several of his front teeth were missing.

"None," Shelo replied, and the very air around them seemed to change. "We are of no use to you. You will not hurt us."

At the sound of Shelo's voice, the outlaw covering Arthur lowered his gun unconsciously, tugging the scarf away from his mouth. He crossed himself just as the boatman had done, upon the snowy riverbank.

Shelo turned. On every visible inch of his skin, inked tendrils curled and writhed. The girl's eyes opened wide and round, but she did not back away, rather leaning closer to stare.

The pale-eyed man held his composure, but Arthur could tell he was shaken. He licked his lips, sweating in spite of the cold, and shifted his pistol to his other hand. There was nothing to stop him firing it, but he seemed suddenly loath to.

"Harpey," muttered the other, "this ain't no natural creature. There's no sayin' what you'll bring down on us, if you kill it."

"What of its com-patriot?" asked the girl, who had raised her own pistol again to point it at Arthur. He had a moment's impression of her suspicious features, before the man called Harpey signalled to her to lower the gun. He looked warily between Arthur and Shelo, before turning his gaze downriver, along the curve of the limestone cliffs.

"I do not know what these are," he said slowly, "nor what we had best do with them. But Barber will decide."

8

Mere Man

Nature had done a strange work in the rock above the high water mark, hollowing out a great gash perhaps sixty feet across. Cedar roots and creepers hid the top of the archway, which was higher than three men stood atop each other's shoulders. Water from tributaries flowing along the high bank plunged down over the surrounding stones, into the deeper waters beneath. Led from daylight into the damp darkness, Arthur kept as close to Shelo as he could. A thick smell of pitch and animal droppings rose to greet them.

The girl was directly in front of him, and he kept his eyes upon her footsteps so as not to fall. She was wearing a pair of man's riding boots, which like her coat were far too large. Every now and then she turned to gawp at Shelo, until he hissed at her, a snarl rippling across his features.

Beneath the earth, the rock was honeycombed by passages. There were crates and barrels stacked everywhere, sacks spilling grain, bundles of timber and spun cotton. Arthur glimpsed an entire herd of sheep fenced into an alcove, a pair of pigs tethered to a post. There were flaming torches fixed to the walls where the daylight no longer penetrated, filling the close air with smoke.

"In here."

He felt the press of Harpey's pistol between his shoulder blades, and ducked obediently to pass beneath a low archway to his right. The feel of the air changed, and he stood blinking, accustoming himself to the larger space. Even Shelo could now stand upright. At the far end of the long chamber, a curtain of water cascaded down, rippling in the narrow shaft of daylight that shone in through a crack in the rock.

The girl, who had hurried on ahead, was now squatting next to a man playing cards upon an upturned crate. He waved her away and she retreated, scratching at her mop of hair like a rabbit with fleas. Arthur's eye was drawn not to the man's face, but to his coat, which was finely tailored and of brightest red, with a silken lining and bronze buttons. His black boots shone as if brand new. Amongst the ragged men against whom he was playing, he appeared like a statesman.

"Mr Harpey," said Benjamin Barber. He flipped the pack of cards through his fingers. "What do you have for me?"

Barber's voice was clipped and refined. His gaze flickered over Arthur, and as it came to rest upon Shelo, his face registered the merest hint of a shudder. Several of the other card players had risen to their feet, hands going instinctively to their weapons. They stared at Shelo, at the burning of his eyes, at the inked forest upon his skin. Arthur saw his lip curl at the corner.

"They were coming downstream, between the islands," said Harpey. "No cargo to speak of. We thought it best..."

Barber laid down his cards carefully, and rose. "Now this," he said, "is a truly curious thing. I believe I heard tales of such a creature." He smoothed his moustache, which was the same light brown as his sweep of hair. "A man hardly a man at all, cast out by his own kind, and an enemy to all. Who are you?"

The black eyes flashed. "I am Shelo."

Barber glanced at Arthur. "And who are you?"

"I am Shelo's dog." He was astonished to hear himself say it – that, in his terror, he even had the breath to speak. Barber let out a sudden, high laugh, which was not echoed by the men around him.

Each was plainly unwilling to step any nearer to Shelo, or even to draw their weapons against him. In the shifting light that shone through the curtain of water, he seemed to fade and then appear again, made of smoke and of shadow. An uneasy murmuring began among them. A small, trim man who had been seated with Barber at the card table rose to speak in his ear.

"Do I shoot?" asked Harpey, who was now sweating profusely. His hand was unsteady upon his pistol. Barber gave a slight shake of his head, moving nearer to Shelo.

"They are afraid of you," he said quietly. Though tall, he still had to crane upwards to look Shelo fully in the face. "But you come here with so little caution. Did you not know, did nobody tell you, that this stretch of the river belongs to me?"

"All the river belongs to you," said Shelo. "And the roads, too, from here to the southern country. It's said that you have a hideout in every county, and put silver in the judge's pockets to keep them from your back."

"Indeed! Rumours spread on these roads fierce as the pox."

"But it is true that nobody knows the land so well as you and your men."

Barber cocked his head to one side, features bright with curiosity. "If you are looking for a part in our enterprise, be warned. I'll have no man who is liable to turn. If you are with us, it is until your last breath. "

"We have searched you out," said Shelo.

Barber considered him, then stepped back, indicating the makeshift table. The men sat around it scrambled out of the way. But Shelo did not sit.

"I have heard," he said, "that there is a place in the southern country where field after field is filled with yellow flowers. Blooms the height of a grown man. And that beyond these fields, built some twenty years ago, there is a grand house of white brick and blue timber, set against a hill."

"A rich man's dwelling. What of it?"

Shelo was silent. There was a pause, then Barber let out a sharp laugh. "You sought me out for your *guide*? We know the place, even my dog-ignorant daughter knows it." The girl, who had been kicking stones into the waterfall, glanced round. "But you are mistaken if you think that we will lead you there, not for any fee."

"You will not so much as direct our steps?" A distinct growl had now entered Shelo's voice. Stood close, Arthur was sure he felt the very hairs upon his arms bristle.

"Not along the routes that I myself keep. No man reaps benefit from them without my say so, and it is plain to me you have some scheme in mind." Whatever amusement had animated Barber, it now faded. A stone-hardness came into his look, and he stood, digging the blade of a pocket knife emphatically into the crate.

"Last man who came to learn the details of my enterprise for his own gain, Harpey here tied a rag over his eyes and set him on his mare over the cliff." There was a nervous snickering from the gap-toothed outlaw. "Then we dashed the brains of his two mewling boys against a tree trunk. Disbelieve me, if you will. I bought my kingship here with blood and with silver, and none shall thieve it from me, not even those who call the land their own."

He took a step closer to Shelo, his eyes narrowed. "I once rode against a whole company of your kind, and for ten years wore a belt made from their scalp leather, until some whore stole it while I slept. Who are you, savage? And why should I not make an end of you?"

A murmur of unease arose from behind Barber, and the small man who had earlier muttered in his ear was pulling at his elbow in dissuasion.

"Enough, Ripstone." Barber waved him away and clicked his tongue, sinking back into his seat. The girl came hurrying to him, carrying a pewter cup from which he took a leisurely drink. She stood at his shoulder waiting to take it back again, regarding Arthur and Shelo with her mouth slightly open.

Barber raised his gaze over the rim. "What do you think, Shelo's dog? They are of the opinion that your master is no mere man. They fear to harm him. And I will not harm him today, for their sake, and that I am loath to spend powder on an animal."

"He called me from across the sea," whispered Arthur. He heard a rumbling in Shelo's huge chest. For a moment, he felt Barber's attention lift from Shelo, and rest on him.

"Did you come here for riches?" asked Barber quietly. "Did you hear that the New World was spilling over with prizes for the taking, sir, that you have journeyed so far from home? You had better keep a watch upon yourself." Unthinkingly, his thumb went to the faded buttons upon his red coat, and began to polish. "A man may drift here, from all he thought he was."

§

They were led back out into the daylight by pale-eyed Harpey and the man called Ripstone. The latter shifted agitatedly from foot to foot as he handed them back the reins of their horse. Afraid to address Shelo, he spat his words at Arthur.

"Take to your boat, and do not think of returning to this place. The second time, you shall not leave with your lives."

They abandoned their vessel upon the bank around the river bend, and made for higher ground. Gone were the gentle green hills through which they had passed on the road from the coast, replaced by pine-strewn cliffs and shadowed canyons. A bruise-coloured column of cloud was blowing in from the east, folding in upon the land like a curtain being drawn. A few droplets of rain began to scatter upon the dusty road, and Arthur bound a handkerchief about his face as the bandits had done.

Shelo was silent, apparently lost in thought. Along the wide road which led from the settlement they had seen on the river, they passed solitary tradesmen, itinerant preachers, livestock drovers. These were not easily alarmed, unlike the larger groups of men and women who banded closely together when they saw Arthur and Shelo approaching. Their dogs slunk back, whining, and their horses came to a stubborn halt, coaxed past with bread crusts and reassuring words. Children sitting upon the back steps of their wagons gawped and pointed at the ink-skinned stranger.

"One girl-child," Shelo said, at long last. "Amidst a whole company of men." He had paused to stare back in the direction they had come, and it took Arthur a moment to comprehend who he might mean.

Their horse's thin flanks were quivering as the rain fell ever heavier. Shelo pulled the beast's nose roughly around, turning his own face to the darkening sky. "We should remain close by," he said, more to himself than to Arthur. "And in the meantime…"

He looked sharply back down the road. Bare feet planted in the mud, he stood drenched in the centre of the path as though he had taken root there. Twilight had stolen the last of the light from the clouded sky, leaving a blue haze of rain, through which it was impossible to see more than a few yards in either direction. When the approaching sound of hooves and rolling wheels began to draw nearer, Arthur made to move aside, but Shelo gave a sharp shake of his head.

The horns of an ox were the first things to emerge from the rain, a laden wagon rolling behind. The man at the creature's side stopped short at the sight before him, throwing out his arm to halt the rest of his party. At first only silhouettes, they became slowly visible through the gloom – another man and two women, all burdened and muddied, three small children sat atop the wagon's front seat. They all gaped wordlessly as the rain lashed down upon them, and Arthur felt chill water seep through each layer of his clothing.

"Unload your possessions," commanded Shelo. "And unhitch your beast."

"Shelo," whispered Arthur, in the dead of night, when they were curled on the hard boards in the back of the wagon. Rain lashed down on the cloth cover above their heads. The small party of travellers had been left helpless in their wake, huddled at the side of the road with their belongings clutched close and their boots sunk in the mud. "How can Barber look and speak so like a gentleman?"

Shelo turned his head, lids still closed, and his ink eyes gazed at Arthur through the dark. "He was a gentleman, so it is said. A merchant, then a militia captain. Then a justice of the peace, no less."

"Then how did he enter his present life?"

"Some say his taxes were hard and his empty stomach turned his heart bitter. Others that he merely took to the taste for bloodshed, in his militia days."

"I cannot imagine that such a man might ever have lived by the law…"

"Come, Arthur. You know the ease with which a gentleman may fall from grace."

This was too barbed. Arthur felt it like a thorn in his flesh, and brooded upon it until his intense discomfort brought on another question.

"Shelo. That woman beneath the bridge, back at the settlement. What did you do to her?" He found himself shivering, but persevered, his body heavy with dread. "Is it your intention to carry on… in Sam's work?"

Shelo's inked eyelids rolled back. The rain outside grew heavier, pelting against the cloth with such force and volume that if he made any reply, it was entirely drowned.

§

The next morning Shelo fixed the blue lantern above the wagon's front seat, and hitched their horse between the shafts. Arthur was certain that the weight would be too great for the bony creature, but Shelo seemed to anticipate his objections. "He is stronger than he looks, Arthur. And he will grow stronger yet."

With Shelo at the reins and the dirt of the road rising from beneath their wheels, they moved slowly along the river, at the edge of unsettled territory. Finding after the first day that he could not cram his long body into the seat beside Shelo, Arthur took to riding on the back step of the wagon, feet brushing the ground. The rough motion made him as sick as he'd been at sea.

Through the hours of darkness, the blue lamp shone out persistently, muted by the fog but not extinguished. Insects were drawn towards it, fluttering erratically until they met the flame and were burned up in an instant.

Arthur thought, though the deep of night made everything uncertain, that natives drew near to their wagon. They gathered at the boundary of the lamplight, curious and cautious. They spoke in their own tongues, gesturing to the rake-thin horse and the hanging blue lantern. Shelo joined them, around blazing fires which sent sparks into the wide night sky. He ate and drank with them, though they never lingered long. To Arthur it seemed that Shelo's outline blurred against the canopy of stars, lost somewhere beyond the smoke. Each morning he would scout the ground near the wagon, searching for ashes and remnants, but found nothing.

Other nights, despite himself, he imagined that he was back in his old bedchamber at Harcourt Hall. Curled at Shelo's feet on the hard boards in the back of the wagon, he attempted to stretch himself out, believing that he lay in a four-poster bed. He grasped for silk sheets and found only a rough-woven blanket. He woke at the sound of the breakfast bell, only to find that it was Shelo, hammering nails into the frame of the wagon with the handle of his knife to fix the wind-torn canvas.

Arthur's body did not take well to these recollections. It retched and shuddered, sweating until his clothes were drenched. When the smell of the wagon's timber filled his nose, he lay catching his breath, making certain of where he was.

He told himself again and again of the distance that lay between him and Harcourt Hall. The Atlantic was wide and it was deep. The litany of all these miles brought some small measure of comfort.

§

At dusk on the third day after their encounter with Barber, Shelo parked the wagon beneath a spreading oak by the roadside, where rain hung in trembling droplets from each leaf. A thin chill mist lay over everything.

They were both sleeping when there came a knocking at the outside of the wagon, and Shelo raised himself so quickly that Arthur was jolted into wakefulness. Shelo pulled back the cloth flap that shielded them from the weather, squinting out into the semi-darkness. He was shirtless despite the cold, his broad inked chest illuminated in eerie blue. Beyond him, tentative and shivering in the damp night, a woman stood wrapped in a thick cloak. She was silver-haired, her frightened gaze fixed upon the dark apparition before her.

"Are you the travellers I have heard word of?" she whispered. "The travellers who stopped beneath the bridge in a town some miles back?"

Shelo looked down upon her, still as one carved from stone.

"I saw your light from the road. I had heard…" She passed her hand across her face. "Forgive me. I have journeyed many days on perilous roads to find you. I had heard a tale so extraordinary I could scarce give it credence."

Shelo's breath misted. He still did not speak, but waited until their visitor had drawn together her composure.

"If you can do for me as you did for the other beneath that bridge," she whispered, "I will pay whatever price you ask."

"No price," said Shelo. And he laughed suddenly, as though caught off guard by his own delight. "No price, if this world has walked upon your back. You must only be willing."

Arthur looked between Shelo and the woman. She seemed to be steeling herself, desperately searching out some trace of mercy in Shelo's monolithic face. "My husband was lost at sea, some months ago," she whispered "My days are empty to me in his absence. I am weighed down by a heavy burden, and can carry it no longer."

Shelo turned his face away, and Arthur sensed that he had not wanted to hear these details. His thoughts already seemed to be elsewhere, and he stepped back into the wagon, rummaging amongst the pile of jars and packages. He straightened the blanket on which he and Arthur had been sleeping, then pulled the bottle of camphor from his pocket.

"Help me lay her down, Arthur," he said, in an undertone. "And then you must sit watch outside."

She sank down when Shelo pressed the camphor cloth to her mouth, and they lifted her carefully, Shelo cradling her head as they laid her onto the blanket. If her limbs had not been thrown out at odd angles, she might have been sleeping. Shelo lit a long taper, and the inside of the wagon danced with shadows. He held it up, the better to see Arthur's face.

"Whatever you hear and whatever fears come to you, do not enter here until sunrise. Do you understand?"

Arthur sat out the night against the base of a nearby tree, watching the back of the wagon, where Shelo had drawn the cloth across once more. The candle within shone dimly through, and he could just make out Shelo's crouched shape in silhouette. Overhead, clouds dashed across the crescent moon. The road lay empty before and behind, snaking its way across the hills.

Tired from the day's travel, Arthur sank towards sleep again despite his burning curiosity. Then somewhere in the branches above him, an owl called shrilly, and he awoke with a start. A crawling sensation began at the back of his neck. Coming from the wagon, low at first but growing ever louder, was a hideous sound.

The woman in Shelo's care groaned like one in the throes of birth. She moaned and shrieked, sending the birds from the surrounding trees flapping into the night. A rabbit grazing in the moonlight froze, ears pricked, then fled for its burrow.

Arthur trembled, torn between obedience to Shelo's words and the urge to burst back into the wagon. Was it possible that Shelo was engaged in some act of unspeakable cruelty? Should he be coming to the woman's aid, or was this the very thing for which she had sought them out?

Whatever you hear, whatever fears come to you.

Obedience won the day. Arthur hunched beneath the oak tree in the darkness, and readied himself to endure the night.

What could possibly be causing her such pain, he could not fathom. He sat immersed in horror, recalling for reasons that were beyond him the sound of his father's cello. Its strings, deep and resonant in their grief, had spoken the things that Jonas Hallingham held silent. Its music had seeped through the walls and corridors of Harcourt Hall, binding them all in mourning long before he, Edward, Harmony and Lucas had even known what they were mourning for.

§

When he finally dared to rise, stiff from having sat against the tree's uneven roots, the new day had come and the woman was nowhere to be seen. Shelo was lighting a fire on the frost-hardened ground, snatching up dry grass for kindling and murmuring to himself.

Arthur, who had barely noticed how cold he was until now, moved over to the fire. He warmed his hands in silence, glancing every now and then to the back of the wagon, half-hoping that Shelo might now offer him an explanation. But none came. When the flames were hotter, Shelo boiled a pan of oats in water, and they ate together. The sun rose above the nearest hill in a haze of blood-red mist. By its light, they could make out a column of smoke from another fire, rising from behind a clump of trees on the opposite hill.

In the boulder-strewn dip between, a clear stream flowed,

a tributary of the nearby river. And even as Arthur and Shelo watched, a fair-haired figure emerged from the trees and picked its way down to the water. The girl's movements, encumbered by a pair of oversized boots, were familiar.

As Barber's daughter approached the stream, Shelo signalled emphatically to Arthur to douse their fire. He crept to the edge of the rise, crouching behind a boulder, and Arthur hurried to his side. They watched as she squatted at the waterside among the reeds, rolling up her sleeves to scrub at her face.

"Amidst a whole company of men," murmured Shelo, with satisfaction. He pulled his flat-bladed knife from his belt.

The girl paused for a moment in her washing, glancing up, perhaps glimpsing something from the corner of her eye. She scanned the hillside, then looked over her shoulder towards the screen of trees, skittish as a deer.

Before Arthur knew what was happening, Shelo was descending swift and silent between the rocks, towards the water.

Part Two

9

There in Darkness

In the close jungle air, Arthur dreamed of England. He tossed and turned in his hammock, and insects came to feast upon him. They crawled across his skin, and drank his blood. Their thin whine persisted into his sleep, like a needle being drawn across his skull.

Hannah Hallingham came to him in his sleep now, always. She stood at the edge of him, and crossed over the moment that he drifted from consciousness. Her cheeks were streaked with tears like rain across window panes. She would not look at him, but turned her gaze sideways, hands clasped together in desperate prayer, greying hair concealing her face. Her nightdress hung from her body and trailed upon the ground, as weeds trail in a river.

He woke in the humid dark, his naked torso dripping sweat. He passed a hand across his brow. The torrid night spilled over with howls and screeches, the cries of a thousand unseen creatures. Beneath the cacophony, he lost the tenuous sound of his own breath.

§

The woman beside the pool had led him from the water, lending him her shawl for his shame's sake. He tied it around his waist. With the damp soil beneath his feet, his eyes still smarting in the daylight after the blackness beneath the world, he had followed her through the hanging branches. Long red flowers brushed against his body, dripping pollen. A different hummingbird droned in the heart of each bloom.

They emerged amongst a cluster of woven reed huts, which were scattered between the trees. Naked children played in the dust, the dappled light casting green shades upon their skin. They stared up at Arthur without fear, their eyes dark beneath high foreheads, black hair bound in braids. At the shadowy doorways of the huts, tall figures appeared, silent as Arthur passed them by. He glimpsed faces which had been pierced and inked, bodies clad with feathers and bright cloths. They whispered amongst themselves.

The woman from the pool did not stop to talk with them. A few hissed between their teeth as she passed, but her bare feet did not falter upon the dirt. Her wet hair hung long and loose. She wore a dull skin garment which was covered in deep stains. As he followed close behind her, Arthur saw that her ankles and calves had been painted with familiar, intricate patterns.

Beyond the little village, she pushed through ferns which grew higher than Arthur's head, glancing behind to check that he had kept pace. For a moment his vision was obscured by leaves, but when they emerged, the strangest of sights awaited him. The clearing beyond was entirely barren. The ground underfoot felt dry, leeched of all moisture, not a single creeper or bloom growing there. On the far side of the dead space, the greenery flourished again, for all the world as though an invisible circle had been drawn.

The only sign that any life had ever taken root there was a solitary tree at the centre, high and broad but skeletal, only a few withered leaves hanging from its branches. Its bark was dark as ash, and cracked all over, as if some poison or intense heat had passed through it. In the shadow of the dead tree was a lopsided hut, dwarfed by the emptiness around.

The woman from the pool watched Arthur as he took in this sight, her face sombre. He was taken by surprise when she suddenly said, in hesitant English, "This is my house. Me, my husband. You will stay with us."

Her voice was low and quiet, weary as all of her bearing. She seemed to read further questions in Arthur's dazed look. "I saw your coming," she said. "I have prepared."

Arthur did not want to go any closer to the dead tree, but he followed her nonetheless, bending low to pass through the doorway of the hut. The space inside was bigger than he had expected, and as scrupulously clean as the Spanish monk's had been, the day he had fled from Ripstone. In the outer room the floor was covered by matting, a cooking fire blocked by stones in the corner and a makeshift hammock hung between two low poles. The room beyond was concealed. All around, suspended from the walls and tucked into clay pots around the walls, were dried leaves and pressed petals, the claws and teeth of beasts. Arthur knew too well their musty, rich-earth smell.

A man sat on the floor, naked from the waist up, his skin the colour of copper. His ears were pierced through many times with thin wooden loops. He looked at Arthur without blinking, but did not seem to take him in at all. His gaze was blank, wholly and deeply resigned. There might have been no life left beneath his skin.

"He does not speak," said the woman softly. "Not in your tongue, not in any. Do not trouble him."

Arthur would not have thought to. The man was stirring the contents of a pot upon the fire, the air in the little room heavy with smoke. Light shone in through a break in the reed roof, splitting into weak prisms.

The woman touched his arm, and he tore his gaze away from her silent husband. "My name is Elia," she said. Her grave eyes settled upon Arthur's face, and he felt that a weight had descended onto his shoulders.

"I am Arthur," he said, then the choking syllables of his whole name. "Arthur Hallingham."

She nodded slowly. "Here is a place for you to sleep, Arthur Hallingham. You will be safe here. You may eat with us. We will give you clothing."

He looked at the hammock, then back at Elia. He wrapped his arms fretfully around his thin, bare torso. The scars that he had gouged into his own flesh aboard the *Head of Mary* were now livid stripes above his ribs. He thought of the darkness beneath the world, where the blind fish swam, and shuddered.

"*How did you know?*" he whispered. "*How did you know I would come?*"

For a moment, Elia hesitated. But then, her face grim, she slipped behind the hanging strings of leaves into the room behind. When she returned, she was holding something, her fingers laced across it. Before she drew them back, Arthur knew what it was, and his heart quaked within him.

"Last night," she said, "he came to me as I slept. He spoke to me. When I awoke, I found this upon my bed. Why should death, why should water, hold him under?"

A black bloom, its dead petals folded in on themselves like sleeping eyelids, sat upon the palm of her hand.

§

In the house of Elia, his thoughts grew hazy. Had it really been only days since he had run from Ripstone, huddled in the cave with Flora, seen Shelo falling away from him beneath the water? In the heat of the night, he breathed in the close air, and breathed out all that he remembered. Had he really sat upon the back step of a horse-drawn wagon, for mile after dusty mile? Had they slept, the three of them, huddled together beneath the stars in the wide wilderness?

Ten, twenty years unraveled in his head like twine. Motherless, he had run with his brother and his sister in Harcourt Hall's overgrown grounds. Little Lucas West, the parson's dreaming son, had been their guide. Lucas knew every pond and climbing tree, every stone which might be overturned to find worms and spiders. He possessed a fishing rod, a pocket knife, and a boundless imagination.

Harmony dirtied her dresses wading with Lucas into stagnant pools of water, pressing through thickets in the pretence of being the first men in a newfound land. They spent hours absorbed in hunting beetles upon tree trunks, while Edward climbed as high as he could, yelling in triumph from the uppermost branches. Arthur, the youngest by some years, lagged behind. Even then, it seemed to him that his body would not obey his simplest desires. He stumbled over every rock and root. It seemed that the true Arthur was not made up of these arms, these eyes, these feet, but rather trapped within the ill-fitting skin of a stranger.

A lake had lain just beyond the sight of the hall's windows, down the hill and behind a screen of trees. Lord Harcourt had fished there, with parties of friends, in the days before sorrow came for him. But the waters had grown green for want of a gardener's care, fat trout multiplying beneath the surface. Lucas baited his hook with worms, and the four of them crouched on the bank in anticipation. On the rare occasions when something bit, Lucas did not take the fish home to the parsonage, but slit it open there and then to examine its insides.

One hot summer, Lucas and Edward stripped to their undergarments and flung themselves into the water, splashing noisily and frightening the fish into the depths. Harmony followed after them in her petticoat, wading in feet first, trailing her hands amongst the weeds. She looked over her shoulder at Arthur, who stood alone upon the bank, shuffling from foot to foot. He hugged his arms to his thin chest, and shuddered.

He had known, even then, that he was not permitted to join them. He knew that his body held the secret of all his shame.

§

He imagined that Hannah Hallingham stood over him, but woke to find it was Elia, tall and solemn, the hanging leaves that hid her sleeping place blowing in the breeze at her back. She knelt down beside Arthur's hammock, her hands folded in her lap. Moonlight touched the silver in her brows and hair.

"You knew him," she said. Arthur nodded. She passed a hand across her face, and he saw that she was shaking with dread.

"He is dead," Arthur whispered. The howl that had broken from him on the bank of the lake caught in his throat. "He is drowned. It is my fault."

Elia made no response, but continued to watch him expectantly.

"He has come to me twice, since then." Arthur sat up, curling himself into a ball. The hammock swayed gently from side to side. "Solid as though he were still living, still wet with the water he drowned in. He led me here."

Elia looked about the little room, as if half-expecting to see Shelo standing in the shadows. "We must be on our guard for him," she said, decisively. "I think that he will never truly leave this place. I think that he will not leave us be."

Outside, the deafening chorus of the night's creatures seemed muted. Arthur could hear the sleeping breaths of Elia's husband in the hidden room, his own thundering heart. Far above their heads, the branches of the skeleton tree were creaking.

"When did you...?" Arthur began.

"Oh, his shadow fell across me long ago." Though not harsh in their shape, her features had a hard look, like a living thing turned to stone across countless years. "I have grown beneath it my whole life."

Elia rocked forward upon her heels, until she was speaking almost into Arthur's ear. "I think that he has loved you, perhaps even as he loved me."

She gripped his shoulders in her cold hands.

"I think that if he could, he would have bound you to himself forever, and never let you go. That is his way. He wants to take what loves, Arthur Hallingham, and trap it between his hands like a fledgling bird. That is his way."

§

Elia gathered growing things from the deep places of the forest at dawn, when the wet reptilian songs of night were replaced by bird calls. Cloud hung in the uppermost branches of the trees, and every inch of greenery dripped with moisture. She bent waist-deep in the thick ferns to pluck seedlings from the earth, peeled strips of bark from the trunks of trees. She tasted everything, casting some back to the forest floor, placing the rest into a basket upon her hip. All of her movements were slow, subdued.

Arthur followed, obediently bearing armfuls of her spoils. In the hut beneath the skeleton tree, Elia and her silent husband crushed and boiled and powdered all that had been gathered. Cautiously, men and women from the nearby village crossed the barren clearing, consulting with her in lowered voices. They did not look her in the eye. She sent them away with poultices and bundles of herbs, taking her payment in cassava flour.

"When I was young," she told Arthur, "my mother had a medicine for every sickness. She helped those who feared her. She bound their wounds, and she birthed their children. She helped those among the women who were with child at the wrong time, if you understand."

Arthur understood. Uneasy, he left them to their work. He wandered alone beyond the clearing, past curtains of creepers and along the banks of lethargic rivers. Insects hovered in thick clouds above the surface of the water. Great water lizards bathed in the midday sun, white birds stepping delicately across their backs.

"*Shelo*," said Arthur aloud, into the close humming tangle of life. "*Shelo. Is there anywhere left for you to lead me?*"

It seemed to him that this was where he would end, whether soon, or on some distant day when his beard was grown long and his memory dim. Creepers would wind around his limbs and bind him to this place, until his body itself set down roots in the soil. He would pass his years forgotten and forgetful, a broken stranger in the house of Elia.

For this, he had crossed the wide ocean and watched his old life burn in Sam's backyard. For this they had defied Benjamin Barber, met with scores of the weary, driven Shelo's wagon and its secret cargo across the stretches of the southern prairies. They had become known from the eastern coast to the west, and this was where it ended. Shelo gone in the water, Flora wounded and fleeing, Arthur rotting in the deep of the forest.

Shelo. You have failed me. You have left me. It had all come to nothing. Arthur was as he had ever been, in the New World as in the old.

§

He cried his impotent fury and his grief to the shifting shadows between the trees. He kicked up the ground, sending birds screeching into the air. As night fell he calmed into shivering

116

resignation, and Elia found him huddled on the riverbank, his skin livid where the insects had fed upon him.

She trailed a toe in the shallows, stirring up the mud. Arthur saw again the elaborate patterns which climbed upwards from her ankles and encircled her lower legs, like a living creeper that had tried to pull her into the earth.

"Did he call you from some far place, too?" he asked her, when she sank down beside him. "Did he promise to you that which never came to pass?"

"I was born here," she said quietly. "In the very dwelling where you now find me, after the tide of blood came washing here from across the ocean."

She held out a hand and pointed through the trees, away from where the sun was now setting, towards the Atlantic. "Long ago, there came over the water a great governor from your land. Newly arrived, he desired to see the country, and was brought here by a band of traders. They were each drunk upon the fruitfulness of the land and the thought of riches. Somewhere along their way, they had forgotten..."

She trailed off. Close at hand, an enormous frog had crawled from the water and begun to inflate its throat. "My mother and some of the village women were out gathering near the water. These men came upon them unexpectedly, and did not hold back from their wicked desires. They were many, and they were strong."

Arthur's breath caught in his tightening chest. The frog began to rasp loudly, its call answered from every side.

"When the men at the village heard cries and struggling, they were fierce in their pursuit. They cut down every white man that day, save for the great governor himself, who made his escape down the river. It is said that he is a man of importance now, in the grassland country. They say that he dwells in comfort and ease, with servants to attend his every need."

She spat into the water, and for a fleeting moment, Arthur saw Shelo's own wrath in her.

"Two of the women were left with child from that day. One was my mother, and I do not know why she did not cleanse herself from it. She had done so for others, many times, and knew the herbs. She chose to give me life." Elia inclined her head, still in doubt, it seemed, that this had been an act of mercy. "The other was young, barely more than a girl, and she vanished in her shame. There were tales that she lived like a beast, that she gave birth alone in a black cave beneath the world. That she raised her child there in darkness, until the day when he was carried by a shallow stream into daylight."

Mist above the river obscured the stars. The bloated sun sank down behind the trees.

"I was bathing alone beside the pool," said Elia. "I was too young to fear him, then. He crawled out of the water, a wretched creature, and I took him to my mother. This is how Shelo came to be raised beneath our roof, away from my mother's people, who believed that neither of us deserved to live.

"You know him, Arthur Hallingham. We were raised together like brother and sister. He did not play, as children play, but was ever filled with bitter fury. He was sure from the first that he had been fathered by that great governor, the man who had done his wickedness in secret and fled without a care. Shelo believed this without reason and without doubt, as though he could not have been born of the seed of any lesser man."

"Elia..." began Arthur, queasy and light-headed with the shock of what was now dawning upon him. But it seemed that, having begun to speak of the unspeakable, she could not bear to stop.

"I was drawn to him in pity, from the first," she whispered. "I pitied him so deeply that in time, I forgot it was pity at all.

Even when I began to fear him, I supposed that I felt something else entirely. By the time we had left childhood, he knew what I bore towards him. It was the nearest to love that he had ever been shown, and like a moth to a flame he was drawn to it... to his destruction, and to mine."

She stared out towards the bend of the long river, utterly lost now in recollection. "They came to this land with such hunger in them, Arthur Hallingham. Some of them lived among us, for the sake of river pearls, or to tell us of their god. Of all the tribe my mother was quickest in her understanding, least in fear, so they stayed beneath our roof. Taught us their tongue. But then she caught the sickness that was her end, and fewer of them came. We were grown by that time, and we were left to each other, Shelo and I.

"He grew wilder, and I was driven further from him in my heart, even as he clung close. My eyes turned to another, the only man in the village who showed me kindness. This man saw beyond my shame, and was willing to take me as his wife." She seemed to be weighed so heavily by these words that her head sank to her chest. "I told you. Shelo holds us, whom he would call beloved, closer and more jealously than his own heart. His anger was boundless."

Arthur imagined Shelo's betrayed howl rising above the canopy, carrying for miles on the stifling air. He imagined Elia and her lover cowering at its sound, shoring themselves up against the breadth and power of his fury.

"Arthur Hallingham, I cut Shelo from myself. In the village I wed the man I loved, who in those days was not silent. But when we returned on our wedding night to the house of my mother, we found that... we found..."

It was apparent that she could go on no longer. She stood suddenly, and Arthur out of nervous instinct rose to his feet too.

The unexpected movement silenced the frog at their feet, which vanished back into the water with a splash. The night breeze bent the reeds. It had grown dark all around them.

In the river below, a great shape stirred, all winding tail and horned skin. A pair of bullet-black eyes broke the surface, and did not blink.

"Stay away from the tree that stands over our dwelling," said Elia. She passed a hand across her weary eyes. "Do not touch its trunk. For it bleeds a poison more bitter than I can say."

§

In the near-blackness Arthur turned in his hammock, restive. A fluttering insect passed close to his head. Moonlight shone in through the break in the roof. It illuminated pools of water on the floor, and a series of wet footprints which encircled him, leading out of the door.

He sat up and swung his long legs over the edge of the hammock, as if sleepwalking. He rose, and padded slowly across the hut, wearing only the cloth wrapped around his waist. In the room beyond, Elia and her husband were sound asleep.

Outside, the trail of wet footprints led away towards the tree that stood stark and bare in the moonlight. Arthur trod across the barren dust. Shelo was waiting for him. Drawing nearer, Arthur saw that he wore a strange, uncertain look. If he had not known better, he might have called it fear.

"Arthur," whispered Shelo. Lake water streamed from his sodden clothes and dripped from between his lips. His inked skin had a wet silver sheen. He reached out a hand, but Arthur hung back. "Arthur. Listen to me."

"What did you do?" asked Arthur. Something dripped onto his

shoulder. He realised that a thick dark resin was bleeding from the branches above him, oozing between the cracked bark of the trunk. It seeped into the dead ground beneath his feet.

"Oh, Arthur," said Shelo. A shudder passed through the whole of his broad body. "What hope is there when the heartbeat of your days is the stuff of smoke and shadows?"

Arthur reached up to brush the resin from his skin. It was the colour of old blood.

"I was born from the belly of the cold earth," whispered Shelo. "I came into this world, like you, out of man's wickedness. We were conceived in shame and born in darkness, Arthur. You and I."

"What did you do?" asked Arthur, again.

Shelo turned away. He cast his eyes out towards the dead ground that lay on every side of them. He spoke half in a trance. *"This I declared over her, and her marriage bed, and the husband she took. Whatever happiness you have, you have built it upon my broken back. And so may everything you touch be extinguished by you, as I have been."*

He turned back to Arthur, and suddenly he blazed with a dark fire that drowned out the night. He placed a hand upon his bare torso, to the left side of the ribcage, where the black bloom unfolded onto his skin.

"I cut out the heart of me," he said, with a dreadful music, "and locked it inside a tree."

Forcefully, emphatically, he lifted his hand from his chest. He placed it flat upon the trunk of the tree, and Arthur saw there, faded with the years but still etched upon the bark, the trace of a bloodied handprint.

"If you don't believe…" began Shelo, and he faltered, clasping at his empty chest again with both hands.

He beckoned Arthur forward, and trembling, he obeyed.

Shelo covered Arthur's hand with his. He pressed it to the trunk of the tree, and Arthur felt an unmistakable pulse beneath his palm.

§

And what would you make of me now, my brother, my sister, my friend?

The villagers looked upon him as some ghost conjured by Elia, a pale and unworldly thing. Passing between the huts, he sensed their accusing gaze. They whispered to one another, and stared with bald hostility.

"They think you are diseased," Elia told him. "They think that you have drunk of the poison of this tree." Her shadowed eyes traversed his face. "They know that you have been with Shelo."

Arthur's stomach plummeted. Before him flashed countless miles of road across the wind-blown prairie, the cries that had echoed through the night. "We did something," he whispered. "Whether it was great, or terrible, I am no longer sure."

Elia looked upon him like a priest regarding a confessor. But she did not place her hand upon his head, spoke nothing of absolution.

"He does not leave," she said, fretfully. "He never left me. The roots beneath the ground and the branches above it are his. And all these years, to my shame and my husband's, I have found myself as barren as this earth."

Of their own accord, her hands passed across her slender belly. Something seemed to groan and then break within Arthur like a bridge bearing too much weight. He turned away, but Elia touched his arm.

"He cannot leave us, Arthur Hallingham. Do you not understand?" Her smile was as empty as the cave beneath the world. "We are such creatures as he is."

He washed himself in the shallow lagoon where he had first seen

Elia, but the dirt would not come off. His beard grew again, patchy upon his face and neck like a moss. He felt that the plants of the forest might sink their roots into his flesh. Half-naked, he slept in the house of Elia, beneath the cursed shadow of the tree where Shelo's heart was buried.

He thought of Flora, and his grief was complete. It was unbearable, that he would never know whether she had made it to safety. He had failed her utterly, just as Shelo had failed him.

He sunk beneath the weariness of Elia, the persistent silence of her husband. His body grew accustomed to the heavy air, the sticky heat. He wandered in the deep of the forest, where clouds hung low in the canopy and great blooms the size of grown men dripped pollen. In the night he thought he glimpsed wet footprints surrounding his hammock, the flicker of an unearthly blue light.

§

What would you make of me now? Would you know me, still?

He could remember little. He supposed that he, too, was faded now from the minds of those he had once known. And then one day hands hammered upon the walls of the house of Elia, and a clamour of voices surrounded them. Elia hurried outside to speak with the villagers, then beckoned to Arthur through the doorway.

"They say that somebody has come for you. A man who has journeyed many miles."

Before he could protest, hands were gripping his arms and shoulders and sides, propelling him forwards. He was bundled into the undergrowth, and towards the village. He found himself pushed through the doorway of a hut by impatient hands. He remembered, from so long ago, the earthquake that had awakened him. The tall outlaw in pursuit, and the small.

Ripstone came to his mind a moment too late, and even as he began to struggle, yelling out in his panic, he caught sight of a wiry figure stood in the shadows at the back of the hut. The villagers forced him forwards.

Then the small man stepped into the light, and upon his familiar face came a look of astonishment, and horror, and wonder.

10

High Country

Shelo took the pistol from Barber's daughter, bound her wrists and ankles, and gagged her with a piece of cloth to silence her ferocious cursing. Arthur hung back, but Shelo was unhesitating, depositing her in the back of the wagon and drawing the flap closed so that her cries were muffled yet further. As they drove in haste away from Barber's campfire, her protestations were still audible.

"She will tire," Shelo assured Arthur, and by sundown it finally appeared that he was right. They came to a halt in the shelter of a wooded canyon, hidden from prying eyes and far from the road. As Shelo unhitched the horse, he signalled for Arthur to check in the back of the wagon.

Nervously he climbed in, and crouched next to the rigid body on the blanket. The girl's eyes were huge above her gag, and she began to wriggle when she saw him, emitting emphatic sounds.

His hands shook as he went to untie the cloth from her mouth, and he snatched them back as soon as it was loose, anxious that she might bite him.

She spat the gag onto the wooden boards, and lay glaring, a livid red mark across her face. "What's the matter?" she exclaimed. "Ain't you never seen a fe-male before?"

He opened his mouth, but had no reply. She cocked her head to one side like an owl. "Loose me of these ties, won't you? I need a piss."

Arthur pressed the backs of his hands to his face, which he knew had reddened.

"You shall be sorry if I am hurt," she told him. "Listen. My daddy's surely comin' for me, and if he finds I have been treated ill..."

He untied her hands first, keeping a tight grip on her upper arm, then fumbled at the bonds around her ankles. She did not struggle or lash out but allowed him to do his work, and to lead her cautiously down the step when she was free.

"She says she needs to relieve herself," Arthur told Shelo, who was beginning to lay their fire. He rose and drew nearer, looming over the girl, who shrunk back. She stared transfixed into his eyes.

"How old are you, child?" he asked quietly. Dusk was falling among the trees, which cast long shadows across the clearing.

"I am Flora Barber. And I am five-and-twenty."

"You are no older than seventeen. And already fallen in with such company."

Her eyes ranged over the loops and swirls of the inked patterns on his skin. She seemed too lost in fearful fascination to respond, scratching at the lice on her scalp. Shelo took her pistol from his belt, watching her as he turned it over in his huge hands. "Take her into the trees there, Arthur," he said, at length. "Do not let her from your sight. If you try to run from here, Flora Barber, I will shoot you in the back."

Arthur kept a grip on her arm as he led her into the undergrowth, but let her move away from him to crouch behind a tree. Contrary to Shelo's instructions, he averted his gaze out of embarrassment, but Flora made no attempt to run. She returned to him tugging her skirts back down again, entirely unselfconscious. When they passed the horse, which had moved to the edge of the trees in an attempt to find edible greenery, she insisted on stopping to look more closely.

"This is the creature what pulls your wagon? This alone? Why, it looks half-dead. It ain't possible."

Preferring not to give thought to this or any other uncanny

126

matter that hung upon Shelo, Arthur did not answer her. She turned towards him, not prepared to surrender her puzzlement. "Are you tradesmen of some sort? I don't see that you have much in the way of wares."

"Climb back in here," said Arthur, "and if you are quiet, I shall not gag you this time."

She obliged, and he helped her back into the wagon, binding her wrists and ankles with the double knots that Silas had taught him. He helped her shuffle backwards so that she could sit up, leaning against the wooden panelling. She watched him beadily as he left her, bundled up amidst the piles of empty jars.

"Once, when Mister Harpey was in jail and awaitin' the noose, my daddy put a torch to the town gate and a bullet in each guardsman. They rode away through those flames, he says, like Shadrach an' Abednego, with the townsfolk up in arms all about them. He don't let useful men go to rot."

Arthur swallowed.

"Won't be long," she insisted. "He'll come for me, an' make an end of you both. Won't be long, now."

§

Arthur and Shelo sat side by side against the wagon as darkness fell. They piled dead wood upon their cooking fire and lit the blue lamp. Arthur grew increasingly tense as the night thickened, convinced that every shadow and snapping twig was a wolf or bear, or perhaps one of Barber's men closing in upon them.

"Will they come after us?" he asked.

The black of Shelo's eyes did not reflect the firelight. He pulled Flora's gun from his belt, and to Arthur's alarm, held it out. "Do you shoot, Arthur?"

Long ago, an ocean away, he had stood in the grounds of Harcourt Hall with a hunting pistol in his hands. His brother Edward on one side of him, Lucas on the other, he had fired wide each time, sending alarmed pheasants screeching into the air.

"Not well."

Shelo pressed the gun into his palm. "Her father may send men. If he cares for her, he will come himself."

Deeply discomforted, Arthur pocketed it. "Shelo," he began, uncertain whether he truly wanted an answer, "for what purpose...?"

"You heard Barber. She knows the roads of this land as well as any of them. It is many years since I passed through the southern country, before the place I seek was even built."

Come the morning, Shelo set her loose. To Arthur's surprise she did not run, but instead returned from out of the trees after going to relieve herself. She lingered, sniffing the air as Shelo stirred a pan of leftover broth upon the fire. When he held out a bowl to her, wordless, she moved near to snatch it away. She ate on her feet, ignoring the spoon and gnawing greedily at scraps of meat. Liquid splashed down her shirt. Her eyes flickered between the two of them, watchful and untrusting above the rim.

"You gonna kill me?" she asked, at length. She wiped her mouth on her sleeve, and handed the empty bowl back to Shelo.

He raised the corner of his lip to show the tips of his teeth, but did not reply. Done with licking out her bowl, Flora looked over her shoulder, taking in the smallness of their wagon before the expanse of tall pines, the sharp rising of the rocks beyond.

"There's bears in this high country," she said fretfully. "An' they do much mischief. My daddy told me, that when a bear catches a cow, he bites a hole into the hide, and blows with all his power into it 'til the animal swells ex-cessively." She turned her lantern eyes back upon them. "Then it dies, the air expandin' greatly between the flesh and the hide."

"Any such creature would smell me out," said Shelo, "and flee."

Flora continued to look at him, and apparently finding nothing here to disagree with, gave a nod. She moved a step closer to their fire, but the whole of her body remained tense. To Arthur it seemed that she was ready to flee at the smallest sudden sound.

Shelo pulled the soft meat from a rabbit leg at the bottom of the pot, shredding it between his teeth. As Flora stretched out her half-gloved hands towards the flames, he shifted himself to face her.

"I have heard there is a place in the southern country," he said, "where the fields are filled with tall yellow flowers, blooms with huge black eyes. Beyond these fields there is a grand house of white brick and blue timber, set against a hill."

Flora drew her hands back to her chest again. "Oh, no. I ain't gonna do what my daddy forbade. I ain't no turncoat."

Shelo laughed, and she jumped. He ran his tongue across his pointed canines. "You are alone," he said, "and you are weaponless. If you run, the beasts will eat you."

Arthur saw her eyes dart over Shelo's great hulking form, then back into the trees again. Trepidation chilled him. He began to hope, with some fervour, that she would simply obey.

§

Her gun sat stone-heavy in his pocket. He rode beside her on the back step of the wagon, a checking hand upon her elbow at Shelo's command. Where his feet brushed the ground, hers dangled in mid-air. She would not stop her restless wriggling, eyes constantly scanning the horizon for signs of her father.

Unawares and barely beneath her breath, she talked to herself.

She craned around to gawp at Arthur when she thought that his eyes were upon the road, which fell away from them with ever-increasing speed. She gnawed at the red-raw skin upon her hands.

Now that there were three of them, they slept out upon the ground around the ashes of the fire. Arthur laid himself at Shelo's feet, and Flora curled in the grass a little way from them. Long after Shelo had fallen asleep, his broad flank rising and falling in slow rhythm, Arthur could see Flora's eyes still wide and wakeful in the glow of the lamp. He realised that she was watching the two of them in expectant fear, and when she caught Arthur's gaze, she turned quickly to face the other way. He could make out the quivering of her body beneath the voluminous coat.

He huddled closer to Shelo, and shivered there on the grass until dawn. When the weak sun climbed up above the line of the rocks, he saw that Flora had now fallen into a heavy doze, but with her arms wrapped protectively around herself. He wondered if she had been expecting one of them to descend upon her in the dark. He did not know how to tell her that, for his part at least, such fear was needless.

§

Upon the road that day, Arthur began to think that he caught glimpses of a rider lagging some way behind the wagon. The figure made no attempt either to draw level or to stay out of sight, but instead lingered on their tail. Flora's head perked up eagerly as she strained for a sight of her father's red coat, but even as Arthur thumped at the side of the wagon to alert Shelo, she drooped in disappointment. The rider was plainly unfamiliar to her, dark-haired and bearded, swathed round in a cloak.

"We keep our speed," called Shelo. "He will not come near until nightfall."

At dusk, he halted the wagon in the shelter of a redwood tree, and lit the blue lamp before crossing to the other side of the hill to snare their supper. It was a damp night, and the fire sputtered, coughing out swathes of smoke. Arthur warmed himself beside it as best he could, half an eye upon Flora, who was slouched against the trunk of the tree. She was staring fixedly out into the gloom, but her head snapped around as footsteps approached.

Arthur scrambled to his feet. The cloaked man had dismounted, and led his horse near by the reins. Man and beast were both flecked with drizzle.

"Are you the travellers of whom I have heard?" he asked. "Can you do for me what the whispers say you can do?" His voice was clipped, careful, but laced with melancholy. His face was all in shadow, save for the languid eyes.

"Who are you?" demanded Arthur shakily. He glanced over his shoulder, but there was no sign of Shelo. Flora stood to her feet.

"I wish to buy your services," said the man. "I will pay whatever you ask if you can truly end my torment."

Coldness ascended Arthur's spine. "Shelo will return soon," he managed to say. "Flora, will you take this gentleman's horse?"

Drawing nearer in cautious fascination, she obeyed. The man let go of the reins without protest, looking upon Arthur and Flora as if they were creatures made from fog and darkness.

"I had never in all my life imagined such a thing as this, until I heard it from the mouth of one who had seen it." He passed a shaking hand across his forehead. "Will this man Shelo wish to hear my sorry tale?"

Arthur thought of the silver-haired widow who had approached them many days ago, the way that Shelo had recoiled as she spoke of her grief. "I do not think so."

"Very well. But it is like bile in my throat. I can barely swallow it down."

"You should sit," exclaimed Flora. Her gaze was fixed upon the stranger's face. He looked back at her dully. "Pull your boots off for a bit, mister. We got a fire."

As Arthur turned to search for a sign of Shelo, she tied the man's dun mare to the tree then led him by the arm towards the flames. He sat rigidly, his thoughts clearly elsewhere. Arthur paced to the brink of the rise, squinting through the darkness, but Shelo was still nowhere to be seen. Afraid to face the stranger without him, Arthur lingered for a time, becoming aware of the murmur of voices from beside the fire.

When he headed reluctantly back, he found the bearded man speaking to Flora in low, lifeless tones. She leant forward to listen.

"… with the militia for eleven years, my child. I have fought many battles, against the natives and the French, and never before doubted my own discipline. I have captained regiments."

"My daddy was a militia man," said Flora proudly. "In his day. With a polished fire-arm, and a bayonet, and a great black stallion, so he says."

"It is a noble calling. Myself, I never gave thought to wife or children. I have never been drawn to look at women, the way that other men do. I believed myself wed to my profession…"

He gave a stiff laugh, but fear flickered in his eyes. Looking up, he noticed Arthur standing close once more, and his hands moved in his lap. "Tell me," he murmured, "have you ever been brought to the mercy of desires which are your master and your shame?"

Arthur froze. He could feel the blood rushing to his face.

"Forgive me. I shall speak plainly, for I must, at last." The man let out his breath with a shudder. "Some months ago, a soldier from another company was sent to me as my second-in-command. He is several years my junior. He is handsome, and courageous, and true. I can think of nothing else. Do you understand me?"

132

At that moment, a shadow loomed beyond the flames, and the three of them turned as one. Shelo had returned, dripping with the damp of the fields, his inked face and body lit in fiery shades. His eyes glinted black. In each hand, he held a rabbit by its hind legs. The two little bodies dangled freely, gaping mouths still straining for their final breaths, necks raw where the snare had closed upon them.

The militia man stood at once. There was terror and pleading in his face.

"You have come to end your torment," said Shelo, assuredly. And he grinned his hook-cornered grin.

§

"Mister," whispered Flora. She shook Arthur by the shoulder. It was the deep of the night, and he had dozed off curled against the warmth of the horse's back. "What's that sound?"

The fire had died now, but her face was faintly visible in the lamplight. Arthur could tell that she had been reluctant to approach him, and she drew back as soon as he sat up. The tip of her nose was pink with cold.

Drifting into the night from the back of the wagon, where Shelo had led the militia man hours before, was a low and abhorrent groaning. It was not so loud as the cries of the widow-woman, but it chilled Arthur to his very bones.

Flora's teeth were chattering. She seemed torn between moving nearer to Arthur, solely for the comfort of another human shape, and retreating as far from him as possible. Then the cries from the wagon rose in pitch, and she sank down next to him.

"My daddy," she murmured, more to herself than to him, "was a militia man. With a great black stallion for ridin'. Led a handful of his company once against a whole clan of hollerin' savages, who killed all but him, and left his comrades' bodies for the crows."

They huddled side by side against the sleeping animal. Flora did not say another word, but her chest rose and fell with shallow, hurried breaths.

Day dawned, drenched in silver mist. Arthur pressed a hand to his aching neck. Beside him, Flora wiped her nose on her sleeve. All was quiet. Arthur found his eyes drawn, with heavy dread, to the wagon.

The lamp had flickered out in the night and now smoked faintly. Dew hung upon the white cover, dripping down into the grass. It was the most innocuous of sights.

"What –" began Flora. But he held a finger to his lips.

There was a sudden thump and a rustling from within. Then the canvas flap at the back was parted.

The man who emerged out into the weak morning sunlight bore the same features as he who had entered the night before. He was dark-haired and bearded still, of stocky build, wrapped in a thick cloak. But there, all resemblance ended. His eyes, which had been moist and dulled with grief, were now blank. His face was set in a look of empty calm, as if he had never known the slightest care.

He blinked, and staggered on unsteady feet as he descended to the ground. His movements were infantile. He was like a being newly created.

The sight of this unnatural creature filled Arthur with such horror that he scrambled instinctively away, almost falling over backwards in his hurry. Shelo's horse, which had risen to graze beneath the tree, tossed its head. Flora, transfixed, took a step nearer.

"Mister?" she called, tentatively. The man did not so much as look round.

Shelo appeared out of the back of the wagon, shirt sleeves rolled

134

up, plainly exhausted. He watched the stranger weave and wind his way back onto the road like a drunk from a tavern.

"Leave him," he commanded Flora, who had made a move to intercept the stranger's path.

"He don't know where he is!" she protested. "What about his horse?"

"Untie it, then, if you wish. But he will not be able to ride."

Flora hurried to lead the mare towards her staggering master, tugging at his sleeve and trying to place his limp hands on the horse's saddle. "She's yours, remember? Don't you want her?"

Shelo watched, expressionless. Though everything in him abhorred it, Arthur moved across to help Flora, attempting to hold the horse still. The mare's eyes had rolled backwards in her head, and her whole body had stiffened, patches of her hide quivering.

Between the two of them, they managed to grip the man by the legs and hoist him up into the saddle so that he slouched there, lifeless as a doll. The horse uttered a stifled scream, prancing skittishly from side to side. Arthur, who had been trying to look anywhere save into the stranger's face, found that they were eye-to-eye as the rider slumped against the horse's neck. The thought occurred that he was not gazing upon any human thing.

They watched the mare and her burden make their meandering way into the distance. Several times it appeared that the rider would fall, but Flora had wrapped the reins around his hands and lodged his feet into the stirrups. From some way off, it simply looked as if he had fallen asleep in the saddle.

Slowly, Shelo descended from the back of the wagon. He smoothed back his oiled hair where it had fallen about his face, and extinguished the smoking wick of the lantern between his fingertips.

"Come," he said, with finality. "It is time for us to go."

§

Arthur was gathering firewood in the trees near to their next night's camp when he heard footsteps close at hand. Afraid that the militia man might have returned to them, he dropped his armful of kindling and tried to ascend onto the broad branches of the nearest tree. As he struggled to pull himself up, he heard the sound of familiar voices. He fumbled in his pocket for Flora's gun.

Harpey's tall form and Ripstone's small one were moving away from him. Their pistols were holstered, and they were not troubling to muffle their speech or their footfalls. Beyond the trees, a thin line of smoke was rising from Shelo's fire.

Arthur lifted the gun, but could not steady his grip. He crept closer, and saw Shelo rise slowly from a seated to a crouching position, like a great cat readying itself to spring. His eyes narrowed to slits. Flora was nowhere to be seen, and Arthur wondered if Shelo, sharp-eared, had hidden her in the wagon.

"Savage!" called Ripstone. He seemed unable to stand still in Shelo's presence, and shifted onto one foot, then the other. "Send forward Barber's girl, and we'll have no more words with you!"

Harpey sucked on the space in his upper gum where several teeth were missing. He dug into his pocket, and pulled out a coin, which he flipped through the air into Shelo's hand. He, like his companion, did not seem to want to draw any closer. "Our master has auth'rised this sum for her return."

"All of this sum?" Shelo gave a snarling laugh. He barely glanced at the coin before tossing it back to Ripstone, who fumbled the catch. The outlaw backed away, unaware that Arthur was now mere feet behind him.

Harpey stood his ground. "As a gentleman, Barber is prepared to offer you re-compense."

"With no urgency, and by another's giving?" Shelo turned away.

Arthur's foot slipped upon the damp ground, and he lurched forward, steadying himself just before he collided with Ripstone. Instinctively he raised Flora's gun, its mouth coming to rest against Ripstone's shoulder. Ripstone froze, as Harpey's pale eyes ranged calmly over Arthur.

"What is your name, man?" he demanded.

"Arthur," he stammered. "Arthur H-Hallingham."

"You speak like a prince, and appear like a madman," said Harpey. Ripstone cursed and wriggled. "What were you before you fell in with this diabolist?"

"The youngest son of an illustrious line," whispered Arthur.

"Illustrious line or none, you've made an enemy of me!" Ripstone flinched away from the gun barrel as though it were burning a hole in his shirt.

Shelo gave a small shake of his head, and Arthur lowered the gun. Ripstone gripped the handle of his own pistol, clearly fuming, but too afraid of Shelo to draw.

"Take the girl, then, and do what you will," he said. He spat on the ground at Arthur's feet. "She is of little use to us."

§

Sent to untie their prisoner again, Arthur found her slumped despondently against the heap of covered jars. She looked somehow diminished there, and averted her face from him, biting at her lip. He tugged free the knots from her wrists and ankles once again, but she did not move, resting her forehead against the wagon's frame. As he turned to leave her, she spoke up.

"I'll do as he asks. I know the way."

He glanced back, and she pulled herself to her feet. Her hurt was written like script across her flat, freckled face. She shook it from herself as a dog might shake fleas, and followed him back to the fire.

11

All You Weary

With the road before him and Barber's gang behind, Shelo whipped their horse hard. It ran with impossible fervour, heaving the rattling wagon behind it, a thick lather on its flanks. He bent over in the driver's seat, whip raised high, cloak billowing about him. He bore down upon rabbits on the road in a fury of speed. Each night when they drew to a halt, he leant close to the horse's ear and whispered into it as the beast's foamy sides shuddered and heaved.

To the southern country. To the southern country.

At every crossroads, Flora raised herself up to hang off the back step of the wagon, hand shielding her eyes as she took in the lie of the land. The wheels spun upon paths that grew flatter as the weeks passed, narrower, fields stretching out in every direction. Flocks of white birds winged overhead.

And each night there came a timid knocking at the side of the wagon, a cloaked figure, a cleared throat. A pallid young woman, a stout old farmhand, a runaway son. *Is this...? Are you...?* Shelo loomed out of the blue-lit dark, offering his hand.

He stood before them like something from a fever-dream, and they looked fearfully behind at the road they had travelled. The sight of Arthur, of his strange body and uneasy bearing, caused them to pale yet further. It was only when their gaze lighted on Flora that they seemed to draw some measure of comfort and courage. Perhaps it was the homeliness of her freckled countenance, the sight of her spindly legs protruding from her oversized boots.

They looked at Shelo and Arthur, and saw grubby crooks like Sam; road bandits, witchery. They looked at Flora, and saw their daughters and their sisters. She seemed unaware of it but Shelo noticed, with the air of man who has bought a cow for meat, only to find that it gives good milk. He let her be, and lifted his eyes to the horizon.

"*Come to me, all you weary,*" he muttered beneath his breath. "*Come to me, you hideous and shameful and desperate. Come.*"

§

Arthur turned over in the night, sleepless. "Shelo," he asked. "Where are we going?"

"*South, Arthur,*" breathed a voice from out of Shelo's great bulk. "*South.*"

His broad chest rose and fell, but even curled close as he was, Arthur could hear no heartbeat. The ink eyes upon Shelo's lids stared ceaselessly up into the night sky, where the plough, far brighter than Arthur had ever seen it, pointed back the way they had come. A month after they had left the hill country behind them, the sky stretched between two low horizons, a speckled canvas of impossible breadth.

He recognised the new angles of the constellations from Lucas's meticulous maps, which they had unfolded upon the library table at Harcourt Hall whenever the conversation turned to the New World. With a sharp pang, he recalled Harmony drinking in these charts, memorising each and every star, asking ceaseless questions and debating with Lucas into the small hours of morning. Arthur himself had been content simply to sit with them, brandy in one hand and the other resting on the parchment.

On such nights Arthur had forgotten, sometimes for hours at

a stretch, what he was. He had sat with Lucas and his sister as they played chess, or pored over maps, joining in at his leisure but more often observing in silence. For once, his skin and flesh had settled upon his bones as though they belonged there. Candlelight flickering upon their faces, senses warmed by brandy and pleasantly blurred by tiredness.

It was the thought of these times, more than any of the horror that had followed, which weighed most heavily upon him now. He remembered the hand that had caught his wrist as he made to leave, and began to awaken with her name upon his lips, crying it into the darkness before he could hold it in. His body quivered and retched as it had done aboard the *Head of Mary*. He wondered, for the first time since he had lain down at Shelo's feet in the attic room, when he would know relief.

"Mister! Mister!" He found Flora bent over him, wretched in the dim blue light. "You're screamin' it again… please…"

Blearily, he sat up, and she backed off. "What?"

"*Harmony*." She was quivering. "You keep callin' it out. *Please*, mister…" Behind her, in the wagon, Shelo's newest visitor was letting out a lung-splitting howl. Arthur realised that Flora had been unable to bear the crescendo of both noises at once.

He could not reply. The howling continued, followed by a sharp outbreak of gasping sobs.

"Is she your wife?" whispered Flora, who looked as if she wanted to bury her head in the silent earth. "What became of her?"

Still halfway between sleep and waking, Arthur answered without intending to. "She is my sister, whom I left behind in England. I have no wife, nor ever shall."

He closed his eyes and saw her, resplendent in her favourite plum-red gown. Her plentiful dark hair fighting to escape its pins. Her oval face full of barely-suppressed humour.

Since the youngest days of their childhood, he could remember only a handful of times when she had not appeared this way, straight-backed and high-spirited. On the night that he fled Harcourt Hall, he had seen the joy drain from her like spilled wine. Her grief had been fierce, her tears defiant. Out of all of them, after the storm of Edward's fury, she alone had dared to suggest the impossible.

Stay, Arthur. Stay.

§

Shapes darting beyond the lamplight brought Flora closer, closer, until she lay just yards from Arthur and Shelo. She crawled nearer on her belly, ever wary. Even when Shelo had gone to the back of the wagon, she did not come to sleep beside Arthur again. It seemed that she was unsure whether to fear him more than whatever lay out in the darkness.

At first he took these shadows for natives, but he soon saw that he was mistaken. The figures were black-skinned, raggedly clothed, leading horses with muffled hooves. They carried bundles of hurriedly wrapped possessions, cooking pots, babies bound to their backs. They moved furtively, and only ever beneath the cover of night.

Shelo pointed out the same constellation which had caught Arthur's attention. "They name it the drinking gourd. They say that it guides them north, to freedom."

By day the wagon passed alongside endless fields of white cotton, tended by bent-backed workers in the midday sun. The men were bare from the waist up, the women in dull blouses, their hair hidden beneath scarves. The air was thick with fibres, which drifted upwards and hung in choking clouds. Sweat shone upon every whip-scarred skin.

Arthur thought of the bodies that he, Silas and the others had tipped into the ocean after the sickness that raged through the *Mary*'s hold. He thought of the figures they had seen leaping overboard from the flaming vessel. His pity for these sunken dead wavered, as the thought came that theirs had been the better lot.

"*Come, all you desperate,*" murmured Shelo. He halted the wagon in a shaded dip at the roadside, and lit the lamp as the golden sun sunk down beyond the cotton fields. He crouched upon a tree stump, his eyes gleaming in the dimness like twin coals, and waited.

A handful of workers came treading through the cotton plants at dusk, glancing fearfully back at the distant plantation house. They approached Shelo with their eyes downcast, unbuttoning their shirts to show him the scars they bore. They muttered to one another in their own tongues, spoke out in broken voices.

Such things we have heard, from the mouths of natives, from swift travellers, from the underground roads where our brothers and sisters have fled north. If these tales are true, we would give anything. But we have nothing to give.

"I ask nothing," said Shelo. His eyes glittered in the falling dark. "You must only be willing."

One by one they entered the wagon, and hours later emerged transformed. They reeled and staggered, mouths gaping blankly. They moved as though there was now nothing within their skin. Arthur, Flora and the waiting huddle watched them stumble away through the cotton field, these blundering infants, these newly made things. Their faces were cleansed of all expression.

There was no question of sleep. Arthur watched Flora's curiosity do battle with her fear as she first tiptoed close to the back of the wagon, then retreated again. Fluttering insects were drawn towards the lamp's blue flame, throwing huge shadows before they were swallowed into the fire. At last, exhausted, she sunk down close to Arthur, at the edge of the cotton plants. She turned her small flat face towards him with a look of pleading enquiry.

He shook his head. He was certain now that he had no wish to understand what took place upon the boards in the back of Shelo's wagon. Flora wrung her hands together in her lap, and drew her knees up to her chin.

"I ain't never been away from my daddy before you took me," she said, after a time. "Not on my own. I never even thought of it."

Arthur tilted back his head and hunted out the shape of the drinking gourd in the sky. Flora looked over her shoulder at the wagon, her voice faint and fretful.

"He makes me think of caymans, you know, great water lizards. Mighty strong jaws they got. I know that if one of 'em takes a hold of you, you gotta push your fingers into his eyes." Violently, she mimed the gesture. "Makes 'em let go."

She turned her gaze back to Arthur again. "Strangest thing is, there are these little white birds what live inside their mouths, pickin' the meat from their teeth, and they won't harm 'em."

He spoke helplessly into the darkness. "He saw me from across the world, when I was a gentleman in a fine house and had never set foot upon this continent. He knew me like nobody else, and he called me to himself."

"For what purpose?" persisted Flora.

"For the purpose of following him," said Arthur. His heart was pounding painfully. It was half a secret, still, even to himself.

Unsatisfied, she let out a heavy breath through her nose. They watched the last of the workers shuffle away from the wagon through the long grass, graceless and bewildered. Insect noise flooded the night.

§

"They will come in flocks," said Shelo. "They will come in droves."

He was not mistaken. As they stopped each night at the edge of the plantation fields, the trickle of workers coming to find them at sundown became a stream. Arthur's lungs grew thick with fibres and with dust. He had the sense of being caught upon the edge of a swelling wave, a force growing unseen beneath them, carrying them ever higher and further.

"We heard of your approach weeks ago," they were told by a tall sombre African with pox-marked features, "and have talked of nothing else." There was a burning look in his lean face. At his back, twenty or so others gathered, hopeful eyes raised towards Shelo. He let them touch the intricate inked lines upon his skin.

"The native," whispered a woman whose belly was uncomfortably swollen. "The Englishman. And the straw-haired girl. We have heard..."

Troubled in the face of their bare desperation, Arthur turned aside. Shelo drove away from the beaten track, the better to avoid the angered overseers who came upon their tail. At the edge of an indigo plantation, they were pursued by a group of worker-women who wept and wailed loudly, tearing at their hair and flinging rocks at the wagon. They lifted their hands to heaven, as though they looked upon spirits from the other side.

Shelo's face closed in upon itself. "Not all are willing," was all he would say, when they drew to a halt near a swift river to see what damage had been done. "There will always be those who are blind and deaf to wonders." Spokes had been snapped on the back wheels, and the canvas torn. He hammered it back onto the frame, refusing assistance, and headed out alone into the fields to burn away his ill temper. Flora flinched as he slashed into the indigo plants with a stick, scattering scented flowers in his wake.

Shadows had deepened beneath her eyes through too many

restless nights. Arthur rolled over in the moonlight to find that the spot where she had last been lying, in the grass some ten yards away from him, was empty. He raised himself from the ground with a growing sense of panic, not daring to imagine Shelo's anger if he were to return and find her gone.

He fought his way through the grass, and to his relief found her crouched at the edge of the water, contemplating how she might cross over. He darted forward and grabbed hold of her.

He was aware of her wriggling ferociously in his grasp, and then of a sharp pain on the back of his hand. Releasing her in his shock, he saw that she had bitten him hard, drawing three fat drops of scarlet blood.

"I'll do worse!" she spat at him. "I done as much to Ripstone before, and others of 'em!"

Her chest rose and fell rapidly as she wiped her sleeve across her mouth, glancing across each part of Arthur in turn as she decided whether to fight or flee.

"I will not hurt you," he managed to say. And then, as she began to scramble back from him, he pronounced more firmly, "*I will not, I swear it.*"

It was plain that she did not believe him. She backed away further, glancing over her shoulder, and he realised that she was about to fling herself into the water.

"I know what you want!" she cried, tugging her coat more closely to her body. "Even if you spare me your witchery, I know you won't leave me be!"

He saw the whites of her eyes, and seized at her wrist. "I do not..." he began. But he lacked the words to speak of this most intimate of matters. "I cannot..."

She seemed to sense that the moment had changed its nature, and fell still. He had never once attempted to explain it before, not even to Harmony, to whom he had told everything else. He had kept this close to himself, always. His strange body did not let him in on its secrets.

"I cannot," he stammered, "cannot feel towards women as other men do."

He found that his hands were shaking convulsively, and let go of her. She did not run, but stood before him holding her wrist. "You ain't never had a girl?"

"No."

"You said, you ain't got no wife."

He shook his head wearily.

Her head tilted to one side, and she began with curiosity: "That militia man, who we spoke with some weeks past..."

"No," Arthur interrupted hurriedly. "I cannot, and have never... towards anybody."

She was silent for a long while. She scratched her tangled mop of hair. "Suppose that ain't usual," she said slowly. "I been around men ev'ry day of my life, mister. I can tell you for certain, they've always been the kind for wantin' what men want."

She raised her eyes to him as though seeing him for the first time. "They been that kind, all right."

§

As the wagon rolled yet further southwards, workers raised their heads, snowy blossoms scattered all about them. The plantation fields fell away, stretches of white-speckled land beneath the clear sky. Shelo sat tall in the driver's seat, wearing a look like a hungry man at harvest.

Flora slung her boots across her shoulder and walked barefoot before the wagon, talking aloud to herself and beating at the road with a stick. She darted towards high ground in search of familiar landmarks, drew out rough lines for Shelo in the dirt. "You got some way to go, still. We ain't close to your grand house until we're deep into the grasslands, not so far from Spanish country."

"You have travelled these roads before?" asked Shelo.

"Oh yes, mister. My daddy found rich pickin's from merchants here, when we came through in years past. I know the way."

The mention of her father tripped from her tongue, and she lifted her eyes to the empty hillside trails, where no red-coated figure rode to her rescue. Shelo had turned away from her to buckle the horse into its harness, but she followed close after him.

"I want to know what your business is," she said. When he ignored her, she tugged on the sleeve of his shirt. He looked back at her, finally, and she drew herself up with new resolve. "I can help."

Arthur expected Shelo to strike out at her, or at the very least to snarl contempt. But he did neither. Slowly, his tongue caressed the tips of his pointed canines.

"What do you think of it, Arthur?" he asked quietly. "Is there another use could we make of this little stray?"

She did not huddle far from the fire as Shelo prepared their food, but sat close, warming her hands. The three of them watched the flames until they began to die, Shelo turning the embers with a long branch. A coyote somewhere nearby started up a thin howl, which was answered from beyond the oncoming hill.

Flora picked at her teeth with a split stick, staring out at the steep rise that would be the morning's journey.

"Shall you be goin' back, Arthur? To your sister, and your own shore?"

"No," he said. He sensed Shelo's gaze upon him. "Never."

"I ain't got sisters," Flora said distantly. "No brothers, neither, that I know of. I guess I got a mother, somewhere…"

Arthur turned away, agitated, but she continued to herself. "My daddy, he says chances are he never saw her face by daylight, which I s'pose is usual. He can't tell me nothing, save that she was prob'ly full of pox and scabies."

She flipped the stick over between her fingers, and began to chew the other end unconcernedly. "Can't tell me the town neither, as he passes through so many, and she left me at the crossroads. I don't recall it, as I was so small, but he says she put me in a box with a label 'round my neck all wrapped in an old petticoat, and a shilling tucked down by my feet."

Arthur imagined the outlaw sat high on a gleaming steed, reining his whole party to a stop at the sight of the little swaddled thing by the roadside. Something about the picture did not sit right. His doubt must have shown in his face, as Flora added, "I sent up such a screamin' at the sound of their hooves that his horse near threw him off. He says he was in half a mind to break my head against a tree, since I was so wrinkled and noisesome. But it came to him that passers-by might willingly stop for the sight of a crying child, the better to be ambushed."

"Such is the way of things," said Shelo unexpectedly, from the other side of the fire. "That men should be so heedless in their fathering."

They both looked up at him. "I figure," said Flora after a moment's surprised pause, "he never needed to give me a share of meat and bread, but always did." She broke her stick in half, and threw it into the fire. "He paid me heed enough."

§

They topped the rise in the middle of the day, and looked out upon an endless ocean of gold. Grasslands stretched as far as the eye

149

could see, from the eastern horizon to the west. Shelo sat back in the driver's seat, breathing in the air expectantly. His great chest rose and fell. Flora lifted her face to the warm wind.

Arthur closed his eyes. The breeze washed over him, and he felt something within him lift, for the first time in numberless months. The scent of the grasses was sweet. He imagined himself far above the entire sight, seeing the white cover of the wagon billowing like a sail amidst the tawny waves.

And for a fleeting, uneasy moment he remembered the tale that Silas had told of the cursed ship *Temperance*, lost upon the sea with its cargo of the blind.

12

Grasslands

They slept beneath the stars together, curled close like an abandoned litter. Flora lay against Shelo's back, Arthur at his feet. On uninterrupted nights, their sleep was long and dreamless, the ground soft beneath them.

The weary came one by one from the east and from the west, from the grassland settlements and the New World's furthest shores. They came following threads of rumour, of barely whispered things. "What you have heard in the night, now call out in the day," Shelo commanded them, as they staggered away from his wagon. "Speak of what has been done for you. Speak of the light of the blue lamp."

He did not follow them along the road, as Flora did, worrying over them like a bird over its flown fledglings. But he began to await their coming ever more eagerly. He lingered beyond the circle of lamplight, stalking back and forth. It was as if he had forgotten how to hold still.

"Your fame goes before you," they were told, by a heavily laden young woman who would not remove the veil that disguised her face. "They speak of you, now, in every town where I have stayed…"

"S'alright, miss," said Flora, taking her by the arm. "Lay down your burdens, now."

The woman looked between the three of them with some trepidation. When her gaze fixed on Arthur, she asked to his astonishment, "Arthur Hallingham?"

His body revolted at the sound of his full name. Baffled as to where she might have heard it, he dug his nails into his palms until they drew blood.

"I met a traveller seeking one of your description," the woman explained cautiously. "Three days past, at a wayside inn. A small man, in ragged clothing."

Arthur wiped his sleeve across his forehead. It seemed that Ripstone, and perhaps others among Barber's men, were still following after them. As word spread of Shelo's endeavours, the wagon was growing ever easier to find.

"What is said of me?" demanded Shelo.

"On the roads, they say that you have a medicine which cures all ills," whispered the woman. "They say that you can bring me peace."

A well-spoken gentleman arrived so weak from his journey that they fed him before taking him to the back of the wagon, watching him spoon stew shakily into his mouth. Shelo sat a little too close, his broad body looming over their visitor, rocking with impatience.

"What brings you? What misfortune have you known?"

The gentleman flinched back from him. "Must I?"

Shelo lowered his head. He let out a snorting breath through his nostrils like a horse, and apparently through sheer alarm, the man began to stammer.

"I loved, sir, as so many others have – fruitlessly. She would not hear me. She has been all of my life and breath. But now my bones are aching. After all…" He trailed off, his lips pressed together, his skin grey with weariness.

Shelo's eyes burned, cavern-deep in his hungry face. "What hope is there when the heartbeat of your days is the stuff of smoke and shadows?"

The stranger looked up. "Yes. Precisely."

Shelo's fingers raked the ground. "She has walked upon your broken back. But it is over now. I promise you, you shall know relief."

"Arthur," said Flora, as they lay back-to-back in the grass. "He likes to listen to 'em, now. No, that ain't right…" She sat up, frowning, and Arthur raised himself too. "He listens to 'em like he's starved for it."

"But before, he never wanted…"

"I know." She looked across at him, her hands twisting together, small face deathly serious in the dark. "I know."

Later, listening to the gentleman's muted groans, Arthur imagined how Hannah Hallingham might approach the wagon. She would hesitate, perhaps for many hours, following them at a distance before making her presence known. She would be tongue-tied from fear and grief. Her white hands clutching at her breast, she would fall on her knees before Shelo.

Please. Do not turn me away. I have done such things…

And oh, I am covered by my shame.

§

It seemed to Arthur that Shelo grew thinner than he had once been. His oiled hair lost some of its sheen. His eyes had a strange feverish brightness. He grew absent in the daytime, neglecting the whip which had once driven them along at a furious pace, allowing the ragged horse to wander and pause for grazing.

He began to mutter in his sleep, sweat breaking out upon his skin. Each morning when he rose, he appeared to leave on the ground behind him a patch of grass grown thoroughly dead and withered – for all the world as though he had leeched the very life from the ground.

"Arthur," he murmured, as they fought their way together through the grasses in search of water. White-capped mountains, bluish above the burnt yellow of the plain, rose to the west. "My Arthur. You would not turn from me, would you? You would not give way to fear, and retreat from me in your heart?"

"No, Shelo. No, of course…"

"If I give you words to say, will you say them?"

Arthur regarded him, willing, baffled. "Words? To whom?"

"The time is coming when I need you to do what only you can do. Only you, of all those I might have called upon." Shelo looked at him as he had once done in Sam's dim attic, hungrily, knowingly. Arthur felt his back straighten, his head lifting high. Shelo brushed a hand almost thoughtlessly against Arthur's face, and he quivered like a praised hound.

"You will speak for me," said Shelo. "In the world that once was yours. In the house whose foundation is built upon bones. You will see it, Arthur. You will see it soon enough."

Because Arthur still did not have the stomach for it, it was Flora who joined Shelo in the setting of snares, the cutting of wild hare skins from the meat. They took down a young doe and stripped the carcass, portioning each part with practiced efficiency. They worked side by side in silence before the fire, the dark head and the fair both bent in concentration, hands stained with blood. They cast the offal upon the flames. When they were done, Flora took in Arthur's distasteful look, wiping her sleeve across her face.

"We ain't all so very high-born," she said.

Shelo turned away, looking out over the swaying grasses. Their horse grazed hungrily close at hand, and the blue lamp burned. "In a land across the sea," he said softly, "Arthur was the youngest son of an illustrious line."

"You come here from your own will," asked Flora, wide-eyed, "or for some crime?"

Helpless, he cleared his throat. "My brother," he attempted, "he could not bear…"

"I should like to see it," Flora interrupted, before he could finish.

"England, you mean?"

She inhaled the steam from the venison stew in a deep, long breath, and her face shone. A smile broke onto her features. "The sea."

Shelo raised himself, his gaze still turned outwards towards the darkness. Wisps of cloud tumbled rapidly across the half moon. It seemed to Arthur that the wind itself replied to Shelo's restless mood, plucking noisily at the canvas cover of the wagon.

"There will be many, tonight," he said, in a low voice. "I will need help."

There was a silence. Arthur looked down at the ground. He had just opened his mouth to form some excuse or other when beside him, Flora rose to her feet. Shelo looked her appraisingly up and down. His gaze flickered over her shoulder to Arthur, with the merest hint of disappointment.

"All right," he said eventually. "Tie back your hair, child. And come with me."

§

Nestled unsleeping in the grass, Arthur was aware of the shapes which flocked from out of the night to cluster around the blue lamp; the weary, the hideous, the desperate. Their groans shook the earth. Their unsteady bodies staggered away one by one into the wilderness.

At sunrise Flora emerged from the back of the wagon. Hair escaped from her long braids, hanging lankly about her face. She stumbled into the long grass and crouched there on her hands and knees, ready to vomit. But she swallowed down her nausea. Deliberately, she wiped her sleeve across her mouth and steadied herself, rising to her feet once again. She squinted at Arthur, and they regarded one another in silence.

He did not ask her what she had seen, because he did not wish to know. Shelo emerged into the daylight behind them, stretching his body like a wintering beast. He yawned, his tongue arched, lips drawn back to show his pointed teeth. His eyes fixed upon Arthur and Flora, and slowly, incongruously, he smiled.

"Arthur," began Flora, later in the day when they rode together on the back step. Clouds above them rolled like a drifting mountain range. He turned fearfully to her, but she did not seem to know how to continue. She stared into the middle distance.

She did not speak again until they had finally drawn to a halt, and Shelo had disappeared over the hill to set his snares. "*Arthur*," she said, more resolutely this time. She grabbed him by the wrist, and he realised that she was shaking. She tugged him towards the back of the wagon, glancing over her shoulder in the direction that Shelo had gone. "I got to show you. No, come *on*."

He resisted her, nameless horror stopping his throat. He could make no sound, but simply shook his head in frantic refusal. Flora's stubbornness, however, outmatched his terror, and she pulled him bodily up the step and into the wagon's interior.

He had not been inside the covering since they had kept Flora tied there, in her first days with them. Now, as then, it was empty save for a dirty blanket laid upon the floor and a heap of covered jars at the back. A few stoppered bottles, filled with a milky, viscous liquid, were tucked into a corner.

"Look," whispered Flora, seemingly caught somewhere between wonder and deep disgust. "Art. You got to see this."

With unsteady hands, she pulled back the blanket which covered the pile of jars. And he saw that many of the containers, unused since he and Shelo had tipped Sam's collection into the harbour, were empty no longer. Fluttering behind the smudged glass were pale, winged forms, for all the world like the insects which flew to the blue lamp in the hours of night.

"They're moths," he said, blankly. His heart, which had been hammering in sickened anticipation, slowed. Puzzlement replaced dread.

"They ain't." Flora's gaze was fixed not upon the pile of jars, but on Arthur's face. She crumpled the blanket between her hands. Her eyes opened ever wider, silently urging him to catch on.

"Then, what?"

Flora picked up the nearest jar. The creature within flapped its delicate wings, then relinquished its struggle, sinking back down to the base of its prison.

"Art," she whispered, so quietly he could barely hear her. "Art. He did something... he does something to them people. He... and then these creatures, they bleed out from..." She swallowed several times, attempting to gesture at her body, but was unable to go on.

His heart had begun to pound again, this time with a laden urgency. To still it he grasped the thought that her illiterate mind – by candlelight and in fear of Shelo – might be compelled to believe all manner of outlandish things.

"They are just creatures, Flora," he insisted. "Just insects, just natural creatures." He reached out and ran his fingertips across the surface of the jar. He took hold of the cloth lid, and began to slowly unpeel it. Flora winced, but appeared too transfixed to stop him.

"Art," she whispered. "I wouldn't..."

Unbidden, Arthur's hands stopped in their motion. Wings quivered within the jar. He became dimly aware, as though he too viewed the world from behind thick glass, that Shelo now stood behind them. The wagon's white canvas cover rippled in the prairie wind.

"They came through their own will," said Shelo.

Flora took an involuntary step closer to Arthur. Shelo's eyes were upon the jar in Arthur's hands. His broad chest heaved with some unfathomable emotion.

"They came through their own choice," he said, "and surrendered themselves. Their very spirit. Their very breath."

§

He showed Arthur how to light the fire, guiding his hands towards the driest kindling, demonstrating how to catch the last rays of the sun with the curved edge of a jar. The tiny sparks, hesitant at first, leapt between the twigs and dried grass. Shelo sat facing Arthur and Flora through the flames.

"Slitwire Sam taught me many things," he said. "I improved my knowledge of certain medicines. Of certain herbs. But it was always my belief that a man less dull than Sam might take their uses further."

Arthur remembered Sam's long-necked wife stood over a bubbling pot, the grimy kitchen filled with steam, the scent of milk and bitter black cohosh. "Further?" he asked faintly.

"You saw them for yourself," said Shelo. "Sick to their souls. Longing for relief."

"You give them medicine. And then what?"

"Then they bleed," whispered Flora. Shelo did not so much as spare a glance for her. His unblinking eyes were on Arthur, and there was a sickness in them. It took Arthur some moments to realise that Shelo's look was one of desperation – that he was longing for him to believe, to understand, to approve. Flora, the quietly grazing horse, the wide night, had all faded to nothing. The two of them might have been alone in a rowboat amidst the vastness of an empty ocean.

"They bleed," said Shelo. "That which they so long to be rid of comes loose from inside them, and bleeds out."

"How?" Arthur felt that he was listening to the babblings of a madman. He felt the kind of ill fascination that might arise from watching somebody die, or copulate.

Shelo traced a line in the ashes at the edge of the fire. "It is different each time. Men often pass it out as they might pass water. Women, as they might birth a child." Arthur flushed. "But sometimes it might be brought up from the stomach, or lungs, or throat. In one instance I saw it crawl from the ear hole."

Arthur's body gave an involuntary twitch, and he tore his gaze away from Shelo. It was not possible and yet, neither was it possible that Shelo had seen him from across the endless sea, called him and carried him to the place where they had met. As the moment stretched on, Flora looked intently between the two of them.

"Arthur," said Shelo, in a low voice. "We are doing a great thing. For so many. In all the ages of man, who could have dreamed it? Before us, how many died crying out for it?"

He mouthed a wordless response.

"How many cut out their own hearts just to ease their torment? When the world broke their bones and walked across their backs?" Shelo leaned forwards, quivering with passion from head to toe. "You see how they come, Arthur. Crawling out of the night. Paupers and whores and kings."

When Arthur still said nothing, Shelo rose to his feet and moved around to the other side of the fire. He crouched, and touched Arthur's face lightly with the back of his hand.

"I cannot," mumbled Arthur, at long last. But he did not pull away. "Please, Shelo, I cannot..."

"I ain't afraid," offered Flora shakily, unheeded.

"But you will stay with me?" Shelo asked. Arthur nodded. Shelo rocked back on his heels, plainly relieved. The flames guttered in the rising wind, and were almost extinguished.

"What happens to 'em?" asked Flora, into the hush. Finally, reluctantly, Shelo turned to her. "Will they die?"

"If they wished to die," said Shelo, "they would not need to find me. No, child, theirs is a new kind of life. They live now without memory and without pain." His chest swelled. "Who would not desire it, when all other comfort is gone?

"And what about...?" Flora pointed to the back of the wagon, where the jars and their strange contents were hidden.

Shelo's expression appeared suddenly glazed, distant. Arthur rubbed his eyes, but his fogged faculties would not clear.

"Foolish to ask," Shelo breathed. "Foolish to wonder. No tongue can tell what they are."

§

There had been little trace of any natives since they had met with Shelo beside the fire, far back in the wooded country. But now Arthur glimpsed them once more. Tall and slender as the grasses, they appeared and vanished again into the haze at the horizon. They floated across the landscape like cotton blossoms. They did not come close until after nightfall, when groups of three or four would be drawn to the lamplight. They whispered amongst themselves. They touched the wagon with curious hands, while their horses stamped and snorted, ill at ease.

The plains people looked through Arthur and Flora as if they were not there. It was only Shelo to whom they would speak, softly and in unknown tongues. One young man with his long hair tied in oiled braids gesticulated wildly, seemingly angered. He spat into the dust and rode away with haste, upright as a rod upon his bareback mount.

"He thinks that we are carrying the dead," said Shelo. "He speaks as though we were doing some kind of wickedness.

Arthur turned over in the night to see blurred shapes gathered around the fire. He heard weeping. An elderly woman was bent double in her grief, howling to the distant stars. In Arthur's mind her cries mingled with the sounds of those who came the next night, and the next. Their weeping flowed together like streams into an ocean.

"I knew that they would be the last," breathed Shelo. "I knew that they would come, in the end."

The natives wept as long and as loud as had all of those who came to the light of Shelo's lamp. They gave up their breath with raw cries. They howled for the wounding of their land, for the passing of better days.

§

"We're close now," said Flora, pointing Shelo towards a far off rocky outcrop. "We'll make it there before nightfall."

Herds of thick-furred prairie cattle raised their shaggy heads as the wagon passed them by. Arthur, who had never seen such a creature in the flesh, raised himself up on the back step for a closer look. The animals were scattered across the land in vast herds, each more powerful than a prize bull. Their young kept close to their sides. A solitary tree, stark against the sky, marked the wagon's progress towards the horizon.

Shelo's ears were pricked, eyes fixed ahead. He looked as though he had caught onto a scent which was luring him forward, driving all else from his mind. Arthur saw that his hands shook upon the reins.

Flora and Arthur looked silently at one another. She had begun to sleep ever more fitfully when she was not helping Shelo in the wagon, kicking Arthur awake. She had grown jumpy even in daylight, gnawing at the skin on her hands and craning her neck to look back the way they had come.

She came running after him when they stopped for water in the afternoon, tugging at his arm and thrusting her freckled face close to his. "Arthur," she hissed, "We're bein' followed."

"We always are."

"No. I mean…" She glanced fretfully over her shoulder to where Shelo was tending the horse, and lowered her voice even further. "I swear I caught a glimpse of it. Once yesterday, and earlier today, when I went for a piss. Just beyond them trees."

"A glimpse of what?"

"His red coat."

Following her meaning at last, Arthur felt a jolt of sickened panic. Even Flora appeared surprised at how much this possibility had shaken her. Preferring to think that she had simply given her imagination too much rein, he did not tell Shelo, who had now torn off his cloak and was sweating profusely. The wagon rattled and jolted its way towards the rocks, and as he gradually saw what was laid out before them, all other thoughts were driven from Arthur's mind.

Yellow flowers, as far as the eye could see, each standing taller than a grown man. At the heart of each bright bloom, a round black eye. And rising out of this spectacle, a house of white bricks and blue-painted timber. Its grand doorway was flanked by pillars, its windows gleaming in the evening sunlight. Beyond it was a scattered settlement, the first they had laid eyes on in many days.

Shelo's face was now so terrible with anticipation, so hideous with unspoken delight, that Arthur had to turn away. His heart descending within him, he looked back down the dusty path across the prairie. The grasses swayed in golden waves.

For a moment, with the haze and the movement of the grass, he took what he saw for a cluster of trees. But then a flash of red caught his eye, and he realized what was bearing down upon them. Filled with an unworldly calm, he seized hold of Flora's wrist.

"Get in the wagon."

"Why?"

"Get in the wagon. Now. And stay silent."

She understood just in time, and flung herself through the canvas flap, drawing it closed behind her. At the sound of hooves, Shelo leapt down from his seat. There was barely time to feel fear, let alone to run away. A sense of unreality settled over Arthur, and he moved to stand at Shelo's shoulder, watching Barber's approach. Unthinkingly, he touched the pistol that he still kept in his pocket.

"We are so close now, Arthur," muttered Shelo. "We need to be rid of him."

"*Creatures!*" Barber's demeanour could not have been more different from the cool detachment with which he had faced them at the cave above the river. His face was set in sour lines, his voice thunderous. He reined in his horse so violently that it almost skidded over onto its side. Ripstone, Harpey and four more of Barber's followers were close at his heels, scarves bound about their faces.

"Creatures, do not think to flee. We will outpace you."

He dismounted forcefully, landing hard upon the ground and straightening up again in an instant. He pulled off his riding gloves and laid them over his arm. A few of his men had drawn their pistols.

Barber did not approach them. He seemed to be on the verge of pacing across to the wagon, but instead merely stared at it, stroking the edge of his moustache agitatedly.

"The roads are alive with talk of you," he began, turning sharply to Shelo. "I have been following your trail."

There was an uneasy stirring amongst the men. Arthur heard the bones in Shelo's back crack against each other as he stretched.

"Well?" demanded Barber forcefully. "What manner of devil's servant are you? What is your intent? And why should you ply your trade on my roads without paying your due to me?"

Shelo licked the tips of his pointed canines. Arthur tried to close his fingers around the handle of the gun, but found that he was trembling too hard.

Without warning, Barber strode across and seized a handful of Arthur's hair. He yanked his head back painfully, thrusting his face close. Shelo's snarl was drowned out by the frightened snorting of the horses, by Ripstone's high laugh.

"*What is your business?*" spat Barber. "And where is the girl? If she is with you by her own choosing, she will pay for her desertion."

"Your daughter left us some days ago," growled Shelo. "She did not have the stomach for our enterprise."

Arthur rolled his dry tongue around the inside of his mouth. His body gave a shudder, and suddenly, his voice left him of its own accord.

"Do you wonder," he said to Barber, "that she did not run back to you?"

Barber's reaction was instant and ferocious. He flung Arthur to the ground, tearing out a handful of his hair, then placed the sole of his boot upon his face.

"Speak those same words again," he said, very softly. "And I will crush your skull."

Arthur could see only the underside of Barber's boot. He inhaled a mouthful of dust, and was aware only faintly of Shelo throwing himself towards Barber, of bullets ricocheting from rocks, of horses screaming. Then the pressure had gone from his head, and Barber was yelling something which became inaudible above the sound of hooves.

In the midst of the stirring dirt, Shelo's strong hands pulled him from the ground. Arthur was so relieved to see him unhurt that it was a moment before he thought to wonder why Barber and his men were fleeing.

Shelo grasped at the front of Arthur's shirt. The dust had turned the whites of his eyes blood-red. He pulled Arthur around to see another, larger group of riders approaching them from out of the yellow fields.

The men wore white breeches and blue coats hemmed with gold, muskets tucked beneath their arms. They encircled Arthur and Shelo before drawing to a halt, cautious where Barber had been bold. Their strong, glossy horses pawed the ground. The rider at the head of the party, whose chest was crossed by a red sash, looked down upon the two of them with unconcealed alarm.

"Are you the travellers of whom we have heard?" he asked.

Beside him, Arthur felt Shelo take a small step back. The riders waited. And at length, Arthur coughed the dust from his throat to reply unsteadily, "We are."

"You are this… apothecary."

Arthur drew himself up, trying to disguise the fearful quivering of his body. "I am. And this is my servant." He indicated Shelo, who bowed his head silently.

Upon hearing Arthur's voice, the refined sound so ill-fitted to the disheveled veneer, the leader of the party was visibly reassured. He glanced at his fellows to the left and right, who nodded encouragingly to him.

"Very well. Then you shall come with us." He clicked his tongue, and his horse turned about. Arthur heard Shelo release a long, elated breath. "The Governor wishes to meet with you."

13

The Bedchamber

They were brought at sundown to the roomy entrance hall, where Flora stood gaping like one led into a strange new land. Shelo appeared diminished indoors, wary and hunched, his bloodshot eyes flickering over the ornately panelled walls and high ceiling. It was clear to Arthur that neither of them had ever set foot in such a place.

As for himself, he remembered. It felt like the walking of a familiar road which was now overgrown. He found himself brushing back his unruly hair with his hands, smoothing it to his head.

"I will take some refreshment," he told the guard with the red sash, "while I wait."

"Certainly, sir."

"For my companions, too," said Arthur. Flora's head tilted to one side as she looked at him, her mouth opening slackly. Shelo's inked face was a mask, his gaze now fixed upon a painting which hung at the far end of the hall.

The guardsman pulled a bell, which rung somewhere far below them. A maid in a neat apron came scurrying in through a side door, and was instructed in lowered tones. Arthur strode to the far side of the hallway, to examine the full-length portrait which Shelo could not take his eyes from. His footsteps echoed on the polished floor.

The painting showed a man in a pea-green silk coat, with heavy features and thick dark hair. He was pictured looking out upon the sea, where billowing white sails were visible amidst the rolling waves. His foot was placed upon a rock, and he held an unfurled map in his hand. Tangled greenery threatened to encroach upon him, creeping in around his feet and hanging from the tree at his back.

The maid entered with a tea tray which rattled in her shaking hands. She placed it upon a table, curtseyed clumsily, and hurried away. Shelo gave a growl, causing all of the guards to glance fearfully towards him. Arthur had the impression that they were itching to tie him up.

"Please," said the man with the red sash, to Arthur. "Make yourself comfortable. I hope that you will not be waiting long."

There were three bone china cups on the tray, set upon delicate saucers. Steam rose reassuringly from the spout of the teapot, which was patterned with red birds. Flora crept to Arthur's side, and tugged at his elbow.

"Like this," he muttered to her, lifting one of the cups by its handle and taking a small sip. The taste almost brought him to tears. Flora cradled a cup carefully in both of her hands, and swallowed a great mouthful of the scalding liquid.

"What are we *doin'* here, Art?" she whispered. Arthur caught Shelo's eye, and quickly looked away again.

"He knows. He will tell us."

"But don't you think…"

"Gentlemen. Lady."

Arthur was the only one who turned around. A manservant had entered through the double doors at the end of the hallway, beneath the portrait. He stood rigidly as he took in the sight of Shelo, whose bare feet had trailed dirt in from outside. Arthur carefully put down his teacup, and cleared his throat.

"Is your master ready to receive us?"

"Yes, sir. The Governor will see you now."

§

In a darkened study in the depths of the great house, a grandfather clock kept time. The ticking of its pendulum was all that disrupted the hush. The lamps along the walls had not been lit. Beside the window, which let in the last of the day's light, a man was bent over a desk.

He did not turn his attention to them until long after the manservant had made an exit, pulling the door quietly to. Appearing to finish the page he had been writing with a flourish, he laid down his quill. When he rose at long last, it was clear that his portrait had not done justice to his great size. He seemed to fill his side of the room, giving the impression of a heavy strength which had barely diminished with old age.

He was attired even more finely than in the picture, in silk stockings and an embroidered waistcoat, his shoes silver-buckled. His eyes were set deep into his skull, half-hidden by shadow. Though his hair was now grey, his movements were still vital and alert.

"The roving apothecary," he said, and smiled. The expression did not spread evenly across his face, but climbed first onto the left cheek, before reluctantly ascending the right.

Arthur inclined his head. "At your service."

"You will pardon me for the wait, I hope. I cannot bear to be disturbed whilst working." He indicated the thick spread of papers upon his desk. "I have spent some years compiling an account of these regions, which I hope will be of interest to parties back in England."

"I have no doubt of it."

The Governor dipped his head in acceptance of the compliment. "You sound to me like a true English gentleman?"

"I am, sir." Arthur's hands convulsed, and he clasped them tightly behind his back. "The youngest son of an illustrious line."

"How wonderful. What an adventure to be so far from home, and pursuing such a singular interest. We shall have to exchange our tales over dinner."

"I..."

"Wonderful. I shall have clean clothes sent up for you. Please do not be embarrassed, I have travelled myself and know that the road is no friend to one's dignity." He reached over, and rung a bell above his desk. "I am afraid my wife will not be joining us. She is indisposed."

There was a pause as the Governor regarded Arthur, his gaze now sharpened. "It has been my hope that you would pass this way. Shall I have my men carry in your equipment?"

Arthur felt Shelo shift at his back. The Governor had not once yet glanced over Arthur's shoulder, or offered any indication that he had noticed the others in the room. "I would not put you to the trouble," said Arthur hurriedly. "My servants will go."

Finally, the Governor's eyes lighted on the two forms at Arthur's back. From his look, it was clear that he had noticed Shelo.

"He does not talk, not in our tongue," Arthur interjected nervously.

"What a strange appearance he has," said the Governor.

"There is no cause to fear him. I keep him for his knowledge of all manner of plants and their properties."

"So many curiosities," said the Governor, "I believe I shall never tire of them. And in my folly I have neglected to ask your name...?"

"Lord Harcourt." Arthur could not summon the will, somehow, for an untruth. He held out his hand. "Lord Harcourt, at your service."

§

He was shown to a lavish second-floor chamber, where a clean shirt and breeches had been laid out ready for him upon the four-poster bed. Here the lamps had been lit, casting a gentle glow upon the deep red of the curtains and thick rug. Upon the walls hung portraits of nameless, distinguished ladies and gentlemen, all framed in gold. As soon as the manservant closed the door behind him, Arthur sank down upon the edge of the bed, and pressed a hand to his racing heart. It was too much.

He groaned beneath his breath, and then leapt up again, running to the window. But even pressing his face to the glass, he could see little of what was happening out in the night. Somewhere below him, he knew, Shelo and Flora were unloading the wagon's strange cargo.

His hands fumbling, he undressed himself. A cloth and a steaming bath had been left for him, and he sunk himself into it, rubbing the dirt hurriedly from his skin. He tried not to look at his thin white torso, marked as it still was with livid scars. He lathered his face and scraped a razor across it before pulling on the fresh shirt, buttoning it clumsily. The feel and the smell of clean cloth came out of another life, a world beyond the ocean.

He might have remained there for hours, hunched over in the centre of the room, running his fingertips dazedly across his chest. But then a bell rang down below, and he rose, bidden by the habit of all his years.

In the dining hall he found the Governor seated alone at the head of a long table. Only two places were laid, and Arthur approached the unoccupied seat to the Governor's left with some caution.

"I trust that you are now feeling more comfortable, Lord Harcourt." He was afforded another half-formed smile, but the Governor's gaze was level and unyielding. Arthur's stomach turned over as he sat down. The room spun around him as the first course was uncovered upon the table, and he could only nod in silent reply.

Before him was a rich pudding of molasses and butter. With the first taste of it, his senses revolted. He forced himself to swallow, battling the bile that rose in his throat. He wished that Harmony were seated on the other side of him, laying a steadying hand upon his wrist.

He wiped his clammy forehead on his sleeve, and forced himself to sit straight in his chair. He became aware that the Governor was speaking to him.

"...all of half a century ago, now. I cannot tell you what changes I have seen in the meantime. And I have never once been back."

Realising what was expected of him, Arthur ran his tongue around the inside of his mouth, frantically searching for conversation. Even at his father's table, with his sister at his side, he had never been good at this. He felt his body begin to quiver beneath his new clothes. "I have been here only months, sir, and should not at all wish to return."

"Quite right. There is enough here to satisfy an entire lifetime, for those with a curious mind and enterprising hands. We have been shrewd, you and I, in our journeying."

This time, his smile was an invitation, a conspiracy. He reached for his wine glass, and raised it. "To a continent of better men."

Arthur mumbled the toast, and took a drink from his own glass. The second course was mutton neck and a game pastry, swimming in thick fruit sauce. He began to feel the wine turning his head, and as he was questioned, spilled a story that was not his own but Lucas West's. It had arrived at Harcourt Hall upon hastily penned pages, each envelope spilling maps and botanical drawings. It was familiar enough that it barely felt like a falsehood to make it his own.

"Quite fascinating. Tell me, what did you make of the equinoctial forests? I journeyed into Spanish territory myself, in my younger days."

"I have not yet been so far south," replied Arthur. "That is where the road is now taking me."

"And how fortunate for me that you should pass this way." The Governor's expression grew grave. He poured Arthur yet more wine, and leaned forward in his chair. The room had become dark, save for the candles upon the table and the twin lamps which burned on the far wall. "May I confide in you, now, the purpose of my summons?"

Arthur carefully laid down his knife. He nodded.

"My wife has suffered with a.... malaise... for a number of years now. I have tried countless doctors. I have jurisdiction over many hundreds of miles of this land, Lord Harcourt, and yet my position has been of no help to me in this."

The candles guttered as the prairie wind rattled the windows. "None can cure her. Now I simply wish to end her suffering."

"I can assure you," said Arthur hoarsely, "that when I am done, she will be at peace."

"Can you tell me anything of your process?" asked the Governor. He ran his finger delicately around the rim of his glass.

Arthur's head was growing ever hazier. The walls and high ceiling of the grand room around him appeared to tilt and sway, like the deck of the *Head of Mary*. He gripped the table with both hands. "That, I cannot tell you. My secrets are... my methods are..."

"I understand entirely." Arthur saw the Governor's eyes glitter darkly. And for a moment which melted away into forgetfulness, it seemed to him that their look was endlessly familiar.

Servants entered to clear away the remnants of their meal, and Arthur felt each mouthful he had swallowed rise sourly in his throat. The Governor poured the last of the wine into Arthur's glass and sat back, arms stretched out beside him. Slowly, he licked the red stain from the corners of his mouth. He watched as Arthur raised the glass to his lips.

"Do you think often of England, Lord Harcourt?" asked the Governor, quietly.

An ocean's width away, Arthur imagined that he could hear his father's cello, echoing through empty rooms. He closed his eyes, and threw back as much wine as he could swallow to drown the noise. "Never," he said.

"I must confess, I can barely recall it." The Governor's eyes bored into Arthur so forcefully that he felt his skin burn. "There is a certain forgetfulness which can come over a man, here. As though the call that first tempted us to cross the sea were the voice of some alluring devil."

Arthur put down his empty glass so hard that cracks appeared in its stem. Nausea climbed in his throat with ever greater urgency, and he stood, unsteady on his feet.

There is something that begins to trouble me, Lucas had written, and Arthur began at last to understand.

"You will excuse me," he managed to say. "I must go and make ready for your wife's treatment. It is growing late."

§

As soon as he had returned to his room, Arthur pulled the door closed and fell to his knees, vomiting copiously into the chamber pot. He was still huddled there, coughing and spitting out the last of his lavish dinner, when Shelo burst in.

"Everything is prepared," he said brusquely. Flora, close on his heels, was wringing her hands together. "We were shown to the lady's quarters."

"Whatever's the matter, Art?" Flora dropped down beside him. Weakly, he wiped his mouth, and sat back to look at Shelo. He was not reassured by what he saw. Shelo's eyes were alight, and every inch of his inked skin was quivering like the hide of a horse before a thunderstorm.

"We need to leave," choked Arthur. "Please, Shelo. Now, tonight."

Shelo looked at him blankly. The light of the wall lamps guttered, and Flora tugged at Arthur's arm. "We'll be out of here real soon." Her voice was tremulous. "C'mon. Let's just do as he says, Art…"

She helped him to his feet, her nose wrinkling as she caught the smell of his breath. On impulse, Arthur fumbled among the cast-off clothes upon the bed, once more pocketing the small pistol they had taken from her months before.

Shelo took the lamp from the bedside table, and led them out into the corridor, around a corner and up a small flight of stairs. Still leaning heavily on Flora, Arthur struggled to find his footing, the sight of Shelo's shadowed form blurring ahead. The house was still and dark now, and they moved through it like phantoms.

"Here," breathed Shelo.

They entered a room hung heavily with dusty drapery, lit by a single candelabrum on the table beside the bed. Propped up against the pillows was a woman who barely seemed to notice their entrance, her parchment-pale face turned towards the ceiling. Fine white hair sprung from her head, her arms protruding from her graying nightdress like withered branches.

"Is that you again?" she asked, in a voice so weak that it was almost drowned out by the noise of the wind against the window panes. "Come back to deliver me, at last?"

Arthur saw Shelo's equipment laid out on the table; the bottles of camphor and of milky fluid, the cloth. The expectant empty jar.

Overcome by sudden horror, he tried to pull back from Flora's grip, but she would not let him go.

"*C'mon, Art*," she begged him, through chattering teeth. "*We got to get this done.*"

Shelo approached the bed, his barefoot tread silent. The skeletal woman looked up at him, beyond all fear and all hope.

"Tell me," whispered Shelo. His hand traced the edge of the bedspread. "What might I do for you?"

"If he called for you," said the Governor's wife, "then it was the first kind deed of his life." She fought for breath, her fragile chest fluttering. "So many doctors! *Malaise*, he calls it... and how am I to tell them? How am I to speak of the man I am bound to?"

Shelo leant in more closely towards her, and she reached a hand to his inked face. "How I hope that the eyes of the Almighty see what I see!" she gasped. "How I hope that judgment comes swiftly!" In the dim candlelight, Arthur thought that he saw tears spill over onto Shelo's cheeks.

"You shall be free of it," said Shelo fervently. "You shall be at rest."

Flora, unbidden, took the top from the bottle of camphor and soaked the cloth. She handed it to Shelo, who bent low over the bed, and pressed the cloth to the woman's mouth.

Her eyes rolled back in her head at once, and she sank back onto the pillows. Flora moved around the bed and tugged away the blankets, while Shelo shifted the weight of the frail body, pulling it down from a seated to a lying position. He tilted back the head so that the mouth hung open in a prolonged, silent scream.

"Shelo," began Arthur. The room still felt unsteady, and he grasped hold of the bedpost to stay upright. "Shelo, I really cannot..."

"Take her arm," said Shelo brusquely. "And hold her down. Her struggles will be great."

"*C'mon*, Arthur," pleaded Flora again, this time with urgency. She had taken hold of the woman's wrist on the other side, and had the other hand on her shoulder, pressing her flat to the bed.

Disbelieving, Arthur could not comprehend the need for restraint. Her arm felt as though it might snap at his lightest touch. Shelo took the second bottle from the tabletop, carefully removed the lid, and then cradled the woman's jaw in his hand as he tipped a few drops onto her lolling tongue.

Arthur saw Flora wince, and was only just prepared. Without warning, the woman's back suddenly arched, throwing her pelvis up at a strange angle. Her spine rippled like a rope bridge in a gale. Her eyes spun beneath their closed lids, and her mouth stretched wide, letting forth a horrendous groan.

"*Hold her!*" hissed Shelo, and Arthur realised that he had almost let go. Shelo tipped a few more drops of liquid onto her tongue, and the writhing grew more violent, accompanied now by a retching noise low in her throat.

It was too appalling to bear. To Arthur's wine-addled mind, it seemed to go on forever, each minute and hour blurring into the last. Retching became coughing, which became a familiar belly-deep moaning, as if she were about to give birth. At first her movements, confined by Arthur and Flora, were the blind thrashings of a dreamer. But gradually the camphor appeared to wear off and her eyes inched open, a sense of crazed purpose entering her struggles.

"Do we have to hold her down?" cried Arthur.

"She'll hurt herself!" Flora was sweating, her face growing red with the exertion. Shelo paced the room, muttering to himself, returning every few minutes to bend close to the woman's mouth. He wrenched her jaw open even wider in his hands, and then peered down into her throat. He held the candelabrum close to try and shed some light, almost setting fire to the bedclothes.

"Close, now," he panted. "It's coming."

The Governor's wife screamed, and her arm twisted in Arthur's grip, her hand bent back at an unnatural angle. Her body snapped forward, and her cry lodged in her throat, causing her to choke. Hurriedly, Shelo tipped her head back again and poured in a few more drops of liquid.

Arthur felt sweat trickling down his back and forehead. Numb with incredulity, he saw a viscous line of blood creeping down from the woman's mouth, dripping onto the bedspread. A second thread slid down from the corner of her eye, and a third from her ear.

Then he saw a searching white tendril appear from inside her mouth, creeping out onto her lower lip. It was followed by another, and Shelo leapt onto the bed, taking her whole head in his hands. He pushed his thumb and forefinger into her mouth like a fisherman removing a hook from his catch.

"*There!*"

The Governor's wife flopped onto her pillows. Arthur staggered back from the bed. A ghost-white moth fluttered in Shelo's grip, its wings veined and delicate, its legs furred. There had been no illusion or trickery, no canvas this time to hide what would have been better hid. It was an utterly unworldly thing.

Carefully, Shelo dispensed the creature into the empty jar, quickly pressing down the lid. Wings flickered behind the curved glass. He stared intently at it, his face contorted.

Arthur cowered back, his head pounding. He felt he was in a terrible dream from which there was no waking. The long dinner table, the Governor's glittering eyes, the taste of wine on his tongue, all seemed a lifetime ago.

"You got it?" asked Flora grimly. There were great grey rings around her eyes, and her hair was drenched in sweat. When Shelo nodded, she wiped her sleeve across her nose, then pulled the blankets up around the woman's helpless form. "Don't look so dreadful, Arthur," she added, wearily. "We done it a hundred times before."

"When will she wake up?" he stuttered.

"In a few hours," said Shelo. "And she will not recollect a thing. Not of tonight, not of all her unhappy years. We have done a great deed."

The Governor's wife stirred where she lay. Her eyelids flickered. She looked blankly at the three of them, and her arms slid down across the bedclothes, as if she had forgotten how to control them. Her mouth hung open, blood still staining her chin. Flora leaned in and tried to wipe it away with the cloth.

Arthur could barely tear away his horrified gaze. His knees buckled, and he composed himself enough to turn towards Shelo. "I cannot remain under this roof." His voice cracked, and he resorted to pleading. "*May we leave this place?*"

The inked shapes upon Shelo's skin seethed with their own life. His black eyes flashed, and Arthur was sure that lamps in the room guttered all at once, caught in a sudden wind.

"I am not finished here," said Shelo.

He pocketed the jar and made for the door. He beckoned, and Flora turned to Arthur, helpless. In her exhaustion, she could barely string together the necessary words.

"We hid 'em all in the master's room, Art. While you was at dinner."

He did not comprehend. She looked at him through the dark, nothing but terror in her face.

§

The master bedchamber was on the third floor of the house, behind a heavy oak door. Shelo stared for a moment into the dimness within, breathing hard. He was alive as Arthur had never seen him before, crouched and readying himself for attack.

They could hear the Governor's even, sleeping breaths. Shelo cleaned his pointed canines with the tip of his tongue.

"You did well, Arthur." He was quivering all over. "My Arthur. As I knew you would. You opened the way for me." The whites of his eyes showed in pale rings, like twin eclipses. "You were not afraid, or dismayed by the form which I take."

"Shelo..." whispered Arthur.

The back of Shelo's hand brushed his cheek. "One last thing for me. Stand guard, and do not enter at any cost. You too, child." Flora raised her head, and Shelo gave her a small nod. He vanished into the bedchamber.

"What did you hide in there?" asked Arthur, through chattering teeth. He heard the soft creak of floorboards. The Governor's easy breathing continued.

She lifted her eyes to him. He saw her waver, her lip trembling, but she bit down on it forcefully. "Them jars," she whispered. "With... you know. Creatures. We hid 'em beneath his bed. And a length of rope."

"*Rope?*"

"Don't ask me, Art." She turned to face the wall, and pressed her fists against it, shuddering. "Please don't ask me nothin' else..."

A cry from within, and an almighty clattering. A snarl, and a series of rapid thumps, as though an untamed beast had been set loose upon the sleeping man. Then a horrible, muffled choking. Arthur's chest tightened, and he felt the blood drain from his face and extremities.

After a few agonised minutes, he laid his hand against the door.

He closed his eyes, and summoned all of his meagre courage. He pushed his way into the room.

For a moment he saw only the empty jars scattered across the floor. His eyes were drawn upward, straining in the dimness, to the two entangled forms upon the bed. The Governor's wrists were lashed to the bedstead with rope, his legs kicking and torso writhing. Shelo bore down upon him, forcing his mouth open with one hand while the other fumbled at the lid of a jar.

Oblivious to Arthur's presence, Shelo pulled out the little winged creature between his thumb and forefinger, then proceeded to force it with slow deliberation down his victim's protesting throat. In the moonlight that broke in through a crack in the curtains, Arthur saw the Governor's back arch, his body convulsing. With Shelo's hand clamped around his jaw and the creature in his throat he could not scream aloud, but his eyes bulged wildly.

Shelo broke open another jar, then another in quick succession. He scooped out the contents, pushing his fingers back into the Governor's mouth, forcing him to swallow. He cast each empty jar onto the floor, and then pulled out another from beneath the bed. All the while he did not say a word, though a violent noise seemed to be trapped at the back of his gullet. It took Arthur some moments to comprehend that Shelo was sobbing.

White wings flapped between the Governor's lips. Shelo shook him until he swallowed again, and again, and the whole floor was littered with glass jars.

The Governor's mouth hung slackly. His eyes rolled up into his head, and then fluttered closed. Shelo sat over him, panting in exhaustion, his great inked head hanging. He moved a clumsy hand across the Governor's face, as though unsure whether to claw at him or caress him.

Then, just as Arthur had begun to wonder whether he was

dead, the Governor's eyes opened. He stared numbly up at Shelo, seeming to see from the depths of a bottomless abyss.

The man with whom Arthur had dined just hours before, the man from the portrait in the hallway, was utterly annihilated. In his place was a ghostly being which gaped unseeingly at its tormentor. Its face was coated in a film of sweat. Its hands clasped its stomach, and its mouth gabbled silently, forming rapid strings of nonsense.

Shelo leant closer, until he was forehead to forehead with his creation. He let out a long, shuddering sigh, and closed his eyes. He whispered something in his victim's ear that Arthur could not hear.

Then there came the sound of raised voices from far below them, and footsteps fast ascending the stairs. Awoken from a trance, Shelo leapt to the floor, and for the first time caught sight of Arthur.

They stared at one another. Before either of them could speak, there came an alarmed hammering at the door.

"*Shelo!*" cried Flora. "*Arthur, please!*"

Shelo seemed unable to move. Arthur pulled back the door, only to be seized upon at once by Flora. Her voice was shrill in panic.

"The guardsmen!" she cried. "They're awoken!"

§

The three of them descended down the back wall of the house by means of a creeper which clung to the bricks. Giddy at the drop below, Arthur faltered upon every branch, Flora cursing beneath him.

"Faster, Art!" she urged, as he hesitated. His awkward body could not keep its balance. Above him, through the bedchamber's open window, he could hear the sound of shouting and of pounding footsteps.

He jumped, and met the ground on all fours. Flora wrenched him to his feet and then pulled him away, Shelo just ahead. The three of them tore across the grass and then vaulted over the fence onto the dusty road.

"Where are the guards?" panted Arthur.

"Searchin' for us inside, they must be…"

They stopped at last by the bole of a towering tree, out amidst the grasses again. Arthur bent over, panting, his hands on his knees. Flora thrashed at the grass with her hand, filling the air with curses again.

"An' we left the horse behind, an' all! Poor beast!" She rounded on Arthur. "What happened in there?"

"Ask – *him*."

Shelo looked at them both, clearly wondering who they were and how he had come to be in their company. He raised himself up to his full height, and for a moment, Arthur thought that he felt the ground itself shift beneath his feet.

"It is over," Shelo said, disbelievingly. "It is done."

The night wind stirred in the grasses, which rolled like troubled waves beneath the silver moon. Shelo's silhouetted form seemed more like that of a great rock than a man, a monolith that had stood for centuries. He turned to look back in the direction that they had come, and Arthur had the sense that he was not really present with them at all.

"Shelo," he tried. There was no response.

"What was that?" Flora stared jumpily out into the long grass. Still watching Shelo, Arthur paid her little heed as she crept around to the other side of the tree.

"Shelo…? It's me. It's Arthur."

"Arthur." The eyes fixed upon him, with the merest flicker of recognition. "Yes. Conceived in shame and born in darkness. Arthur Hallingham. From across the sea."

"You called me," whispered Arthur, reaching to wipe flecks of blood from the front of Shelo's shirt.

Shelo stared unblinkingly at him. Then, unaccountably, his face crumpled. He seized Arthur's collar, and leant close to whisper in return.

"Arthur Hallingham. Will you leave me now?"

Before Arthur could answer, a cold laugh shattered the night. Turning, he saw a man in a blood-red coat stood waist-deep in the grass beyond the tree. His pistol was pointed at Flora.

"I must confess," said Benjamin Barber, "I am a little surprised."

Bewildered, she tried to back towards Arthur and Shelo. Barber stepped forward onto the road. His polished boots gleamed in the moonlight.

"*Daddy?*" said Flora.

"Seventeen years I have acknowledged you as mine, though no doubt the whore who birthed you had more men than she could count. And now to find you in such company..."

Barber drew in a hissing breath, a smile playing about his thin lips. "I should have broke your head open where I first found you."

From sheer force of habit, Arthur turned to Shelo. But he was staring vacantly away. Flora's freckled face was milk-white.

Arms seized Arthur from behind, and Ripstone's voice was laughing in his ear. Instead of a steel blade against his throat, he felt this time the mouth of a gun, pressing between his shoulder blades. Beside him, pale-eyed Harpey had taken hold of Shelo, who did not so much as struggle.

Barber pulled back the safety catch, and turned again to face his daughter.

"You know that I have never taken kindly to deserters," he said. The smile faded, to be replaced by a hard, hollow look. "I have my name to think of."

Not once, in all of his years, had Arthur's body felt strong. But in the lengthening seconds that followed, as Barber's finger hesitated upon the trigger, it finally knew itself.

In one quick, twisting move, he was free from Ripstone's grasp, and had plunged his hand into his pocket. In long gone days, in the grounds of Harcourt Hall, he had once stood with Lucas and Edward at his side, and attempted to shoot at game birds.

His hands remembered.

14

Two Bodies

In the aftermath of the two shots, there was nothing in the world but cavernous silence. Then Arthur became aware, first that his whole right side had been numbed by the firing of the gun, and then that two bodies had fallen in quick succession. Directly ahead of him, Barber had been flung against the trunk of the tree, still half upright, his face frozen in numb astonishment. And thrown sideways into the grass, a red stain spreading rapidly across the front of her shirt, was Flora.

There was a snarling beside him, and Arthur realized that Shelo had awoken from his stupor to cuff away his captor. Harpey staggered backwards, cursing in shock and pain, and Shelo rounded on Ripstone.

He seemed to suddenly tower, made of darkness, made of smoke. A fierce wind blew through the branches of the tree above him, and clouds swept across to cover the moon. He opened his mouth in a bellowing, bestial roar, and Ripstone and Harpey were gone, fleeing like wild dogs into the night.

Arthur collapsed onto his knees beside Flora. Her wide eyes darted to and fro across his face, and he tried clumsily to pull her near, her blood soaking into his shirt.

"Arthur," she whispered. "Arthur, help me." Her hands searched her chest, baffled, trying to locate the source of her agony. He saw it as he lifted her into his lap, a small round wound at the centre of the spreading stain. It seemed that in the crucial moment Barber had misfired, and hit her not in the heart, as he had clearly intended, but some inches lower.

Arthur's mouth gaped. As he sat in useless indecision, her life leaked away into the grass.

Shelo was at his shoulder, pulling him aside. He took Flora in his great hands and lowered his head towards her wound, nostrils flaring. She did not seem to want to let go of Arthur, but Shelo prised her hands away impatiently. "Go to him," he commanded, nodding towards Barber. "If he is not dead, finish him."

Horrified, Arthur approached the form slumped against the tree. At first he was bewildered as to what had brought Barber down — he could see no sign that his bullet had found its mark. But then, close-to, he realised that the scarlet coat was drenched in blood of the same hue. He had hit Barber in the stomach, and the outlaw was not yet dead. Thick blood dripped from the corner of his mouth, and though his eyes had closed, he emitted a choked gurgle.

Shaking, Arthur reached for the buttons on the front of Barber's coat, half thinking to check the wound. But suddenly, the dying man's rigid hands had seized upon him.

Barber's eyes snapped open. His bloody mouth widened in a laughing leer, and he pulled Arthur up against him, until he could actually feel the throb of escaping blood against his own belly.

Then, as unexpectedly as it had risen, the life in Barber died. Arthur felt him stiffen, and saw his eyes glaze over as he departed for some distant place. His hands continued to grip and his blood continued to soak into Arthur's own clothing, but he was gone.

Arthur wrenched himself free with a cry of disgust, and found that he was on his knees at the base of the tree, vomiting for the second time that night. There was little left in his stomach, but he retched and heaved nonetheless, sour bile stinging his throat. Tears streamed down his face.

"We must go." The sound of Shelo's low voice brought him back to himself. Flora was still lying in the grass, but Shelo had moved away from her, staring back in the direction of the house. "The guardsmen are coming for us. And it will not be long before Barber's men return."

Arthur stood. He made to wipe his mouth across his sleeve, but then saw that his hands were coated in Barber's blood. He was overcome with weakness again. "What about…" he began, shakily.

"She will not see dawn," said Shelo.

Flora was silent, still save for the stilted rise and fall of her chest.

"We cannot…" he choked. "Do you mean to *leave* her?"

Shelo's inked face was an unsearchable mask. "She will not live," he said. "There is no time. Come, Arthur."

He rose. But he found that his legs did not carry him to Shelo's side, instead leading him back to the crushed patch of grass where Flora lay. Her eyes were closed, her skin pallid. It was the first time she had truly looked to be the child that she was.

Arthur looked up at Shelo. The firm voice that left him did not seem to be his own at all, and neither did he understand the words that he found himself speaking.

"She was our little sister, Shelo. She was *entrusted* to us."

He tucked one arm beneath her back, the other beneath her knees, and then lifted her from the ground. She was not heavy, but nonetheless he buckled beneath the load.

Arthur and Shelo looked at one another. And then, unmistakably, Shelo's gaze turned downwards. The surety drained from his broad body. He nodded.

§

Arthur stumbled with every step, progressing through the grass with painful slowness. His back ached and his arms cramped, but he held her as close as he could. It was the only way to be sure that

187

she had not slipped away, and several times he was forced to stop, checking that he could still feel her breath upon his face.

Shelo made no secret of his impatience, pressing ahead and then falling back each time Arthur lingered. They had not gone far before he took it upon himself to lift Flora out of Arthur's arms. He laid her across his wide back, her head flopping down onto his shoulder, and moved away again without a word. He was not slowed by her in the slightest.

Then there was only the moonlight upon the swaying grasses, the sight of Shelo before him, Flora's tangled hair hanging in a curtain across his back. They were far from any settlement, now, and the night was filled with the calls of unseen creatures. Arthur quivered at every bark and howl, and many times mistook the movements of a fox or rat for approaching human footsteps. It barely occurred to him to wonder where Shelo was fleeing to.

At long last they staggered out of the grass and into a hazy, dew-damp dawn. The plain lay featureless behind them, not a soul in sight. Ahead lay a wooded hill, overlooking a valley where a stream wound between smooth rocks.

"Into the trees," panted Shelo. As soon as they were beneath the cover of the canopy, they collapsed to the ground. Shelo laid Flora down on a blanket of fallen leaves, and they sat on either side of her, catching their breath. Arthur buried his bloodied hands in his hair.

"Have we outrun them, do you think?"

"There is no telling how persistent they will be," said Shelo. He turned Flora onto her side, his hands almost gentle. For a moment she appeared limp, unresponsive, and Arthur's heart leapt to his mouth. But then she let out a groan, trying feebly to pull away.

"You said she wouldn't see dawn," said Arthur. Shelo looked at him, expressionless.

"Wood, Arthur. As dry as you can find."

The first of the day's misted sunlight broke through the trees, but it brought no warmth. Arthur's eyes blurred, and he gathered branches into his arms with feverish effort. He felt that they had been pulled through the bottom of the world into another, shadowed place.

He closed his eyes, steadying himself against a tree, and felt again the numbing jolt of the pistol as it fired. He heard the twin shots, and Barber's leering face swum before his eyes. It was entirely clear that he, Arthur, had been the first of them to pull the trigger.

He found his way back to where Shelo was crouched beside Flora, and as he approached, saw that he had torn strips of cloth from his shirt to bind her wound. His cloak was wrapped around her. He chewed on a handful of berries, spat on his fingers and then rubbed the resultant paste upon the bandage.

Arthur tipped his armful of wood to the ground. Wordlessly, he took the other end of Shelo's bandage and they tied it together, pulling it tight around Flora's shivering chest. She let out a moan, seizing at the front of Arthur's shirt. Her face was now alarmingly flushed, damp with sweat.

"Is there nothing more you can do?" he demanded of Shelo, who had moved away to light the fire.

Flames flickered in the dimness, and he saw that Shelo's eyes had been drawn skywards. He was gazing out to nowhere again, apparently arrested by some thought or recollection. The fire took hold, and Shelo shuddered, his face closing in upon itself. When he finally spoke, it was in a strange flat tone, his voice dredged up from the dead space inside him.

"*Why do I feel no change, Arthur? Why do I feel no peace?*"

§

Arthur passed in and out of sleep at the edge of the fire, jumpy at the thought of Ripstone, and Harpey, and the whole crowd of Barber's men, bearing down upon him . He imagined that he heard them baying like hounds upon the scent.

He thought that he saw natives slip from between the trees to speak with Shelo in unknown tongues, and bend over Flora's fallen form. Smoke blurred their bodies. Their voices were low and soporific. The scent of unknown herbs reached Arthur's nostrils, and he stirred fretfully. When they were gone, he crawled to Flora's side and lay down against her back.

Her breath came in laboured gasps. She had already bled through her bandage, and now groaned at intervals, her teeth locked together. Since the other side of the night, she still had not uttered a word.

Shelo roused Arthur when the fire had died, and lifted her again, cradling her in his arms. They pressed on into the daylight beyond the wood, exhausted. Arthur cast frequent glances over his shoulder, wondering how far they had really come, and whether it had been wise to rest.

They followed the river into the valley, and found themselves looking upon a great lake, its waters still as glass. The surface reflected the overcast sky, and Arthur shuddered, imagining the chill in its iron depths.

Shelo carried Flora through the reeds, mud splashing onto her shirt, and then lowered her gently down on the bank. He scooped water into his palm, and then wet her hair and forehead. She stirred, her lips moving incoherently.

Shelo sat back, Flora's hands gripping weakly at his shoulders. His head drooped, his mane of oiled hair hanging about his face. For a moment, the pair of them were still at the edge of the black water. Then Shelo turned to Arthur, his look empty of all feeling.

Arthur felt his heart sink to his churning stomach. He looked further down the valley, and far in the distance, saw a thin rising column of smoke.

"Come on," he said thinly. He barely expected to be obeyed. "Come on. This way."

§

Deep in the valley, arid rock and dry grasses gave way to fields of lushest green. As night fell, Arthur and Shelo pushed their way through ripening corn which rose to the height of their shoulders. Cattle grazed beneath sheltering trees, and wildflowers burst from every bank.

Shelo held Flora close to his chest, her blood soaking through the bandage into his shirt. Her complexion had turned to lifeless grey. Shelo stopped in his tracks when he saw the little farmhouse, from which smoke had begun to rise once again into the evening sky. His lip rode up over his teeth.

"Not here, Arthur," he murmured. "Into the wilds."

Arthur looked from the front door of the farmhouse to Flora's limp, fading form. Then he darted forward and hammered forcefully at the door. "*Please!*" he cried out. "*Somebody, please help us!*"

There was a momentary silence, before footsteps shuffled within. Then the sound of a lamp being lit, and a pause, the stranger thinking better of his decision.

"*Open up!*" pleaded Arthur, knocking again. He had no more courage, no more resolve, and was about to fall back when a bolt snapped.

The door was pulled open the smallest crack. In the glow of the lamplight, a black-skinned face peered at them, eyes growing wider and wider. The young man behind the door looked upon

Arthur, upon his strange body and disheveled hair and bloodstained hands. Then his gaze was drawn over Arthur's shoulder to where Shelo stood, Flora in his arms, his hideousness written upon his very skin.

"Where is your master?" demanded Shelo, in a low, guttural growl.

"I have no master save God in heaven."

"Then where is the owner of this house?"

"I am the owner of this house," said the young man, raising up his lantern so that Shelo cringed back from its light. He pushed open the door a little wider.

"*Please*," Arthur interjected, his weak voice betraying him. "*Please*. She is grievously hurt."

The young man came slowly down the steps, his eyes now upon Flora. He held up his lantern above her, and leant close, lifting up her bandage to examine the wound beneath.

"Who are you?" he asked. "What has happened to her?"

Arthur swallowed. "We are – we were attacked on the road. They took everything we had. Their leader, he shot... he shot my sister."

The farmer looked levelly at him, and Arthur knew that he was not deceived. But then Flora stirred, letting out a groan between her rigidly clenched teeth. The stranger's brow furrowed, and he pressed her bandage down again.

"You." He pointed at Shelo. "Bring her inside."

§

The night passed, and she breathed, still. Arthur's impressions of those hours grew scattered – the bronze glow of Shelo's eyes as he crouched upon the hearth, wood-smoke rising into the chimney, the whistling of the kettle. Flora's face was ashen in the lamplight as the farmer's hands propped her against a pillow. He plunged a sharp instrument fearlessly into her wound.

Her ragged cry would not fade from Arthur's ears, even when he lay exhausted on the floor beside the bed hours later. The farmer remained calm, cleaning her side before binding her in fresh bandages. Arthur's hands shook as he held out a bowl of reddening water for the stained cloths.

"I have done all I can, now," he was told, when Flora at last lay sleeping fitfully. The farmer wiped his hands. "It's too late, I figure. Could you find no physician?"

Arthur was silent. In the room beyond, the fire crackled, and Shelo murmured to himself. The farmer held up his hands in resignation.

"Very well. But there'll be no help for you if you bring trouble my way." He looked back to Flora again. "May I ask her name?"

"She is Flora." Arthur swallowed. "And I...I am Arthur."

The man gave a small nod, and held out his hand. When Arthur merely looked at it, dazed, he tucked it into the front of his apron. "Robert. May I ask..."

He gave a nod in Shelo's direction. Arthur buried his hands in his hair, and shook his head. He felt weary beyond words.

"He will not harm you," was all he could bring himself to say. "Please. Do not turn him away."

He lay upon the hard floor, every inch of his body aching. But sleep eluded him. Some hours before dawn he thought that Robert came back into the bedroom, pressing a cool cloth to her forehead. All the while, Shelo rocked back and forth on his heels in the room beyond, muttering aloud.

"*Lost. All is lost. All is lost.*"

193

§

Flora faded further from them, ghost-pale, already beginning to pass from the world. Arthur dozed on the floor, helping Robert to spoon sugared water into her mouth every few hours. When Robert left, Arthur crawled onto the bed beside Flora, listening to the sound of her thin breaths. The lamp on the bedside table sputtered.

"I came so far," he told her, "because I thought that if I was to find relief anywhere..." He rubbed his eyes with the heel of his hand. "But it will never be made right, and it will never be well."

Her eyes did not open. It came to Arthur that she would die here, shrouded in her ill-fitting clothes, her father's body barely yet cold out on the prairie. The thought was so heavy to him that he could bear it no longer.

"Flora," he said, beneath his breath, and the unconscious girl made no response. She could not hear him, and she would not wake.

"Flora. I can remember being born."

He closed his eyes. Her dying breaths fell upon his cheek.

"Flora. I can remember floating in the dark. A place of coldness. I can remember... knowing, even then, that I was unwelcome."

Part 3

15

Cool of the Day

It had been whispered to him in his cradle. And then, as he grew, each time that he was bathed and dressed. His nurse, Mrs Walmsey, murmured it to him over and over again, like a favourite nursery rhyme. *Oh, Master Arthur. What a strange creature you are. What a curious child. No small wonder, that you were the death of my lady!*

"Truth be told, 'tis a mercy Lady Emily never lived to see you grow," she told him, with affection. She did up his buttons and tied his laces. She combed his rust-coloured hair. "She would not have known what to make of you! God-fearing soul as she was."

He remembered entering the world, sodden and bloody and screaming. He remembered arms which had not held him close, but shuddered when they touched him. He supposed that this must have been his mother: that Lady Harcourt had received him in fear and disgust, from the first. Within a month of his arrival, she had departed.

Edward, who had been six when Arthur brought sorrow upon Lady Harcourt, spoke of her often. In the way he spoke, it seemed that she had merely gone to take a walk about the grounds, and would come back through the door at any moment. He made drawings for her, and in moments of forgetfulness, asked after her whereabouts. Lord Harcourt's face would turn pale, and he called for their nurse, who took them away to play in some quiet room while he sought out his cello. At such times Jonas would tolerate only the company of his sickly sister, Lady Hannah.

She had been sent to Ireland for her health at fourteen, and returned some years before Arthur was born, still delicate as a china doll. She persisted in wearing black, as though she had never left mourning for her sister-in-law. In the absence of Lady Harcourt, she sat with Jonas in the darkened drawing room, and read to him beside the fire. She embroidered dresses for Harmony, and helped Edward assemble rows of dominoes, smiling tentatively, a little colour coming to her thin cheeks.

Whenever she tried reading to Arthur, or went to lay a hand upon his head, it seemed that she found herself overcome by fear. Her white hands trembled and withdrew into her sleeves. She flitted about the edges of his world, but like his father, never came too close. He came to understand the kind of creature that he must be.

What sorrow you have brought upon us all. Mrs Walmsey was left to scrub his narrow knees, to thread his awkward limbs into his clothes. Her ruddy face smiled lopsidedly upon him, and she crooned the old lullaby, laying him down each night in the nursery. *Strangest of creatures. Curious child.*

§

He was not yet seven when Edward began to creep into the nursery while he slept, snatching away his blanket. At first he was unable to determine what was missing, or why it had gone. Then he awoke one night to find his brother sat beside the bed, watching him shake in the cold. Edward clasped Arthur's blanket to his chest, features puckered angrily. Defiant tears coursed down his face.

This happened time and again, and Arthur did not yet have a mind to comprehend it, or the words to speak of it to anybody. Then Edward changed the game. He came into the nursery with scissors stolen from his aunt's sewing box, and began night by night to cut away little tufts of Arthur's hair, close to the skin. Mrs Walmsey examined Arthur's scalp in puzzlement. Then one night Edward surpassed himself, hacking away a generous handful, and her suspicions were aroused.

"Who done this, Master Arthur? Speak plainly, now."

Lord Harcourt was not told of the crime, but Edward was sent to bed without supper. Arthur could hear his snuffling sobs through the wall, and tentatively raised a hand to his mutilated hair. He rubbed his fingertips against the hot, prickly patches of bare skin which had been left. Mrs Walmsey carefully kept him upstairs and out of his father's way for the weeks until it had all returned.

For a long while afterwards, Edward was docile, even timid. He brought Arthur his most prized possessions – a box of wooden soldiers, a picture book, a rock that their father had carved into the shape of a monkey. He pressed these upon his younger brother and then played diligently with him. He cast anxious glances at Arthur's rust-coloured hair, which had grown back in ugly tufts.

Edward's rages came fitfully, and he lashed out at Arthur unprovoked, broke the very toys that he had so generously given. He cried easily. He did not seem to understand himself. He urged Arthur to stand before the portrait of Emily Hallingham, and then grew furious when he did so. *You are not allowed. You do not deserve to see her. Only me and Harmony and Father are permitted to look.*

"I remember," Arthur tried to tell him. "I remember being born. It was dark inside her, and then I came out into the cold. They put me in her arms."

Edward sneered at this, but he looked suddenly wounded, alarmed. Arthur woke that night coughing, in the midst of a haze of brightness. He saw his brother through the smoke, stood in frozen horror with his candle before the flaming curtains. The box of wooden soldiers on the floor was alight, but the fire had climbed, and as Arthur sat up in bed the rail came crashing to the ground.

The noise awoke Mrs Walmsey and the rest of the servants from their quarters below, and the fire was doused within minutes. The memory of Jonas Hallingham entering the charred scene in his dressing-gown, stone-faced and with his belt in his hand, would remain with Arthur down the years. His father passed him by with barely a glance, and crossed the room towards his eldest son. Edward stood with the burnt box of soldiers at his feet, his face pale and smudged.

He did not cry as he was beaten, but afterwards when Lord Harcourt was gone, sobbed his heart out. Mrs Walmsey brought him warm milk and a blanket, but still he cried, babbling his apology to Arthur over and over again. He was finally carried back to his own bed, having exhausted himself.

By the time the morning came, Edward had been utterly changed. A silence and a sullenness had come over him, as though he had taken the choice to withhold himself from the world. He no longer ran through the grounds with Arthur and Harmony, and their friend Lucas, the dreaming boy from the parsonage across the lawns. Edward took to secretive indoor pursuits of his own, haunting his father's study, and began to learn the running of the house. He had the servants call him *Lord Harcourt*.

§

The fire shook Jonas from his waking slumber. He hired a tutor for his sons, and did not notice that his daughter and Parson West's small son sat in upon each lesson. He took on gardeners to tame the overgrown expanse of the hall's grounds, much to the chagrin of Lucas and Harmony, whose expeditions into uncharted weeds and woodlands were curtailed. The household staff dusted every room. Hannah Hallingham sat with the cook to draw up dinner menus, and they ate at the long table in the shadowy dining hall each night. Arthur caught his father's dinner guests staring sideways at him, and stared back, strange body itching in his starched clothes.

Mrs Walmsey did up his shirt buttons, gently folded down his collar. She tried to smooth his unruly hair. "There, Master Arthur," she said. "Let 'em look all they want. To my eyes, you're as handsome as they come."

He did not yet have the words to speak to her of his hidden sickness. Nor would she have begun to understand. But Harmony, who sat beside him at the table, cast him small smiles between courses. Silently, she cut his meat into smaller pieces, nudged him when he used the wrong fork or chewed with his mouth open. She was the image of her mother's portrait, her dark hair framing her long face. She looked upon her father's guests with clear, level eyes.

"They'll be coming for you soon, and all, Miss Harmony." She came to sit in the nursery, and Mrs Walmsey plaited her hair before the fire. "Make no mistake. It shan't be long now, and you with such striking features..."

Harmony wrinkled her nose at Arthur. But Mrs Walmsey tugged her hair firmly into its ribbons.

"Mark my words, Miss. Give it a few more years."

It began when she was fifteen, when she had grown tall, and Mrs Walmsey began to tame her heavy hair with pins. They were the sons of Lord Harcourt's acquaintances, young men with impressive words and more impressive fortunes. Harmony listened politely to them, whilst in the seat beside her Arthur wriggled, struggling to bite his tongue. Sometimes wordless sounds would burst forth from his wayward body, unexpected grunts or barks, and Harmony would bite her napkin to keep from laughing.

Guests stared in alarm, while Jonas coughed into his wine. Lady Hannah toyed with the food upon her plate, birdlike, devoid of appetite. Edward grew red above his stiff collar.

When all had departed, Harmony pulled down her hair and laughed freely. Her eyes sparkled with mischief. She touched Arthur upon the arm. *Oh, my brother. If you had not, I think I should have done so, simply to break the tedium!* When their father had at last retired to bed, they let Lucas in through the tradesman's entrance. They sent the servants to bed, and stayed up late into the night, eating cold leftovers at the kitchen table.

It was on such nights that Lucas first began to speak of far continents – of Africa, of the Indies, of the New World. He had grown lither since childhood, and bolder, but his grey eyes still wore the same dreamer's look. The three of them broke open the pantry window, and leaned out of it together, staring up at the stars. Lucas whispered tales of ships with white sails, of virgin shores, of greenery that grew with the speed and vigour of animal life. Arthur could feel him shaking with excitement, while on his other side, Harmony quivered with the same emotion.

Think of it, whispered Lucas. *Think of a land of waiting wonders. Calling all brave pilgrims to itself.*

§

The parson, Henry West, preached to the frozen air of the chapel, his breath emerging in shining clouds. Harmony folded her hands demurely in her lap, but her eyes were brightened and alive. Lucas smiled over his shoulder at her from the foremost pew. Her singing was full-throated, her face raised fearlessly to the daylight. Beside her, Hannah Hallingham withdrew nervous hands into her black lace sleeves. Arthur hunched over, gnawing distractedly at the skin on the underside of his wrist.

And they heard the voice of the Lord walking in the garden in the cool of the day, and they hid themselves from his presence. He knew, even then, that he was beyond the reach of the Almighty. As his body changed, it only became more hideous to him. His brother and Lucas seemed imperceptibly to become men, their voices deepening and their shoulders broadening. But Arthur's strangeness grew with him, wrapped tightly around, like a weed upon an ear of corn.

He hid his body from all save Mrs Walmsey, who still patiently buttoned his shirt, combed his hair. She had grown slow and blurry-eyed with age, and patted him fondly upon the cheek, murmuring the same old choruses. *Black day it was that you were born, my child! My poor boy, my poor Arthur. And it never shall be made right, it never shall be well.* She poured pans of boiling water into the copper bath, and steam rose into the air.

He lowered himself into the cloudy water, submerged his white body into the deep of the tub. He bowed his head and wrapped his arms about his knees as she poured water onto his tousled hair. Beyond the window, an uneasy wind stirred the tops of the trees. The warmth of the water did not penetrate beneath his skin.

When Mrs Walmsey had gone, he ran his fingertips across the length and breadth of himself, up the protuberant bones of his long spine, and felt nothing. A chill washed over his heart, and he knew, even then, that some part of him was missing.

§

Lucas took a boat to Africa, promising his soon return. He packed up his collecting jars and notebooks, traced tentative lines across maps with the point of his finger. Henry West, after long months of trying to dissuade him, sighed and wrote letters ahead to the missionaries and merchants he knew there. *My son has taken it upon himself to see the whole of creation within his lifetime. I beg that you will show him hospitality, and when his curiosity is sated, send him back to me intact. May the Lord preserve him.*

Harmony crept into Lord Harcourt's study, closing the door behind her. Arthur could hear their raised voices through the floor for many hours, and knew what she had requested. But there was no question of Jonas relenting, as the parson had, and allowing his daughter to roam so far afield. She watched Lucas depart in the brightness of a March morning, then picked up her skirts and headed back to the house. She spent the summer walking the grounds alone, or sat in the library with Arthur, tapping her fingers impatiently upon the spine of her book.

He returned with a whirl of autumn leaves, his hair turned fair in the sunlight and his skin nut-brown. For Harcourt Hall he had brought back a lion skin rug, a glass-eyed beast which was laid in tawny splendour upon the floor of Jonas's study. To Harmony and Arthur, he also gave ivory horns, carved with native patterns. He had purchased these, he told them, from an old tribesman, who assured him that elephant flesh was the sweetest meat of all.

The great elephant! The round river-horse! The lion, and the black panther, and the howling hyaena! He could not stop talking of all he had seen. His collecting jars were full of red beetles, of bright-winged butterflies, of curious seeds and berries. Petals and branches spilled from between the pages of his notebooks. He showed them drawings he had made of river boats and indigo fields, of elegant deer and banana fruit trees. Harmony drank in each detail of his tales, but laughed in entire disbelief when he tried to convince her of the appearance of the giraffe.

"Now," she said, "Mr West, this is a fiction. Would you mock me because I was not permitted to go with you?

One rain-washed November day, promising Arthur and Harmony a surprise, he ushered them into a carriage and gently tied a scarf around Harmony's eyes. He grinned at Arthur, pressing a finger to his lips as they drew into the grounds of a house even grander than Harcourt Hall. Between them they helped Harmony, still blindfolded, down the steps of the carriage, and led her through wrought-iron gates into the most curious gardens that Arthur had ever seen.

Palm trees burst from between moss-covered rocks, and huge flowers bloomed in hothouses. Lucas led Harmony into a walled menagerie, where birds filled the chill air with their screeches, and dull-furred monkeys stared from behind their bars. Towering above the scene, with its legs planted in an enclosure but its impossible neck stretching high as the surrounding trees, was the very fiction that Lucas had described.

As Harmony tugged away her blindfold with exclamations of delight, Arthur moved away, to where a great black cat paced restlessly within its cage. Its head was level with his hip. The tip of its tail flickered, and its yellow eyes slid closed as it regarded him. It licked the tips of its pointed canines.

The rain came heavier than ever, but Harmony was far too enchanted to care. Arthur would remember, long after, the sight of her walking beside Lucas through the gardens as he held his umbrella above her head, the two of them laughing together. She did not notice the small heels of her shoes sunk into the mud, the hem of her green dress trailing through each puddle.

§

Her suitors came, still, and with each passing year she seemed to grow wearier of them. She attended her father's dinners, attentive and polite in conversation, resplendent in her finest gowns and with Emily Hallingham's jewels shining at her throat. But her smile wavered. Arthur saw her turn aside, the candlelight catching half of her suddenly sombre face, her dark brows lowered. Edward, whose own friends were now amongst those who came to call upon her with hothouse flowers and hopeful glances, made no secret of his disapproval.

You cannot hold back forever, as if they were each unworthy of your notice. He rounded on her when guests had left them. *You cannot scorn every offer, when you are already past the proper age.* Clearly riled by his father and aunt's inattentiveness, he took it upon himself to see that all of the hall's doors were locked after dark, and the lamps extinguished. Arthur and Harmony took to letting Lucas in through the library in the east wing, far from earshot of their brother's chambers.

As a boy Arthur had had only noises, incoherent barks and howls to fight her cause, but now his tongue awakened. It surprised him, aflame with sharp insults. It interrupted dinners with curses that made Hannah Hallingham blush and drop her glass to the floor. Harmony's suitors stared in shock, many so taken aback that they never returned.

Arthur's wayward body shuddered with pleasure at the sight of their horrified faces. He found that an unexpected viciousness lay low in him, waiting to be roused.

Lord Harcourt was ordinarily too lost in himself to care much for his children's conduct. But when Arthur's tongue took against a wealthy acquaintance of Edward's, in the midst of distinguished company, Jonas had a rare fit of temper. He had never quite been able to look at his youngest son directly, but he drew Arthur aside into his study and raged until he was hoarse, back turned all the while.

Arthur stared into the glass eyes of the lion-skin rug, which lay with its jaw grotesquely stretched, dust settled in its mane. He barely heard a word. When his father had finished, he burst out of the front door and ran down the lawn to the woods beyond. It was late in the evening, and clouds at the horizon threatened rain.

Harmony found him some hours later, beside the overgrown fountain in what had once been Emily Hallingham's rose garden. She sat down beside him, and discreetly pulled the twigs and dead leaves from his tousled hair. She straightened his collar, brushing dirt from the side of his face. They sat in silence for some while, the green water in the base of the fountain burbling behind them.

"He has shut himself away upstairs. Aunt Hannah went to console him." She laid a hand on his arm. "Come inside, Arthur." She was wearing her favourite plum-red gown, little jewels shining like stars in her dark hair.

He turned away. Staring back up at the distant lights of the hall, he said, "Promise that you will never leave me."

She smiled, and leant close to whisper to him. "Here's a secret, little brother. I am quite resolved never to marry. I shall become an old maid, and live in the attic. I shall come downstairs only at Christmas, in order to frighten Edward's children." She brushed back an unruly strand of hair from his face. "Now come inside. You cannot sleep out here."

"I shall if I wish to."

"I often wish to, and never have." She stood, and beckoned to him. But he did not move. The night wind rustled in the dead stems of the roses.

"Harmony," he said. "There's something wrong with my body."
Her smile faltered.

"There's something wrong with my body. As though I am trapped inside myself. As though I do not know myself."

She stood there in the starlight, silent. He dug his fingernails into his palms until they bled. "Why am I not — *made* — like everybody else?"

"Arthur, please... you are frightening me..."

He looked up at her pleadingly. She shook her head, looking at him as if she were seeing him for the first time. "Do not talk that way. There is nothing *wrong* with you, Arthur. Whatever anybody might say."

The rest of his words died on his lips. He huddled on the edge of the fountain, but Harmony would not leave, standing beside him in the falling of the night. Resolutely, she gathered her skirts, and held out her hand.

"Come inside. It looks like rain."

16

Hideous Creatures

Jonas Hallingham's hair began to turn silver with his years and his grief. The music that he made rung through the floors and seeped into every curtain and tapestry. It hung heavy on the air. It weighed down upon Arthur's heart, and he was sure he had once heard the same songs played in some sad circumstance. But no memory returned to him, save for the old recollection of sliding from darkness into the cold world. The cello's strings sung out, their sound deep and rolling as the ocean. Hannah Hallingham, each time she heard the music begin, would pause in her occupation and bow her head.

Her small white hands worried at her black lace sleeves. She moved timidly about the house, as if anxious she might be stricken again by the illness that had once sent her from the house. When her brother shut himself in his study, or played for hours on end as if trying to drown all other sound from his ears, she was the only one who went to sit with him. They could rarely be heard speaking, but seemed bound by a silent understanding. To Arthur they appeared like a pair of corks bobbing in troubled water, carried on a current which drew them together, drew them on.

§

With Jonas drifting ever further from his duties, Edward stepped into his father's place. He arranged the dinners that brought Harmony's suitors, who persisted still, though fewer in number now. In the autumn, when the pheasants had grown fat, he instigated a shooting party in the woods. Arthur stood beside Lucas, his hands sweating upon the handle of his rifle. He fired wildly, and the birds rose above the trees, their cries echoing across the misted hills. He brought nothing home that night. From Edward's hand hung a clutch of bloodied birds, their beaks open, their black eyes glazed.

Edward did not trust the servants to put out the lamps at night, and patrolled the house himself like a policeman. Tall and imposing, with his unsmiling mouth and sweep of dark hair, his firm hand was upon all of the hall's affairs. But in his night-time wanderings he did not venture as far as the library in the east wing, where Arthur, Harmony and Lucas spent the late hours amidst shelves of silent tomes.

Peace lay over the dusty pages and moth-eaten furnishings. They sat around a low table hidden in the corner beneath the window, slowly drinking down a crystal bottle of brandy which had been there for decades. Harmony, often still dressed in her dinner finery, wrapped a blanket about her shoulders and pulled up her knees to her chest. Lucas lit candles upon the table and the windowsill, dealing cards or pulling down books from which he would read aloud until his throat grew hoarse. Wax dripped onto the wood, and on many nights they would not even notice the midnight chiming of the clock.

§

Harmony and Lucas mapped the stars beyond the window. They squabbled agreeably about how this arrangement would vary upon different latitudes and longitudes, how the heavens might appear if one stood upon the line running round the earth's centre. And Lucas's grey eyes began to cloud once more with their dreamer's look. He began to mutter of far-off white shores, of pine forests, of wide skies. He began to whisper of the New World.

§

Arthur lay awake, some nights, with a cold sweat upon his skin. Rain pattered against the tall windows. In the dark hours his mind wandered, and he knew that things could not long remain as they were. The coming years were without candlelight in the quiet library. They were without Harmony's smiling eyes, without the familiar sight of Lucas's wiry form striding across the lawns from the parsonage. Whatever she said, she would marry, because she must, and he would cross oceans that were fathoms deep, miles wide.

And what shall become of you, Master Arthur? Mrs Walmsey hobbled to hang wet bed sheets before the fire. She rocked back and forth in her chair, and shook her grizzled head. She lay the back of her rough hand against Arthur's forehead. *What shall become of my poor boy, all grown? Who shall care for him when I am gone? Not his addled father. Not Lady Hannah, sick as she is.*

There would be no place for him, he knew, in Edward's house. He watched his brother with the young ladies who came to dine, all self-conscious laughter and hands fussing at the back of their curled hair. Edward did not thaw for them, but the promise of his inheritance seemed enough. He regarded them with detachment, his choice a matter of sober duty. He showed more concern about Harmony's prospects than his own.

When will you stop this stubbornness? Will you not think of this house? Of our honoured name? Her eyes flashed, and she made no reply to him. One warm night in late August, after she had once more politely declined all invitations to dine and dance with Edward's friends, he caught her by the wrist as she made to leave.

"What is your intent, Harmony?" he asked, in a low voice. "Tell me. How do you think you might live through the years ahead?"

She tried to pull away from him, but his grip only tightened. Edward thrust his face close to hers, a flush colouring his cheeks. Arthur drew back against the wall.

"You think it will always be summer, Harmony. But your winter is coming, and you have stored up nothing for yourself." She turned, but he pulled her roughly back. "They will come no more, these suitors, and you will be left to care for our father in his old age. Believe me, you will look back in bitter regret at those you once cast aside!"

She drew herself up, her height easily matching his. But her voice shook. "I shall not care," she declared. "For Arthur will stay with me. And Lucas."

Edward's laugh was unexpectedly fierce. "Arthur! Do not speak to me of Arthur." He seemed to collect himself, and his voice grew softer, more urgent. "And Lucas? His infatuation will fade – listen to me, Harmony!" The colour had drained from her face. "*It will fade*, and he will marry some village girl. He will give up one day, and soon. You will glimpse him in church each Sunday and turn aside, mortified that you ever allowed yourself and this family such an intimacy with him."

Arthur's ears rung. When Harmony had fled upstairs to her bedchamber and Edward had stalked away to douse the drawing room lamps, he sat alone in the empty dining hall. He did not even think to go and let Lucas into the library. He gnawed at his nails, and rocked back and forth.

Late in the night he knocked at his sister's door, and she answered wearily from the other side. "What do you want, Arthur?"

He dug his toes into the carpet. He heard her sigh, and she pulled the door open a crack. She was in her nightgown, her hair impatiently tugged down from its pins, her eyes red-rimmed. He blinked at her.

"It's all right," she said, more gently. "Go to sleep, little brother. It will be all right."

He wrapped his arms around himself, shivering. The lamp upon the bedside table behind her flickered and guttered. Harmony reached out, and took his cold hand.

"Whatever comes to pass," she told him quietly, "I shan't leave you."

§

Lucas took his ship to the New World, at long last, later that same year. His departure came after strange months in which he came to the hall only in daylight, conducting himself with formality. He and Arthur fished beside the lake, speaking little through the blustery autumn afternoons, unaccompanied by Harmony. Arthur trekked up the lawns at nightfall, but Lucas headed back down to the parsonage. *There are so many preparations to make. Send my apologies to your sister.*

"You will write to us?" she asked him, when he came to bid his farewells. He shook hands with Lord Harcourt and with Edward, kissed Lady Hannah upon the cheek. When they had gone, Arthur and Harmony accompanied him to the front of the house, and the three of them stood looking out upon the grounds.

"I have been happy here," said Lucas, soberly. "I do not quite know who I shall be when I am gone from this place."

He embraced Arthur, and hesitated before taking Harmony's hand. He kissed it quickly, then stepped back, inclining his head to both of them. "I shall return a year hence, be sure of it. Even for the riches of the New World, I could not stay away longer."

They watched him depart, growing smaller as he crossed the lawns in the gathering dusk. Harmony's face betrayed nothing, but she drew near to Arthur, threading her arm through his. She did not move, long after Lucas had vanished from sight.

"That's that, then," she said. "That's that."

There were fewer dinners, that winter. Jonas barely emerged from his own rooms, sending down for food from the kitchen. Harmony and Arthur took to sitting in the library together, a fire lit in the grate, reading as the wind howled through the woods outside. Every now and then Arthur cast a glance at his sister's face, and caught her staring blankly at the page before her, eyes unmoving.

Bad weather kept correspondence away. When Lucas's first letter finally arrived, it was bundled along with the second and third. Edward read these slowly and joylessly at the breakfast table, refusing to yield them until he had perused every last page. When he finally finished, Arthur and Harmony stole the papers away to the library, where she spread them upon the table with hands that shook. Amongst the closely written pages were myriad charts and drawings. While Harmony's forefinger traced the loops of Lucas's bold handwriting, Arthur examined sketches of the black and white *racone*, of deer with great branching antlers.

The flora and fauna were not skillfully drawn, but something about their very inexpertness gave them a life of their own. Lucas's beasts seemed to stare out beadily from the pages, his flowers and trees springing up with indecent vigour. Where he had drawn scenery, he had tried with some earnestness to convey the majesty of the skies which overarched all he beheld. Lakes and forests and hills were dwarfed, confined to the bottom inches of each page, beneath the hugeness of the heavens.

Oh, Harmony, he wrote. *Oh, Arthur. This is God's own land, made from the finest of His materials!* His ship, the merchant vessel *Benefactor*, had come upon the shore in brilliant morning sunshine, the dew-soaked land lit gold before them. His shipmates had laughed as he stumbled from the deck, burying his hands in the grass, breathing in the shimmering air. *From my earliest youth I believe that such a place has taken root in my imaginings. Glories overflow on every side of me. I have seen such wonders here, that I do not know how I shall tell you of them.*

§

They bundled his letters together with string, and kept them stacked upon the bookshelves, amidst their father's musical scores and dusty volumes of verse. Arthur knew that Harmony slipped in amongst the shelves when he was not there, and turned the pages over in her hands. Sometimes, in her absence, he did likewise. He held the paper close to his face, and fancied that he inhaled the dust of the far continent. To think of all the miles that the papers had travelled made him feel giddy and faint.

As a boy, Lucas had fought his intrepid way through Harcourt Hall's overgrown grounds, butterfly net and fishing rod over his shoulder, penknife in his hand. Arthur pictured him now, fighting through forests which grew high above his head, wading through pools that were thick with darting fish. Picking strange fruits for the eating.

Do you not think he writes too eagerly? As though he may choose not to return?

Some nights Harmony fell asleep beside the library fire, her head nodding forward onto the pages of her book. Arthur shook her gently awake, and watched her come to in momentary distress, as if she had thought herself to be somewhere else. They walked together through the grounds in the deep of winter, among Emily Hallingham's skeletal roses and beside the frozen lake. They wrapped themselves about with coats and scarves, while Edward had the servants gather firewood to hold off the chill from the hall's dim chambers.

Each time I look at the ground, I see some plant I have never seen before, and am forced to call the entire party to a halt. The letters came fortnightly, smudged and crumpled, spotted with ink and with mud. *I have enclosed another drawing of snow upon the pines, and of a native boat, or Canou, which is made from the hollowed bark of the birch. I have been thirty leagues a day down the river in one of these vessels, and once seen a glimpse of the brown bear, which is taller than a man and feeds upon fish.*

Harmony lifted her skirts from the icy ground, and strode across the lawns to meet the postman as he approached upon his horse. She tucked the letters inside her coat before Edward could request them. It was not long before the pile in the library grew so thick that she bound the pages together in a makeshift volume with leather and thread.

I must confess I have been seized with something of a wondrous terror. I do not think we have begun to conceive how much still lies beyond the borders of our knowledge. I do not know how it is that the Almighty is yet mindful of us.

§

Winter bled into spring, frost thawing to rain, and Lucas wrote less frequently. Edward took to staying up even later into the night than Arthur and Harmony, wandering the halls and corridors. Arthur saw the light of his lamp burning beneath the door of his chambers in the small hours, heard the restless shuffle of his feet. The sound of a cello wove in and out of earshot as doors opened and closed. Half-asleep, Arthur was left somehow with the impression of a growing darkness within the house, and Edward a helpless watchman, chasing it down in empty rooms and along dusty passageways.

I cannot think so clearly as I once did, wrote Lucas. His handwriting had diminished to a barely legible scrawl. *I have been enticed further and deeper into this country than was my first intent.*

Arthur's body shivered beneath his sheets. He dreamed of branches through which no light could penetrate, of a blackness beneath the world, and when the heat of summer came, awoke sweating, his bed linen soaked through. Mrs Walmsey worried over him, pressing a cool cloth to his forehead and murmuring absently. *My poor Arthur. My poor boy.*

As Lucas journeyed southwards, he drew swollen red fruit, snakes which hung in sinuous coils. *There are fields here,* he wrote, *where men are made to work like beasts. I am told that their wives and brothers and children have perished on the voyage from their homeland. I am told that this land is to be built upon their backs.*

Arthur caught glimpses of himself, from time to time, in the long mirror which hung upon the wall of the drawing room. He drew back in alarm. The face before him, always so pale, was moon-white beneath its shock of rust-coloured hair. And the eyes, the awful eyes, darted evasively away. Even his own reflection could not bear to look upon him.

§

There is something that begins to trouble me, wrote Lucas. *I shall say no more of it here. But my heart is strangely heavy. I think of you often. I think of my return.*

He came back unannounced after fourteen months, and was met by nobody, as the whole household was at dinner. He had left his bags and travelling clothes at the parsonage, and crossed the lawns in the twilight, coming in through the servants' entrance. The cook made him bread and jam and sat him in the drawing room, where he remained quietly until Hannah Hallingham went in to fetch her sewing.

He had brought no gifts, this time. He was thin and worn, and though he accompanied Arthur and Harmony over to the library, he did not seem eager to talk. The sight of all his letters, stacked high and bound together, barely raised a smile. He rubbed his eyes with his knuckles, and Arthur saw a look pass between him and Harmony, filled with weariness.

I am glad to be home, was all he said. *Glad to be home.* He passed in and out of the house, in the weeks that followed, but never stayed long. He had been trailed back it seemed by some shadow, which crept up the lawns and began to seep between the bricks of the hall.

Dread sat heavy in Arthur's stomach. Kept from sleep one November night, he stood with the book of letters in his hands, turning each page fretfully as fresh images rose in his mind. Lizards the length of a grown man, sunk low in the water. Insects that lit the night like drops of pale fire. He shook his head as if trying to rid himself of an intruding sound. Beyond the window, the wind howled through the trees, buffeting against the glass.

Suddenly the pane was thrown open, the wall lamps spitting and guttering, and the papers in Arthur's hands were scattered from their binding across the library floor. White sheets flew around him, maps and paintings and letters caught on wild torrents of air. And a strange scent was carried in out of the night, with a whirl of dead petals and leaves. A smell like buried remains and deep-forest earth. An ancient, acrid musk.

§

And it came, at last; that for which he had waited his whole life. The howl, ringing through the corridors of Harcourt Hall, telling him what he had always known. That something was wrong beyond all rescue.

He was in the entrance hall with Harmony, bidding farewell to Lucas as he made to leave them at the end of the evening. Lucas halted in the act of pulling open the door. The cry echoed from somewhere high above them, wild and bleak and broken.

"*ARTHUR!*" bellowed Edward's voice, and there was no fleeing from it.

He followed the sound of his name, up the stairs and into his father's bedchamber, where he had never once set foot before.

"*Arthur!*" cried Edward, upon the sight of him. He raised a violently shaking hand to point in savage accusation. "*Oh, I have always known it!*"

He was weeping as he had not done for nearly twenty years, since his father beat him for setting fire to the nursery. His whole body convulsed with great, boyish sobs. Behind him on the bed sat Jonas Hallingham, white as chalk, fumbling with the buttons on the front of his nightshirt. Lady Hannah stood beside the window, nightgown hanging from her shoulder, fragile little fingers clutching a blanket around her body.

Arthur stared between her and his father, uncomprehending.

"I have always known it!" gasped Edward, as Harmony and Lucas came stumbling into the room on Arthur's heels. "Ever since I was a boy... in the manner that small children know... not completely, but as in a dream..."

"Edward," began Jonas faintly.

"That such a thing could happen... behind the closed doors of this house... that such a thing has been happening these last thirty years..."

"Edward, *what* in all the world are you speaking of?" Harmony stepped forward, and tried to place a hand upon his arm. But he flung her away from himself so violently that he caught a vase which stood upon a nearby chest of draws, sending it to noisy destruction upon the floor. Eyes and nose streaming unchecked, he turned upon his greying father.

"Shall you tell them, Lord Harcourt, Sir? Or shall I?" His voice cracked and broke into sobs again. "When did it begin? Before I was even born, perhaps? When she first returned from across the sea, and she was a stranger to you, not like your flesh and blood at all?"

Harmony froze in the act of trying to lay a hand on him again. Jonas did not seem able to move from the bed, or to speak a single word.

"Or perhaps even before that, when you were barely more than children yourselves? Before she was sent away… for her *sickness*…"

"Please," whispered Hannah Hallingham. "Please." She was weeping too, now, with a fathomless, weakened grief. Her hair fell across her face as she hung her head.

"Did he force himself on you?" demanded Edward. And then, when she only wept all the more, seized her by the wrist and bellowed in her face. "*DID HE FORCE HIMSELF ON YOU?*"

Arthur's heart sat in his throat. Slowly, her tears raining down onto the carpet, Hannah Hallingham shook her head. "I have desired him too," she whispered. "From the beginning of it."

Jonas rose at last, arms raised across his chest in readiness to defend himself from blows. "Who else knows?" demanded Edward, with sudden hard coldness. "Is there anybody else who knows?"

"Just the nurse," whispered Hannah. "And no other living soul."

"Fetch Mrs Walmsey," Edward fired at Harmony. She was gone in an instant, leaving a gaping silence in her wake. Lucas hovered in the doorway, too stricken either to stay or to go. Edward strode to the fireplace and kicked the smouldering logs, which gave off a puff of ash. Arthur felt as if he were viewing the scene from outside of his body, which had grown numb from head to toe.

Jonas moved towards Hannah, but she turned away from him,

her breath misting on the window. He looked desolately across at his sons, his lined face drained of all life.

"But I ain't to speak of it, Miss Harmony, not ever!" They heard Mrs Walmsey outside in the passageway, the shuffling of her slow gait upon the carpet. She was still protesting when Harmony steered her into the room. "I swore it to the master, and to the lady herself, God rest her…"

Her half-blind eyes blinked round at them all, and lighted on Arthur. "There now," she mumbled. "There's my poor boy. Such sorrow upon us all!"

"Mrs Walmsey," said Edward, loudly and tremulously. He loomed over the fireplace, hair in wild disarray, shirt collar torn open in his distress. "Pray tell us, under what circumstances Arthur came to be born."

The old woman's mouth grew round in surprise and trepidation. She looked to Lord Harcourt for guidance, and he gave her a resigned nod before covering his eyes with his hand.

"Poor Lady Emily," she whispered to Edward. "'Twas the shock and the disgrace of it what killed her. God-fearing soul she was. Your mother, and Miss Harmony's."

A rushing noise filled Arthur's ears. And he saw the image of Lady Harcourt, looking imposingly down on him from the far wall of the portrait gallery.

Such sorrow. Such sorrow you have brought upon us all.

"T'was easy enough to hide it, Lady Hannah being so small. The master, he put it about that she was sick, and she kept herself upstairs. My Lady, she…" She mimed the padding of her belly. "With rags. Was only the four of us ever knew…"

Unwanted, even then. Floating in the cold darkness inside her. And then entering the world that had dreaded his coming, sodden and bloody and screaming.

"Such a look he had," whispered Mrs Walmsey. "Such a devilish look, my poor boy. T'was no wonder she couldn't take to him. No wonder it was the end of her."

Dimly, Arthur became aware that all eyes were upon him. A prickling, cramped sensation spread through his chest and limbs. At the corner of the room, he could see Hannah Hallingham, black hair curtaining her face, shaking with silent sobs. For several long minutes, nobody said a word. Then Jonas finally lowered his hands from his forehead, his shoulders hunched in lifeless defeat.

"It occurs to me," he intoned dully, "that we shall be damned for what we have done. Hideous creatures that we are."

"*Father?*" There were scarlet patches in Harmony's cheeks. "*Father, is this…?*"

"Every word of it true," he said.

She did not gasp, or cover her mouth with her hand. Instead she seemed to absorb the news into herself, her back straightening, her jaw set. Edward, however, combusted again.

"*GET – OUT – OF – THIS – HOUSE!*"

His spittle flew into Arthur's face, his arms waving wildly, his eyes bulging. And he was not to be denied. He seemed to fill the room in all its dimensions, the storm of his rage flattening them like saplings in a gale. Arthur felt his knees buckle, and a wail rose up from somewhere within him, a piteous thin howl like a dog left out in the rain.

"*GET OUT!*" Edward leapt towards Arthur, fists flying, but Lucas flung himself between them. "*Out of my sight… away from this house… away from here… before our shame is known by all…*"

He was taller than Lucas, lent strength by his wrath. He broke through, and landed a blow upon Arthur's head, then another. The world tilted sideways. There was only pain, and shouting from all sides, and the sound of Edward sobbing. And still, that strange, remote ringing in Arthur's ears.

"Edward! EDWARD! I'll take him. Listen —" Lucas was panting, his arm locked across Edward's chest. "I'll take him far from here. *Just don't hurt him.*"

Mrs Walmsey was wailing incoherently. Harmony had Edward by the arm, and helped Lucas to pull him back, leaving Arthur crumpled on the ground. He could taste blood between his teeth.

Neither Jonas nor Hannah had moved a muscle, transfixed by the scene before them. Edward finally fell quiet. He shook off Lucas's hold in a single movement, then stepped forward towards his father. He spat forcefully at Jonas's feet. When he spoke again, his voice was low and utterly commanding.

"We shall never again speak of the deeds done under this roof. Nor of their consequences. It will be as though he never lived."

"Get up, Arthur," muttered Lucas, an unmistakable edge of fear to his voice.

"*Get him out of my sight, out of this house, out of this country. And may he never return.*"

Lucas raised Arthur up by his elbow, and tugged him towards the doorway, out of Edward's reach. Hannah gave a small whimper, but seemed unable to speak. Jonas was still staring at the spittle on the floor before his feet. It was only Harmony who, as Lucas pulled him past, reached out to hold him back.

"Stay, Arthur." He saw that she was crying too now, stormily, defiantly, wiping her tears away as fast as they came. "Stay."

Uncomprehending, he flinched away from her hand.

§

The night was black, the candles in the entrance hall unlit. He had packed no belongings. He stood before the open door waiting for Lucas to bring the horses, his split lip throbbing. He could still taste his own blood upon the tip of his tongue.

Outside in the grounds, the lawns rippled in the moonlight. He became aware that somebody had slipped quietly from the shadows behind him. The curtains rustled. Hannah Hallingham stood at the back of the hall, still in her long nightgown, which trailed upon the floor. She looked small, and ragged, and lost.

"You were taken from me," she said. Her voice echoed in the cold chamber. "Given over to her before I could so much as hold you."

Her eyes pleaded for absolution. But there was no feeling in him, only a resounding hollowness. Her pale face crumpled. Lucas called urgently from outside, and as Arthur turned to leave, she whispered to him through the darkness.

"If they had placed you in my arms instead of hers, I would have held you close, and never let you go."

17

Orphans

"We rode through the night, Flora. Lucas and I."

She was still breathing. Light broke in through Robert's curtains, illuminating her pallid face, her sweat-soaked hair. Blood had oozed through her bandages yet again, staining the bedclothes.

Arthur lay alongside her, throat hoarse from talking. His body ached with grief.

"We rode through the night to the sea, where the ships were waiting. He gave me letters for his friends in Africa, asking for sanctuary." In the drizzly dawn, the boats in the harbour had loomed huge as dragons. "He paid my passage on a merchant vessel."

Arthur rubbed his hands across his face. Lucas fell away from him in the early morning light, silhouette marred by mist, hand raised in dazed farewell. The iron-grey waves rolling below.

Flora stirred, muttering inaudibly. Brought back to the present moment, Arthur brushed the hair from her face and laid the back of his hand against her forehead. She was still feverish, but cooler, he was sure, than hours before. He sat up, startled. And even amidst his relief the thought crept upon him that she had been conscious all the while.

"Robert!" he called, sharply. "Robert!"

§

"She's going to live, Shelo. He says she's going to live."

The shadow beside the stove stirred, growling deeply. Shelo looked up at him, empty-eyed. He did not rise, but turned his broad back.

Arthur ate with Robert at the table, bread thick-spread with butter, cornmeal, salt pork. The farmer chewed slowly, not once turning away his watchful gaze. Exhausted from the long night, Arthur found his head nodding forwards, his eyes sliding closed.

"Rest," said Robert. "I'll stay with her."

It came to him, as he bedded down in the barn behind the farmhouse, that if Robert had passed by the bedroom in the night he might have overheard all manner of things. Curled in the straw, Arthur shuddered. A stream trickled by outside, and a sparrow chirruped in the eaves.

He thought of the weeks he had spent upon a cloth ship, bound for the coast of Africa. That voyage, his first, had passed in a daze. Stepping out onto the hot shore, the sun had blinded his eyes. *Ask at the port for these names,* Lucas had told him, *for these places. There will be refuge for you.* There had been no will in him even to try.

He had lived beneath the harbour, eating what was tossed away from the crates when the ships came in. The port never slept. In the night the lamps had ever been lit, spewing out thick smoke, while the scorching sun beat down in the day. Endless shouting in foreign tongues; the great crash and rumble of ships being unloaded, loaded, sent forth again. The chattering of monkeys and lowing of livestock. And the smells. Meat rotting in cases, sweat on bare skin, sour brine, spices from a hundred far lands.

Sick at heart, Arthur had forgotten the images which had so arrested in him the pages of Lucas's correspondence, the strange scent of the wind blowing in through the library window. These came back to him only when he saw a boat with billowing white sails and a woman's head carved at its prow, being loaded for a voyage to the New World.

Here, mister, it's plain that some trouble's befallen you. A shadow lingered in the doorway of the barn. It was around midday, the light shining in through the slats over his head. *Even inexperienced hands will be of use. Any willing hands, with a cargo of this kind.*

"Shelo," he said. The shadow in the doorway moved reluctantly towards him. "Shelo. Why did Silas leave me?"

"Silas."

"The old sailor, Shelo. He was good to me."

Shelo seemed barely to hear him, his thoughts far away. His foot trailed through the dust, the edge of his lip lifting up over his teeth. "She paid her price long ago," he said, nonsensically. "Turned from me in her heart, and for that her years covered with shadow." A strangled laugh escaped him. "Body as dead as her ground."

Shelo had left himself behind in the governor's dreadful chamber. His head with its mane of oiled hair hung low, the fight and the ferocity drained from him. Arthur, wearied to his bones by all that he had relived in the night, could summon little curiosity for anything else.

Shelo's teeth ground together, his eyes darting furtively about. His hands kneaded absently at his empty ribcage. The dappled light shone down upon his inked skin as though he were underwater.

§

Art, Flora whispered weakly. *Art, is that you?*

She could not yet raise herself from the bed, and her smile was a grimace. But she had returned to the world. He hovered anxiously in the doorway, dozed upon the edge of the bed. He could not shake the fear that she would remember all he had whispered to her. He would never have spoken it, had he not been sure that she would carry it to her grave.

"Lie quiet," he muttered to her. "Do not distress yourself. Lie still."

I think I can recall... She tossed and turned, clutching the blankets to herself. She stared wide-eyed at Robert when he came in to clean her wound. *Was we in a dark wood, Art? Or a grand house? Certain I can recall... my daddy was there...*

And then, as it returned to her, she grew subdued again. She lay facing the ceiling, hands resting upon her bandaged chest.

"Where's my boots?" she asked Arthur eventually. Obligingly, he fetched them, and she sat up. Uncertain what she had in mind, he helped her to pull them on, her arm slung about his neck. The farmer had dressed her in his own shirt and breeches, which hung loosely on her.

"Shelo still with us?" she asked weakly. Arthur nodded. "And that man..."

"Robert. His name is Robert."

She flinched, freckled countenance paling as she swung her feet to the floor. Leaning heavily on Arthur, she raised herself from the bed.

"Are you certain..." he began nervously.

"I got to breathe some air."

They sat together on the damp earth in the vegetable garden, amongst the sprouting sweet potatoes and cassava. A few chickens scratched amongst the weeds near the wall of the house. Mountains rose on either side of them, shrouded in mist, the river flowing close at hand. Flora wrapped her blanket about her shoulders, breathing unevenly, and looked at Arthur.

"It was him," she said. "Weren't it?" Her fingers traced the bloodied bandage bound across her chest. She wiped her hand violently across her eyes, but there appeared to be no tears. Her shoulders hunched.

"I am sorry," said Arthur.

"I figure, he was took down before he shot. He'd have hit his mark for sure, otherwise. I seen my daddy shoot apples down from trees and a whisky glass from a man's hand. He said to me, he once hit a sparrow at fifty yards."

Arthur clenched his fists tightly closed, and watched her face, uncertain how much she could remember. "He took a bullet in the stomach. He died at once."

"At once, huh?"

He nodded. She gazed up towards the cloud-capped mountains, her eyes closing as her face turned to the light. She flinched from the sun, but after a few moments seemed to warm in it, letting out a long breath.

"I told you. Ripstone and the others, they always were the kind for wantin'... you know. And he never did rebuke 'em for it."

She was looking at Arthur, suddenly, with clear and unblinking eyes. There was a tenderness in it that he could not bear, and he turned away. Flora's fingers began to comb peaceably through her knotted hair. He tucked his hands beneath his belt to conceal their trembling.

§

Robert laboured through the daylight hours, bent-backed in the fields. He murmured to his cows as he milked them, returned at night with his hat in his hand and his tools slung over his back. He was careful towards the strangers in his home. He changed Flora's bandages with steady hands as Arthur hovered in the doorway, faint with the sight of the wound.

"My mother's master was a physician," Robert explained, washing Flora's blood from his hands in a bowl on the bedside table. "When I was a boy, he allowed me to assist."

"An' you ran away?" asked Flora.

"No, miss." He smiled. "No, I had no need to run."

He appeared entirely unused to company. He sat by the fire in the evenings, his brown dog curled at his feet. He asked no further questions, not even regarding Shelo, who had taken up residence in his barn.

"She will need to rest days, at the least, before she can travel any distance." He pulled closed the bedchamber door after Flora had drifted into sleep, and addressed Arthur with wary formality. "Sir. Might you travel to the next town to send a message ahead? It's a mere day's ride back down the valley..."

"No," said Arthur. "No, there is nobody."

"No companions, or relatives?" Robert looked back through the crack in the door, to where Flora lay asleep in his bed. Her overlarge boots were propped against the wall.

Arthur shook his head. "We have no living family."

Flora brightened gradually, strong enough to eat bread, oatmeal, stew. She requested that the window be opened, and sat with the breeze blowing across her covers. The light in the valley was gentle and mild. Some nights, rainclouds would become trapped between the surrounding mountains, thunder reverberating round and round until it finally wore itself into silence. Each morning, the air was clear again.

When she thought herself alone, Arthur caught Flora gazing enraptured at the clouds which cast their passing shadows across the room. She had not yet once complained of any pain. And neither, for one who had been her whole life upon the road, did she appear restless. She sat still and quiet upon the pillows.

Arthur washed his hands and scarred torso attentively in Robert's water barrel each night. He could not bear the possibility of Flora recollecting, even dimly, what he had spoken to her when he had thought she would not wake. It was too late to unsay the words, or to stem the flood of memories they had brought; all was laid bare, the heart of it as rotten as it had ever been. It was time, at last, to bring it to an end.

§

Shelo.You saw into the very heart of me.You called me across the sea.

Shelo had divested himself of his shirt and coat. Barefoot, oiled hair hanging down his back, he sat in the doorway of the barn. He opened his mouth to catch the droplets of rain which came dribbling from the roof. He slept in the straw, hands covering his inked lids. He murmured fretfully to himself.

"*All lost,*" he muttered. "*And still no peace.*" He watched the sparrows in the eaves with hungry eyes. Arthur slept at his feet, as ever, but this no longer brought any sense of safety. The strength in Shelo's broad body seemed to have seeped away. The twisting tendrils upon his face, chest and limbs appeared to encircle him ever more tightly, strangling the life from his flesh.

Shelo. Now that I have aided you… do you think…

Arthur could not bring himself to speak it in full. When Shelo only looked blankly back, clearly struggling to recall who he was, panic began to fill him. For so long, he had fought to keep them from these shores – his father, Edward, Lucas and Harmony. Hannah Hallingham. But now their faces were before him every waking hour. His body groaned for the ending of it.

"You recall me, Shelo," he said, tentatively. "Arthur Hallingham. Conceived in shame, and born in darkness."

He dreamed that the knot of grief inside him was drawn up through his chest, choking him as it rose into his throat. His body convulsed with birth-pangs. As it unfolded in his mouth, he felt the strange sensation of tiny legs, of wings against his tongue. And then it had escaped from his lips, fluttering up towards the moon, silver-white and delicate.

Numbness descended upon him, an empty and endless forgetting which dissipated when he awoke. His pain returned in all its measure.

"Shelo," he whispered brokenly. "I am so very weary. Is it not yet time...?"

I desired him too. Hannah Hallingham's small white hands retreating into her sleeves. *From the beginning of it.* Arthur groaned aloud. *I am afraid that we shall be damned for what we have done.* He lay close to Shelo, listening in vain for the pounding of a living heart.

If there was to be no relief, he had come to the ends of the earth for nothing. He imagined that he felt the ground shuddering beneath him, rock straining on rock, deep in the belly of the world.

§

He felt that he had been hollowed out on the inside, scraped clean like a cooking pot, like the carcass of a fish. He imagined himself suspended in liquid blackness, the pieces of his body coming together over long hushed months beneath the gown which concealed him. He wondered if she had tried concoctions like Sam's. If she had sat upon the edge of her bed pulling down her skirts with shaking hands, praying for the bleed. He ought never to have brought her name to his lips.

He watched Flora as the colour returned to her cheeks, as she moved awkwardly from the bed, still clutching at her side. She leant trustingly upon Robert, did not struggle against him when he came to clean her wound.

232

Arthur ventured in when he thought that she was sleeping, and stood beside the headboard, watching the rise and fall of her chest. In the quiet of the room, his thoughts were in turmoil. He felt profoundly shamed, as if he had allowed her to catch sight of him unclothed. He did not know what was to be done.

He had turned to leave, to rejoin Shelo in the barn, when he felt her hand grasp lightly at his wrist.

"Art," she said sleepily. "He's kind. Ain't he? He's been awful kind to me."

"He has been generous."

"Art. I'll go with you, if you like. Back to Eng-land." She released him, and smiled faintly. "I always figured I'd die on some dirt road, or with my neck in a noose, but it ain't come to pass." A sigh escaped her. "I should like to meet 'em someday. Harmony, and the rest."

His heart gave a lurch. Her eyes began to flutter closed again, but he found that he had shaken her roughly by the shoulders, jolting her awake.

"Do you think I have a plan?" he demanded, more vehemently than he had intended. "You really think I have some... *home...* to go to?"

Her peacefulness had turned to puzzlement. She raised herself onto her elbow, one hand over her wound. "Arthur..."

He spat the bad taste out of his mouth, his words turning to mockery. "And I suppose you'd want to marry me as well?"

She looked up at him, plainly shocked, and laid herself bare without hesitation. "No one else ever gonna want me. Ain't that so?"

It was a plea, and he did not answer it. He shook her grip from his sleeve and pulled away, making for the door. He hurried down the passageway, and then almost collided headlong with Robert, who was coming in from the garden. The smell of turned earth filled the muggy night. He tried to avert his face, but Robert paused, blocking his way.

"Forgive me." Robert raised an arm to lean against the doorframe. It was not a threatening movement, but Arthur recoiled. "I been resolved not to concern myself..."

Reluctantly, Arthur met his gaze. He realised that his raised voice must have been audible through the bedroom window.

"What fearful trouble," asked Robert softly, "has brought you to my door?"

Arthur swallowed, and again shook his head. There was a sad ache at the back of his throat, an overwhelming longing to confess all. But it would not do.

His face must have betrayed him. Robert lowered his arm, looking at Arthur with bafflement through the dark.

"I told you." Arthur swallowed. He gestured weakly back towards the bedroom door. "We are, the three of us, nobody but orphans."

§

Shelo. Shelo, it is time for us to leave. Wake up, Shelo.

An uneasy wind stirred the skies. Shelo groaned and turned over in the straw, hands covering his ears. But Arthur shook his shoulder. "Come on. Time to go. We've no more business being here."

Out into the night; out once more into the unsheltered wild. It seemed to Arthur that the shape of Shelo shifted constantly in the moonlight, one minute a man running alongside him, the next a towering column of smoke and mist. Shelo snarled, and approaching thunder in the clouds snarled back. They stumbled away down the valley, panicked, directionless.

He had ridden with Lucas through a rainstorm towards a silver dawn. Arthur heard a sob escape his throat, and close by heard Shelo howl, caught in his own secret grief. They came to a copse against the side of a mountain, and retreated beneath the trees as lightning lit the sky bone-white.

Shelo's lips were drawn up over his pointed teeth. Every inch of his skin was alive and writhing with terrible shapes. His eyes burned like coals in the heart of a furnace.

"All finished," he gabbled. *"All over, and still no peace."*

"Shelo..." Arthur could barely speak, his chest heaving, his body quivering with terror and with strangled hope. "Can you not find the herbs here? To make your medicine one last time. For me, and for you..."

Shelo looked at him, sorrow and fierce pity in his gaze. "Oh, Arthur," he said, very quietly. His inked lids slid closed, and Arthur was regarded by a second pair of eyes, cold and dead and pitiless. His body fell still. And dread, as deep and cold and wide as the ocean itself, flooded into him.

"I know it now," said Shelo. "There is no rest for you and I. There is no relief to be found, not on this side of the world, or the other."

Arthur choked upon his own breath. "But you... you *called* me! Didn't you? You promised me... you promised..."

The ink eyes were unblinking. Shelo gave no reply.

The wind had risen, buffeting the treetops and driving black clouds across the moon. Arthur could have sworn that the very ground beneath him was shifting, snarling like a living beast. He had to raise his voice to cry his protest, fighting to be heard above the din.

"I should never have come with you! I should have taken that ship with Silas!"

"Silas who left you?" asked Shelo. His voice was low, still, sinuous, but audible nonetheless. "At your very hour of need?"

Something was amiss. Arthur turned aside, gasping for air, his mind racing. And he recalled, as from a long-faded dream, how he had left Sam's attic for the harbour that morning. Shelo absent when he awoke. A bright planet hanging in the sky, ringed in red among the last faint stars. And in a dim alleyway nearby, the sound of two men fighting fiercely.

"He came to find me," said Arthur. "Didn't he, Shelo? He came to find me at Sam's place, before I was even awake. But you... but you..." He choked.

"I needed you," said Shelo. His eyes had slid open again, and now there was terror in their depths, and pleading. "I did what I had to do. Arthur..."

"What did you do to him?"

"Arthur... my Arthur..."

"What did you do to him?"

Shelo's hand strayed, involuntarily, to the flat blade that he kept in his belt. Countless times Arthur had seen him skin rabbits with it, cut through stubborn undergrowth. And now he saw, vividly, Shelo holding it to Silas's throat. The old man crumpling, blood pooling from his slit jugular. Breathing his last wet breaths as Arthur stood waiting for him in vain beside the harbour, the scarlet sun rising over the sea.

It was with an animal cry, with feral strength, that he flung himself upon Shelo. And where there should have been a wall of muscled resistance, there was nothing. They tumbled backwards together out of the shelter of the trees, into the spitting rain. Rolling head after heels, he felt Shelo meet him with a half-hearted blow, and responded with renewed ferocity.

Shelo bellowed like a wounded bull, goaded now. Locked together, they tripped over a ridge, and went tumbling down a

236

slope towards the bottom of the valley. Below them lay the great lake, its black surface a chaos of waves, lashed by rain.

Stones skidded beneath their feet, and lightning lit the world again. Scrapping like rats, biting and kicking, they tumbled backwards in a whirl of limbs and shivering droplets. They hit the surface of the seething water with an almighty splash.

They sunk still half entangled, Shelo's hands clawing for Arthur's neck, Arthur kicking with all his might. For a breathless moment it seemed that they would pull each other into the depths, each the other's dreadful end. But then, suddenly, mystifyingly, as though in the surrendering of all hope, Shelo let go.

His broad body went limp. His hands unlocked from Arthur's limbs.

And Shelo fell away from him for the rest of his life, suddenly limp in the dappled underwater light. Shelo fell away from him through the water, sinking deeper, his black eyes open and clear as glass. He was swallowed by darkness.

§

Some secret strength carried Arthur up the muddied bank, crawling on all fours consumed by bitter weeping. The storm swelled all around. And there he lay, his body wearied beyond all words, until the coming of the earthquake.

18

To Sea

*A*rthur. *Arthur. Can it be you? When I have searched so long and so hard?*
A hand upon his. A face from a long-forgotten world.

Arthur, do you know me?

"I know you." His voice, so long unused, emerged cracked and hoarse. The natives at his back shuffled their feet and muttered to one another. Dappled green light blurred the edges of every shape and shadow. "You are... you are..."

A long-forgotten world. The deep, resounding lament of a stringed instrument in the corridors of a grand house. Steam rising from a copper bath. A wiry figure beneath an umbrella with a woman in a green dress.

Something rose out of the fog that filled his mind. And with faint surprise he found that there were tears upon his cheeks, rolling down into his tangled beard.

"I know you. You are Lucas West."

§

He had forgotten that he was almost naked. He looked at the cloth tied around his waist, and ran his hands through his tangled hair. His feet were bare, his thin body stained with dirt. He had forgotten his own name.

Arthur. To have found you...

He found himself weeping often. He found that something had changed in his body, as though the inside of his skin now faced outwards. He felt tender and raw.

For some days, he could barely speak. He sat with Lucas on the bank of the river, and neither of them said a word. In the evening, glowing insects danced low over the water, and reeds bent in the soft breeze. Arthur and Lucas looked at one another, remaking their acquaintance slowly, silently. Lucas bore all the marks of a long expedition. His clothes were ragged and the bones in his face stood out starkly, an untidy beard covering his chin.

"How did you find me?" breathed Arthur, when at last he could summon words.

"Oh, Arthur. What a journey! What a dance you have led me!" Lucas laughed. "Through the deep of these forests, along paths only the natives knew, to the edge of my own endurance…"

Arthur echoed his mirth shyly.

"Even from the English shore I wondered whether my search was not in vain. And then some time ago I passed through a green valley. I met a young freedman-farmer. And a girl…"

Arthur nodded. Tears arose in him yet again, and he did not hold them back, bending over to rest his chin upon his knee.

"…a girl who was a guest beneath his roof. I had been looking so long, Arthur. So many months, and only whispers of you. The strangest whispers. And then to find one who knew you, who had journeyed with you…"

Arthur's weak chest drew in the damp air, and expelled it shakily. Flora had limped and stumbled back down the valley, to the place where she had known kindness. He had not been the death of her, too.

Stars blazed in the velvet sky, vivid as bonfires. He remembered leaning out of the pantry window, Lucas on one side of him, Harmony on the other. He looked up from the water, and found that Lucas was watching him searchingly.

"She told me such things, Arthur," he said quietly. "Such things."

§

I was a terrible coward, Arthur. For months after I put you on that boat, I hardly dared return to the hall. The natives gathered in curious groups, pointing and muttering behind their hands at the sight of the two white men walking together. *The very air of the place felt poisoned. Your old nursemaid had been sent away too, to France. Lady Hannah sat in a chair before the window, and would not say a word, nor eat a single morsel. Your father and your brother were as men carved from stone, unfit for the running of the house. All fell into disorder.*

And your sister... your sister...

Sometimes they were followed by naked children, who hid in the hollows of tree trunks and padded through the undergrowth alongside them. Lucas examined his hands in the dappled green light. He looked sideways at Arthur. *I kept my distance for so long. Then I began to receive letters from my friends in Africa, some months after they had been expecting your arrival. I began to fear...*

Arthur closed his eyes. For a moment he felt the motion of waves beneath him, smelled the stench of the *Mary*'s hold.

And then... Arthur, I do not know how to tell you. There was news from the hall. It had been a long winter. I believe your father had little strength left for living. I believe he welcomed the darkness, when it came.

Jonas's end had crept close while he slept, bitter as a December wind. There would be no more music, now, drifting through the corridors of Harcourt Hall. Arthur's grief caught him by surprise, cold in the humid air, beneath the equinoctial sun.

§

"I returned in the thaw," said Lucas. "I returned when it seemed to me that the trees were shaking the snow from their branches, and the ice had melted in the lake."

Arthur pictured Harmony, sat alone at the table in the library, her father's ledger before her. Her brows were knotted with weariness. When she caught sight of Lucas in the doorway, returned after the lonely winter, she let the book fall shut. A room of dust and quietness lay between them, a world of lost and longed-for things.

Arthur imagined the rebuke in her face. But then he saw that beneath the interlacing shadows of the trees, Lucas was smiling, smiling.

"Have you ever been outside on the morning after a storm, Arthur? To find that everything is destroyed, and new, and clean?" Lucas covered his mouth with his hand, as though afraid that the breadth of his smile would split his face in two. "And then suddenly things seem possible which have never been possible before."

The two figures in the library came to Arthur's mind again. He saw Lucas moving closer, tentative. And even as Harmony rose to her feet, a light blazing behind her tired eyes, Lucas sinking to his knees. Taking her hand in his.

Beneath the trees, Lucas uncovered his smile once again. Brightness broke out onto his face like sun through cloud. He was looking expectantly at Arthur, who realised what her reply had been. Her grief and her joy mingled in her tears.

I cannot marry you . . . not because of your station, or mine, or Edward's displeasure. Not any more. But because I cannot accept such happiness while my brother is still out in the world somewhere, lost and alone.

§

"She longed to come herself, Arthur. You know that she would have come in a heartbeat. But she could not leave Edward. He took your father's death so very hard."

Lucas pulled a crumpled envelope from inside his shirt. On the front, in Harmony's large, deliberate hand, was Arthur's name.

He slept many nights beneath Elia's roof with the unopened envelope cradled close. For the first time in as long as he could remember, he ceased to dream. He breathed the heavy air deep into his lungs. He woke, finally, with a sudden sense that everything was clear. He read Harmony's letter sitting in the doorway, by the light of the rising sun. As he slipped outside, he caught Elia's gaze from where she lay on her back beside her sleeping husband.

Barefoot, he padded across the dead ground and then through the undergrowth to the village. He passed between the silent dwellings and then down the bank, beneath the hanging creepers and past flowers as high as his hip. The pool lay still and green below him, delicate ferns trailing in the water. The languid light glimmered upon its surface.

His body trembling in anticipation, Arthur untied the cloth from around his waist. He stood naked in the warmth of the morning. Beads of moisture formed upon his skin.

He dived inexpertly, enveloped by the water. He slipped beneath the surface, and for a moment, all was dim and blurred.

Then he rose. His head emerged first, arms, shoulders, torso. He broke out with a great shower of shimmering droplets, with a grateful gasp for air. He stood waist-deep in the pool, water streaming from his hair, his nose, his mouth. He turned his face up towards the light.

§

My stubborn brother. My dearest Arthur.

You are so very far away, and we have been in strange correspondence with stranger people to find out where. Rumour has it that you have crossed to the New World. That you have journeyed deep into the wilds, in the most mysterious company. How I wish that I could see your face, or at least receive a letter in your hand! How I wish I could be sure that I have not been deceived; that you really did make it across the sea alive.

You may think that there are things too awful to be spoken of. Clearly, for you, they are too awful to be borne, or you would not have vanished so suddenly from the face of the world. I will tell you that it is difficult for me, still, to write of them. But I am certain now that things no less sinful pass through respectable heads and out of respectable lips every day. As you know I am not in any case given to blushing or to delicacy. Lord knows my heart is strong enough to pull this load.

Edward is made differently, and I know that you have much to forgive him for. Perhaps it was the exhibition he made of his shock and disgust that has driven you beyond our reach. But he knew, in his way, long before we did, and the weight of it must have been dreadful to bear. Understand how, beneath all of his pretence, he had always adored Father. And more, perhaps, how he knew Mother — the woman we all called our mother — far better than we ever did. What he uncovered was enough to madden him. Do not despise him for it.

He is to be married now, Arthur, and is a calmer man than he who chased you from our midst. He is also — and here I must break to you that which I hoped would not happen until you were safe back with us — the new Earl of Harcourt. Father's passing was not unexpected, as he had been wasting both in body and in spirit all winter. But it leaves us changed. I wish so much that you could have been here. I think it would have comforted him to see you, before the end.

Hannah is still here with us, and I will not have it any other way, though

243

she asks me weekly if I would not rather that she returned to Ireland. There is nothing for her there, and I will not have her sink into her twilight years abandoned to her ghosts. She is bound inside her grief for Father, but I believe that in some ways it is a release. There will be grand-nephews and grand-nieces for her to dote on, in time. I pray that life will reclaim her, piece by piece. I pray that one day soon, she will see her son again.

And what of you, Arthur? I have a map on my desk and can trace your voyage to the tip of Africa. And then the journey of your second ship, that vessel where you and countless other souls endured unspeakable horrors. Why would anyone board such a ship out of choice, Arthur? I cannot make head or tail of it. Neither can I understand the whispers that reach us of your time in a traveller's wagon, upon the dusty roads of the New World.

You have run so very far. As though if you ran far and fast enough you could leave your very body behind! But Lucas will find you. Of that, I am sure. Whatever you have done, however low you may have fallen, he will bring you back to me.

Come home, Arthur. It will not be easy, not for any of us. Come home as you are, in whatever rags, and as long as you wipe the mud from your boots, there will be a bed for you here. No, better. There will be rejoicing and a feast.

Whatever you may think, there is nothing lost which cannot be found. You were born into this world with the same curse and the same choice as the rest of us.

Though it may be half the truth, I sign myself wholeheartedly,
Your sister,
   Harmony Hallingham.

§

"The girl, Flora, spoke of your companion." Lucas seemed hesitant for the first time. "A man, she said, who was hardly a man at all.

Forgive me, but I can hardly believe..."

Arthur could give him no answer. Shelo as he had first appeared, looming in the doorway of Sam's attic room. Made of ashes, made of smoke, leading him between the darkened trees. *If you do not believe, then touch me.*

Had Flora and Elia not seen him, known him too, he might have been part of some feverish imagining. In the face of Lucas's uncertainty, Arthur began to doubt.

"She said that he had been drowned. That he fell into the water, and there was an earthquake, and a storm. Who was he, Arthur? What hold did he have upon you?"

"No hold," muttered Arthur. "Not any longer. Not now."

Whose had been the groans and screams, echoing from the back of a wagon in the heart of the wild? What had become of those nameless weary? When Arthur closed his eyes they passed before him, stripped of themselves like winter trees of their leaves. For them there would be no returning. And for the Governor in his grand house, who had swallowed their griefs like poison, no relief.

When he thought of them, it seemed to Arthur that he had followed Shelo in a dream, stumbling like a sleeper, empty of reason. He had not once held up a warning hand to any approaching the wagon, spoken words of caution. *Turn back. This is not your rest, this is not your peace. Turn back.*

"I fancied that a voice called me from across the ocean," he whispered. "That is all. That there was one who saw me, and knew me, and had called me to himself."

Walking back at dusk from the home in the village where Lucas was staying, Arthur glimpsed a shifting shadow from the corner of his eye. The shape followed him, flickering in and out of view, melting between the twilit trees. He smelled deep-forest earth. The hint of an ancient, acrid musk upon the breeze.

At the night's meal with Elia, he saw that she seemed alert, expectant. Her husband swept away the dead petals that blew in through their doorway.

"He has returned here," Elia said softly. "Risen from the deep. I know what he is seeking."

Arthur turned over from sleep to see that a trail of wet footprints led around his hammock and out of the door. A dim shape lingered near his feet. When he swung his bare legs down over the side of the hammock, it backed warily away.

A scattering of leaves whirled across Arthur's feet, and he rose to follow them, out through the door and into the heat of the night. Wet footprints led across the dead ground towards the tree. The broad form of Shelo was silhouetted beside the trunk, against the stars.

Arthur drew to a halt, overcome. He could not see Shelo's face but was certain to his very bones that it was turned in his direction. Eyes fixed piercingly upon him.

Shelo reached out his hand, and there was a loud splintering of wood, followed by a moment of hush. Shelo lifted something from within the tree and took it in both hands, cradling it to himself.

Then a long, low sigh sounded from out of the air. Arthur was aware of Elia rushing to his side, arms wrapped about herself, feet bare upon the earth. .

And then Shelo was gone, melting into darkness just as he had been born from it. Arthur ran forward, too late to see anything but the shallow pool of water upon the ground. His eyes were drawn upwards, towards the trunk, where at the level of his chest he could make out a bloodied handprint upon the wood.

If you do not believe...

He reached out and laid his palm against it. All beneath the scarred skin of the bark was silent and still.

§

Lucas did not hurry him. There were no seasons in the equinoctial forest, save for the frequent coming of the rains, which pelted down through the canopy and drenched the ground beneath. Petals and leaves sagged beneath the weight of fat droplets, bright fungi swelling indecently at the base of each tree trunk. Birds shook their shimmering wings. The children in the village ran with their heads tilted back, mouths open, yelling and splashing excitedly.

Elia raised her eyes to the light above the canopy. She was no longer listless, as though all her will had been drained from her. She took to stepping in the night through the tangled groves, amid a cacophony of noise. Her careful feet trod ancient paths, and returned her before dawn, damp with dew.

She held her arms open to the sky, her hair loose at her back. She licked the raindrops slowly from her lips, thirstily, like one awakening from a long slumber. Her husband sat upon a stool in the doorway of their home, absently carving a fallen branch. He hummed softly to himself beneath his breath, the sound almost drowned out by the din of cascading water.

And what of you, Arthur? Harmony's letter grew grey and crumpled with much reading. *What of you?* He could not so quickly leave behind the stench on the *Head of Mary*, the wailing of the weary, the Governor's dreadful bedchamber. The blood of Benjamin Barber, the eyes of Shelo falling away from him in the dark.

Come home. He imagined her stepping through the greenery, skirt hitched up about her ankles, brushing aside creepers and errant insects. Arthur knew just how she would look, breathless and brightened, colour high in her cheeks. Her eyes turned smilingly upon him.

He shook the lethargy from himself as if shedding an old skin. He imagined climbing out of the shell of himself, leaving it upon a rock in a sunny clearing. Feeling the air against his tender face and limbs.

§

When they left, there was blossom upon the branches of the tree that stood above the house of Elia. The ground that had been hard and dead was softened by the rains. Elia bade them farewell from the doorway of her home, one hand extended towards Arthur and Lucas, the other resting upon her rounded belly.

She burdened them with bundles of scented herbs, with roots and pressed petals. Lucas took her gifts eagerly. Arthur knew that they would soon spill out onto the table in the library at Harcourt Hall, filling the room with their deep-forest musk.

Elia inclined her head gravely to them. Her look, the winding ink about her ankles, the swollen curve of her stomach, stayed with Arthur in the days that followed. The night before his departure she had lingered at his bedside, her eyes upon him as he drifted into sleep. Her murmuring had eased him into dreamless rest. *Not for nothing, Arthur Hallingham, has been your coming. Has been his leading. As though we are all now being remade.*

After some days they passed the village among the reeds where Arthur had fled the house of the monk. They stopped for fresh water, and Lucas handed three letters to a young native, conversing with him long and carefully in Spanish.

"The first is for your sister," he explained to Arthur. "The second to ensure our passage upon a vessel which sails tomorrow. As to the third, he knows the place of which I speak."

Arthur did not think to question him. They journeyed along the bank of the sluggish river, Lucas leading the way, his scant possessions bound to his back. They slept wrapped in creepers amongst the bloodwood roots, beside plunging waterfalls whose mist rose towards the low moon. Often Arthur would wake to find his companion risen before sunrise, strolling barefoot amongst the dew-drenched blooms. Phosphorescent stars hung close to the world.

§

And then at dawn, the thinning of the trees. The widening of the river's mouth, into an ocean lit cool silver by the pale light. The rippling of white sails.

Arthur breathed the salt air deep into his lungs, breeze lifting his hair. The vessel before them was being readied for its voyage, men hauling great bundles of timber onto the deck. His feet carried him towards the shore.

The water dashed up the beach and soaked his boots, trickling away again with a rush and a sigh. The sailor's calls echoed down from the deck, loud and urgent with the need to catch the fair wind. One of them beckoned animatedly to Arthur and Lucas, miming the lifting of the anchor.

"One moment!" cried Lucas, who had lingered on the road. Arthur, hearing the sound of approaching hooves, turned around. "Stay, one moment!"

Some distance away, beside the rocks at the top of the beach, two figures were dismounting from a horse. One, tall and dark-skinned, raised a hand to Arthur from across the sands. The other, small and fair, shielded her eyes from the sunrise. And then, catching sight of Arthur, kicked up a storm of sand as she came tearing down towards him.

She was dishevelled as ever, skirts held near her knees. Her mouth slackened as she regarded the sea over Arthur's shoulder. She was entirely wonderful to him.

"Are you coming?" he asked breathlessly.

She smiled and smiled, but she was shaking her head. "Not this time, anyhow. Not yet." She grabbed his arm and spun him giddily round with her to face the ocean. "But the *sea,* Art! The sea! I had to see the sea!"

The breeze snatched their breath away. Flora laughed lightheadedly, still clinging to his arm. He turned her to face him again, her freckled face squinting up at him.

"I am glad to have known you, Flora Barber." Gently he tucked a strand of wind-blown hair behind her ear, and bent to kiss her forehead.

"And I you." She straightened the collar of his shirt, and then regarded him beadily, her head tilted to one side. "Go safe, won't you?" She wiped her nose upon her sleeve. "And Art..."

"What?"

"All is well," said Flora, suddenly serious. "It is well. *It is well.*"

He looked out to sea. And it seemed to him that he could already see a figure running to meet him across the lawns of Harcourt Hall, running, running, arms open wide.